HOW THE FINCH STOLE CHRISTMAS

I took a settling breath and started up the remaining flight of thin-carpeted stairs to the top-floor attic apartment.

"Kim?" I called out softly from the top landing. "Are you in here?" The only door visible up here was ajar. I pushed it open with the palm of my hand. "Kim?"

A small globe light above the door on the inside glowed yellow. The only other illumination came from the strings of lights twinkling on the outside of each window.

"Amy!" Kim scrambled to her feet from the braided rug she'd been seated on and rushed at me. "You're here!"

"Yes." I squeezed her. "I'm here. Now," I said, grabbing her by the shoulders, "tell me what is going on!" Kim's hair stuck out in several directions from her black knit cap. She was bundled up in a hip-length, houndstooth-wool duffle coat and black corduroy slacks with knee-high black leather boots.

"Don't you see him, Amy?" Kim was practically hysterical now, as if my coming had opened a tap of panic that she had heretofore been holding in check. "Don't you see him?"

"See who?" I replied, trying to hold her in place.

Kim pulled away and pointed. "Right there!" she shouted. "See? It's Mr. Finch!"

The living quarters had once been the home's attic. What I saw was a vaulted room with a convenient beam running lengthwise down the middle—convenient if one wanted to hang oneself, that is.

Because Franklin Finch was hanging from the center of the beam by a rope tied around his neck . . .

Books by J.R. Ripley

DIE, DIE BIRDIE
TOWHEE GET YOUR GUN
THE WOODPECKER ALWAYS PECKS TWICE
TO KILL A HUMMINGBIRD
CHICKADEE CHCKADEE BANG BANG
HOW THE FINCH STOLE CHRISTMAS

Published by Kensington Publishing Corporation

How the Finch Stole Christmas

J.R. Ripley

LYRICAL UNDERGROUND
Kensington Publishing Corp.
www.kensingtonbooks.com

LYRICAL UNDERGROUND BOOKS are published by

Kensington Publishing Corp.
119 West 40th Street
New York, NY 10018

All Kensington titles, imprints, and distributed lines are available at special quantity discounts for bulk purchases for sales promotion, premiums, fund-raising, educational, or institutional use.

Special book excerpts or customized printings can also be created to fit specific needs. For details, write or phone the office of the Kensington Sales Manager: Kensington Publishing Corp., 119 West 40th Street, New York, NY 10018. Attn. Sales Department. Phone: 1-800-221-2647.

Lyrical Underground and Lyrical Underground logo Reg. US Pat. & TM Off.

First Electronic Edition: November 2017
eISBN-13: 978-1-5161-0314-0
eISBN-10: 1-5161-0314-9

First Print Edition: November 2017
ISBN-13: 978-1-5161-0315-7
ISBN-10: 1-5161-0315-7

Printed in the United States of America

1

A commotion of some sort was brewing on the street below, but I chose to ignore it. I was happy.

"Isn't it wonderful this time of year, Derek?" I reached out the bottom of the double-hung window and carefully slid the plastic tray from the feeder so I could refill it with sunflower seeds. It felt cold in my bare hand. I had promised Derek that I would give him a bird feeder for his apartment—and further promised to come by weekly to refill it for him.

"Everything is so peaceful, so quiet." I admired the sparkling tinsel lining Lake Shore Drive. "So festive."

"I agree," Derek said lazily.

"For a while there, I was beginning to wonder if I would ever truly settle in here." Since returning to my home in the Town of Ruby Lake, North Carolina, things had been anything but normal and peaceful. And rarely had things been quiet. Finally, things had settled down.

And with Christmas just around the proverbial corner, my life couldn't be more perfect.

I inhaled the chill morning air. The sweet smell of baking coming from C Is For Cupcakes, located across the street and a couple of shops upwind from Derek's second-floor apartment, was making my mouth water. I looked hungrily at the pink-and-blue bakery shop sign and considered stopping in for a midmorning treat. This time of year, I heard Connie added vanilla and peppermint cupcakes to the lineup and I was dying to try one.

"You moved into a new house, opened your Birds and Bees store. What did you expect? There were going to be some bumps in the road, Amy," Derek said patiently. "I had some bumps of my own when I moved here."

"I know. Thank goodness we're past them." Birds & Bees was the bird-watching and bird-feeding supply store I had started up on returning to Ruby Lake. I operated the business out of the house I owned on Lake Shore Drive, the town's busiest street. I didn't know much about business and I wasn't the world's foremost ornithological authority, but, so far, I was making a go of it.

"I'm looking forward to a bump-free future," I said with a grin.

Derek laughed as his eyes skirted to the muted television screen facing him. Some morning sports-recap show was airing. He had moved to town around the same time as me. He wanted to be nearer his daughter, Maeve, who lived with his ex. He also wanted to be nearer to his father, Ben. The two men shared a law office directly downstairs from the one-bedroom apartment Derek called home.

"It was hard there for a while," Derek agreed. "But I feel a change in the air and it isn't only the coming of winter. And it's nice being near Maeve."

A house finch clung to the red brick several feet to my right, one curious eye on me as it attacked the mortar with is stubby beak.

"The sense of home and family. That's a big part of the reason I moved back to Ruby Lake in the first place." Being nearer to my mother and farther from my ex-boyfriend had definitely played a significant role in my decision to move back home.

I turned and looked at Derek as he snorted. "I thought it was so you could meet me," he said with a grin. He sat with his feet up on the green sofa, hands behind his head, eyeing me. He wore a pair of loose-fitting jeans and a rumpled heather sweatshirt, and he still looked gorgeous to me.

As a lawyer, Derek is all suit and tie during business hours, but when he's off duty, he prefers to go casual.

"Very funny." I pushed a wavy lock of brown hair from my eye.

He wiggled his stockinged toes in reply.

The bird feeder was held to the glass via four strong suction cups. The frame of the feeder was made of recycled plastic. It had a sloped roof and a perching tray of clear plastic. The tray slid out, making it easy to bring in, refill with seed, and replace on the window.

I picked up the small tote bag of mixed birdseed, reached my hand inside, and refilled the tray one handful at a time. I carefully slid the tray back into the feeder, dusted off my hands, and closed the bottom sash.

The minute I did, the finch alighted on the tray. Its toes clung to the edge as the bird rooted around in the fresh layer of seed. "It looks like you've got a friend."

Derek squinted at the bird. It was a mere six inches long from the point of its beak to the tip of its tail. "That bird or one just like it is always pecking away at the bricks." He sat up. "In fact, I think he, if it is a he, prefers it to the birdseed."

I smiled. "You don't know much about birds, do you?"

"Nope." He rose and kissed me quickly on the lips. "That's what I've got you for, Amy."

I tapped the end of his nose with my index finger. "I believe you are more interested in my weekly visits than you are the birds that are attracted to your window, Mr. Harlan."

"You won't get any argument out of me, Counselor."

"For your information, that little bird is a house finch. And this one," I explained, pointing through the glass at the bird, "is a male. See all the red?" Our bird sported a red forehead, rump, and chest.

Derek nodded.

"The females are paler, with more of a gray-brown plumage."

"And they like to eat bricks?" Derek whispered, not wanting to spook the bird. I could feel his warm breath on my neck and smothered a sigh.

"There is lime in cement, and lime is a good source of calcium. If you'd rather they didn't eat your mortar, you could try putting out broken egg shells. The birds might eat that instead."

Derek pulled away. "That's okay. There's enough mortar on these old walls to last longer than I'll be living here." He picked up the remote and turned off the television.

"Are you thinking of moving?" Not that I would mind too much, just as long as he remained in Ruby Lake. In fact, if he wanted to move out of the apartment, I would help him pack. His ex had recently partnered in a bridal boutique right next door. I could read the shop's sign from the window: DREAM GOWNS.

It was more of a nightmare, if you asked me.

"No, at least not anytime soon."

I nodded. "What *is* going on down there?"

Derek rejoined me at the window, placing one hand on the ledge and the other on the small of my back. "I'm not sure."

Together we watched as what had started as a small crowd on the sidewalk now spread out onto Lake Shore Drive.

As many as twenty people had gathered in a loose crowd. Passersby slowed to watch. Several in the group held makeshift signs.

"Can you read what the signs say?" Derek pressed his nose to the window and cupped his hands over his forehead.

"No. Maybe it's a gimmick. Christmas House Village might be running some kind of a midweek sale." Opposite the brick building housing the offices of Harlan and Harlan, Attorneys, sat one of Ruby Lake's oldest and most popular attractions, Kinley's Christmas House Village.

"Say, isn't that Kim?" Derek asked.

"Kim? Where?"

"That blonde on the right in the long red coat."

I followed the imaginary line of Derek's index figure. It led to a pretty, long-haired blonde with a shiny, black patent-leather purse over her left shoulder. "I wonder what she's doing there."

"If it is a sale, maybe she's shopping."

"Maybe." But I didn't think so. Several persons in the crowd were carrying cardboard boxes, others toted bags. Some were empty-handed. All appeared agitated.

A man in a black suit soon came down the sidewalk bisecting Kinley's Christmas House Village. A security guard wearing a holly-green uniform joined him. Kinley's Christmas House Village was a collection of six houses, three on each side of the narrow cobblestone sidewalk connecting them.

The small cluster of multistory Victorian-era homes were original to the location. The houses sat on postage-stamp-sized lots and had been home to some of Ruby Lake's earlier residents. The charming enclave had been constructed by a small group of immigrants in the late eighteen hundreds.

Families came and went and, after World War II, Owen Kinley moved into the second house back on the left. Sometime in the 1950s, he had turned the first floor of his house into his business, Kinley's Christmas House.

It was to become the beginning of a small-town empire. Kinley's Christmas House grew from first one house, to two, and then three, until finally it became Kinley's Christmas House Village as Owen Kinley and his family purchased the remaining houses in the enclave to expand their holiday-themed business.

"Look! Somebody just took a swing at Kim!" Derek said in astonishment. "That woman hit her in the side of the head with her purse!"

I gasped. "That's Mrs. Fortuny. What's gotten into her?"

"I don't know," replied Derek. "But it appears to be spreading." He clamped his hand on my shoulder and pointed with the other. "Look."

I looked. The street had erupted in mayhem. Kim was now surrounded by an unhappy crowd. I saw Kim pull out her cell phone. She dialed, talked quickly, and then dropped the phone into the front pocket of her coat.

So much for my bump-free future.

"We'd better get down there!" I pulled away and ran for the apartment door.

We grabbed our coats and Derek fumbled into his sneakers. The door to Derek's apartment opens at the rear onto the alley. I led the way down the narrow metal steps with Derek right behind me.

We went around to the main street and had to wait for a line of traffic on Lake Short Drive to move past before we could cross over. "Kim!" I shouted, signaling with my arms as we approached. "Over here!"

Kim turned and looked at me. She was in the midst of a heated discussion with an elderly woman with silver hair tied in a tight knot behind her head and dressed in a big black coat that fell to her knees. Kim said something to the woman, then hurried toward us.

Mrs. Fortuny was huddled with a stout older gentleman who appeared to be consoling her. It wasn't her husband. He'd died years ago.

On the opposite side of the street, I noticed a smaller group that included our mayor, Mac MacDonald, Gertrude Hammer, and a man whose name I didn't know but recognized as the head of our town's planning and zoning commission.

"Amy." Kim gave me a quick hug. "What are you doing here?" My best friend is a long-legged blonde with devilish blue eyes. She is thirty-four, like me, but likes to brag that she's younger—three months, big deal. I'm taller. We'd known each other practically forever.

Kim had loaned me some startup money for the business. In return, I made her a partner and part-time employee in Birds & Bees.

She turned to Derek and said hello. Derek nodded in reply.

"Me?" I said, looking over her shoulder at the mini protest. "Shouldn't I be asking you that question? And let's assume I just have. What's gotten into these people?"

"Them?" Kim waved her hand in frustration. "They're just upset. I called my boss. He's on his way over."

I arched my brow. "I can see that. But why?" There was no sign of the police. I hoped that was a sign they would not be needed.

"Ms. Christy!" A clear, sharp voice rang out over the murmurs of the crowd. It was the tall man in the black suit. He had a long face, dark brown eyes, and a sallow complexion. The younger man next to him in the green uniform stood at attention, his arms crossed over his chest. "I'd like a word with you, Ms. Christy!" He beckoned her with his hand.

Kim sighed. "Sorry, I've got to go." Her hand brushed my sleeve. "We'll talk later, okay?"

"Okay," I agreed, though I was dying to know what was going on. "Wait." I reached for my best friend's hand and held her back. I nodded my chin in the direction of the man in the black suit who, at the moment, was checking his gold watch. "Who is that man?"

Kim shot a quick look over her shoulder. "Him? That's Franklin Finch."

"Franklin Finch?" I asked.

Kim's phone chimed before she could respond. She retrieved it from her coat. "Hello, Mr. Belzer," she said quickly. "Yes, that's right." She twisted her neck and looked at the crowd gathered on the sidewalk outside Christmas House Village. "Yes, I know. Okay."

Kim turned her attention back to me and Derek as she once again dropped her phone in her pocket. "I'd better get back."

Kim turned to go and I grabbed the bottom of her coat to prevent her slipping away without further explanation. "Franklin Finch?" I repeated. "Just who is Franklin Finch?"

"You'd better tell her, Kim," Derek chided, "or she might never let go. You know how stubborn Amy can be."

Kim rolled her eyes in a *don't I know it* fashion. "Franklin Finch," she said hastily. "He's the new owner of Christmas House Village."

Kim swatted my hand and I lost my grip on her coat. She disappeared into the crowd, moving toward Mr. Finch and his security guard.

"New owner of Christmas House Village?" I looked at Derek in wonder and surprise.

I tilted my head up in the direction of Derek's apartment window. A trio of nuthatches danced around the window feeder, taking turns. "If only the folks on the street were behaving that orderly."

"What?"

I pointed to the birds. The small but large-headed birds skittered happily upside down along the brick, hopping in and out of the feeder for seeds. "No pushing, no shoving. Peaceful coexistence."

"What kind of birds are they?" asked Derek, squinting to see.

"Those are nuthatches," I replied. "And those," I added, pointing to the agitated cluster of folks on the sidewalk, "are nutcases."

Derek chuckled. "What do you say we get out of here?"

"What about Kim?"

"I'd say Kim has her hands full."

Kim stood in front of Franklin Finch. His hands were gesticulating toward the men and women swarming around the perimeter. A three-foot-tall white picket fence separated the sidewalk from Kinley's Christmas House Village. Finch, Kim, and the security guard stood on one side. The guard appeared to be unarmed except for a walkie-talkie.

The rest of the protesters stood on the street side of the fence. However, there were more people watching from the front porches of the houses inside that comprised Christmas House Village—shoppers, employees, or both. Kim stood stiff-backed, taking it in. Even in profile, I could see the frustration on her face.

I felt Derek's hand on my elbow. "Can I buy you a cup of coffee?"

I took one last look at the crowd. Mayor MacDonald and the man from the planning and zoning commission had disappeared. Only Gertie Hammer remained—a distant observer. Her hands gripped the handle of a Lakeside Market shopping cart laden with stuffed plastic grocery bags. Had she had something to do with all this commotion or was she simply a curious bystander?

The crotchety old woman had sold me my house, then tried to buy it back again. When she couldn't buy it from me, she tried to snatch it by other means and had failed.

I'd had little to do with her since then and preferred to keep it that way. "Only if it comes with a cupcake," I said in response to Derek's offer of coffee.

"Deal." Derek and I started down the block. "Don't worry about Kim," he added. "I'm sure she can take care of herself."

I swiveled my neck for the second time to look back at the scene, as we strolled hand in hand ever closer to the smell of freshly baked cupcakes.

I nodded. "Kim's tough, all right." But little did I know how tough her situation would prove to be.

2

Derek stepped to the side and pulled open the glass door of C Is For Cupcakes.

I moved inside, enjoying the scent of sugar and cake as much as I enjoyed getting out of the cold. I unbuttoned my coat and draped it over a hook on the coatrack near the entrance. Derek did the same.

"Welcome to C Is For Cupcakes!" An exuberant young man wearing a blue hat and apron behind the counter waved to us. A woman wearing a pink hat and apron stood behind him filling a plastic to-go tray with cupcakes.

We approached the sales counter. The pine-topped counter was flanked by two long glass cases filled with every flavor of cupcake imaginable and then some. The bakery's walls were painted in stripes of pastel pink and blue. The floor was wide plank yellow pine.

"Do you know what you want, Amy?" Derek asked.

"Vanilla peppermint," I replied without hesitation. I pointed my finger at a particularly thick-frosted one near the front of the glass case.

Derek ordered a pumpkin-spice cupcake with maple cream-cheese frosting and two large coffees. The ever-smiling youth filled our order and placed it on a plastic tray. Derek carried the tray to a small round table on the far wall.

I rose and crossed to the serving station that held napkins, utensils, and coffee additives. I added some sugar and cream to my coffee and picked up a wooden stir stick. Derek was drinking his coffee black.

I returned to my chair and peeled back the wrapper on my vanilla peppermint cupcake. I carefully removed the lower half of the cupcake, broke it into two pieces, and popped one in my mouth.

"What are you doing?" Derek watched in wonder.

"What?" I licked my fingers.

He pointed to my decapitated cupcake.

"I always eat my cupcake like this. I like to save the part with the frosting for last." I eyed his own half-eaten cupcake. He'd taken a man-size bite out of the side. "Primitive," I quipped.

Derek chuckled. "It seems there is a lot I don't know about you yet, Amy Simms."

I plucked the second chunk of cupcake and popped it in my mouth. "Consider that a good thing."

"Believe me, I do and I . . . uh-oh." Derek stopped as his eyes shifted to the door.

"Uh-oh what?" I turned, catching a frigid blast of air in the face. Mrs. Fortuny and the elderly gentleman who'd been consoling her outside Kinley's Christmas House Village had stepped inside the bakery.

Though why she needed consoling after knocking my best friend upside the head with her big purse was beyond me.

Irma Fortuny was a small, thin woman with a bowl of silver hair on her head. I knew her to be in her upper seventies, but she was still sharp as a tack—and apparently still packed a mean punch, albeit with her purse. Her blue eyes were equally sharp.

She spotted me, patted the arm of her companion, and walked slowly to our table like the world's most sluggish bird of prey.

Up close, I noted her owlish features—the rounded skull, big eyes, and flattish face. "Good morning, Mrs. Fortuny." I extended my hand across the table. "Do you know Derek?"

The corners of her thin lips turned down. "I've not had the pleasure." Finger by finger, she pulled off her brown suede gloves and draped them carefully over her pocketbook.

Derek stood. "Pleased to meet you, ma'am."

Mrs. Fortuny nodded. "You're Ben Harlan's boy, aren't you?"

"The one and only. You know him?"

"Sit," Mrs. Fortuny said with a wave of the hand. "Are you a lawyer, too?" Derek sank back into his chair. "Yes, ma'am." He winked at me. I gave a small shrug in reply, hoping Mrs. Fortuny wouldn't notice.

If I remembered correctly, Mrs. Fortuny had been widowed some years ago. "I hear that Christmas House Village has a new owner," I said, putting some cheer in my voice. My fingers toyed with the upper half of my cupcake, the thick frosting beckoning. "That must be quite exciting."

"Huh!" snorted Mrs. Fortuny in reply. "Is that what you think?" She shook her head side to side. "But then again . . ." She paused to snatch her gloves, which had been in danger of slipping to the floor. "But then again, you would, considering you and Ms. Christy are friends."

"Kim?" I drew my brows together. "What's Kim got to do with this?" "Why don't you ask your friend Kimberly Christy? She and her boss are the ones who are destroying this town!"

Mrs. Fortuny's companion sidled up to her, tray in hand. On it were two coffees, one carrot cake cupcake, and one dark chocolate cupcake. "Hi, folks." He nodded to us. "Ready, Irma?"

"One moment, William," Mrs. Fortuny answered. "This is William," she said for our benefit. "He works in the Christmas House Village stockroom. At least he did."

Her companion, William, was a broad-shouldered man of about seventy years. Big brown spectacles rested on a nose that would have looked at home on a former prizefighter. He carried a burled walnut cane in his craggy left hand. William managed a small smile as he settled the tray against his stomach.

"Isn't that right, William?"

"Yes, Irma," he said, his voice low. "But do try to stay calm. You remember what the doctor said about your blood pressure."

She nodded curtly and the elderly gentleman moved to an empty table near the door and sat with his back to us.

"Oh my gosh," I gasped, thinking I had finally figured out what Mrs. Fortuny was saying between the lines. "You haven't been fired, have you, Mrs. Fortuny?"

"Fired?" Derek said.

I nodded. "Mrs. Fortuny works at Kinley's Christmas House Village." I turned to the woman. "How many years has it been now, Mrs. Fortuny? Thirty?"

"Twenty-seven," she answered, clutching her gloves in both hands. "It would have been my twenty-eighth Christmas season, too." The poor dear looked angry and upset.

"I was fired once myself," I said, reaching out and patting her arm. "I know exactly what that feels like."

Mrs. Fortuny drew herself up. "Young lady, I was not fired. I quit!"

My eyes grew wide. "You quit? Why?"

"Because I have always worked for the Kinleys. I will not work for some New York incomer."

"I'm sure the new owner will be fine," Derek bravely interjected. "If you'll just give him the chance. I'm something of a newcomer myself."

"That may be, Mr. Harlan, but you are not intending to rename the town after yourself now, are you?"

"I don't understand . . ." Derek turned to me for help, but I had none to give and could only throw up my hands.

"What are you trying to say, Mrs. Fortuny?" I inquired.

"Mr. Franklin Finch—"

"The new owner," I interjected.

"Yes," Mrs. Fortuny said with clear disdain. "Mr. Finch intends to replace most of us with younger, cheaper help."

"I am so sorry," I said. Derek echoed my sentiment.

The corners of her lips turned down. "He had the gall to offer us thirty days to stay on with pay if we help train the new staff. After that, he's letting us go. Well, I, for one, will not give him the satisfaction. I quit today." She slapped her gloves against her leg. "And good riddance to him, I say!"

"That's terrible!" I squawked. "I wish there was something I could do. Derek?"

Derek threw up his hands. "It's not illegal to hire new staff. In fact, it's not uncommon for a new owner to want to bring his own people in."

I frowned. "I never dreamed Kinley's Christmas House Village would not belong to a Kinley."

"Oh, it won't be Kinley's Christmas House Village any longer," Mrs. Fortuny said with a touch of bitterness.

"What do you mean?" I asked.

"It is going to be Finch's Christmas House Village." The elderly woman arched her brow at me. "And this is all your friend's fault."

"I don't see how Kim—"

"I don't know how the woman can live with herself." Mrs. Fortuny turned without further ado and took a seat beside her companion, William.

I picked up my mug. My coffee had gone cold and I'd lost my appetite.

Derek reached across the table and patted my hand. "Are you okay, Amy?"

"Finch's Christmas House Village?" I said with a pinched voice. "It just doesn't sound right."

In fact, something was very wrong.

3

That evening, after closing up Birds & Bees for the day, I locked up, climbed into my minivan, and drove to Kim's house. I had not heard a single peep from her the rest of the day, despite having left her two phone messages.

It was time for the personal touch.

The sun sets early in western Carolina this time of year. It was long past dark as I pulled into the steep drive behind Kim's sapphire-blue Honda.

The front-porch light was off. The curtains were pulled and there was no light visible inside the house from the street. Kim lives on the opposite side of town from me in a Craftsman-style bungalow in her parents' old neighborhood. An expansive front porch with white square posts atop chestnut redbrick piers rising to slightly above the white porch railing was a great place to while away a warm summer's afternoon.

An ever-empty red flower box attached beneath the triple attic window held the occasional bird's nest but never a flower. The bungalow, with its stone-colored weatherboard, white trim, and deep red front door, reminded me of the house I'd grown up in.

Though Kim's car sat in the drive, she could have been out on a date. My gut told me she was home.

I turned off the motor, dropped my keys in my purse, and pulled my collar tight as I marched determinedly around back to the kitchen door. I didn't bother knocking. When Kim was in a mood, she wouldn't answer anyway, not even for me.

I bent and reached for the spare key she keeps hidden beneath a flowerpot on the back stoop. I didn't get a chance to use it.

The door shot open. Kim stood at the entrance in a pair of brown corduroy jeans and a billowy cream-colored sweater. "Come on in," she said rather wearily.

"That was my plan," I quipped as I replaced the key under the pot. Kim turned and walked to the kitchen table against the far wall. Furry yellow slippers covered her feet. When she moved, it looked like two baby chicks following her around.

"Can I get you anything, Amy?" A crumpled package of pecan sandies and an open bottle of rum sat within hand's reach of her.

"Are you okay?" I removed my coat and hung it over the back of an empty chair.

"Everybody hates me," Kim said, wrapping her fingers around a crystal tumbler with a splash of dark liquid at the bottom.

"Don't be so gloomy," I replied. "Things can't be that bad." I pulled a cookie from the protruding sleeve and took a nibble.

"Are you kidding? The entire town hates me." Kim brought the glass to her lips and polished off her drink. She reached for the open bottle of rum.

I grabbed the bottle and set it out of reach atop the fridge. "How about if I make us some coffee?"

Kim pulled a face but did not protest. She reached for a cookie, put the whole thing in her mouth, and clamped her jaws down on it like a vise.

"How's your head?" I called as I grabbed the glass carafe and filled it from the tap.

"What?"

"Your head. I saw Mrs. Fortuny clobber you with her purse."

Kim made a face as her hand went to her ear. "You saw that?"

I nodded. "Half the town saw it. It was kind of hard to miss."

Kim rubbed her ear once more, then dropped her long locks over it. "Mrs. Fortuny didn't miss, that's for sure," she muttered.

I couldn't help but laugh.

"It isn't funny, Amy Simms."

"Amy Simms?" I poured the water in the chamber of the machine and popped in a fresh paper filter. "Now you sound like my mother." I scooped a half-dozen spoonfuls of ground coffee into the filter, closed the lid, and hit the brew button.

I pulled out a chair and sat across from Kim. "I ran into Irma Fortuny at C Is For Cupcakes. She told me that the new owner of Christmas House Village is getting rid of all the employees and replacing them with younger, cheaper help."

Kim groaned and held her head in her hands. "He promised he would keep everything the same." Kim looked up at me. Her eyes were red and bloodshot. "So it's true?"

Kim shrugged. "Pretty much."

"Is it true that he also intends to change the name of Christmas House Village to Finch's Christmas House Village?" The coffeepot hissed and burbled in the background. I rose, pulled two mugs from the mug tree, and filled them. I set one in front of Kim. I added cream and sugar to mine.

Kim dunked a pecan sandie in hers and let it sink to the bottom. I tilted my head as she did so, thinking that it might actually be quite flavorful. I plucked a cookie from the sleeve and followed suit. "Franklin showed me the rendering for the new sign." Kim tugged at a strand of her hair. "It's true."

I brought my cup to my lips and drank. "Why didn't you tell me that Kinley's Christmas House Village had been sold?" I set my mug on the teak table. "I didn't even know it was for sale."

Kim picked up her spoon and stirred it slowly around the lip of her mug. She fished out the sodden cookie and popped it in her mouth. She chewed and swallowed before answering. "It was a secret. Mr. Belzer said the Kinley family insisted that everything had to be kept confidential."

Ellery Belzer, Kim's boss, was the owner of Belzer Realty. Ellery was a widower himself and worked seven days a week at his business. Kim worked for him on a part-time basis. After graduating junior college, she had started selling real estate in the office of Mac MacDonald. But he had closed his office after becoming our town's mayor.

"Why the secrecy?"

Kim leaned back in her chair. "It was meant to ensure that the sale went through without a hitch and without creating any disruption to the business."

"I'd say that plan backfired."

"Big-time," agreed Kim. She rose, fetched the rum from atop the fridge, and poured a splash into her coffee, giving me a look daring me to admonish her as she did so. She tilted the bottle my way.

"No, thanks." Coffee, rum, and pecan sandies did not sound like a winning blend.

Kim replaced the bottle and sat. "I still don't get it. The entire time the sale was being negotiated, Franklin repeatedly assured Mr. Belzer and me that he was going to keep Christmas House Village just the way it was. Then, the day he takes over . . ." Kim threw her hand in the air. "Whoosh! Everything goes out the window!"

"I'm surprised that the Kinley family agreed to sell. It has been in the family forever."

Kim nodded. "Yes, but when Tyrone died last year—"

"Tyrone?"

"Tyrone Kinley." I nodded and Kim continued. "Anyway, when he died a widower, that left only his grown kids: two boys and a girl. They all live out of the area and had little interest in running the business. I guess they have careers of their own."

As Kim talked, I borrowed her spoon and used it to fish out my own submerged cookie. I lifted it carefully and popped it on my tongue. It was delicious.

"The kids decided to sell?"

Kim managed a small grin. "They wanted to. They contacted Mr. Belzer and asked him to try to work it out with Virginia, but she absolutely refused to sell."

"Virginia?"

"Virginia Kinley Johnson. She was Tyrone's sister. She was married to Chris Johnson. He passed some time ago, leaving her a widow."

"With no children of her own?"

"That's right. Virginia owns, or owned, ten percent of Christmas House Village. Tyrone's children owned thirty percent apiece."

"And she wouldn't sell her share?"

Kim shook her head. "The nephews and niece reached out to her several times. Each time, she steadfastly resisted the idea of letting Christmas House Village out of the family. Finally, Tyrone Kinley's children contacted us. Belzer Realty, that is." She pouted and took a drink. "The rest is history."

I fingered the handle of my mug. "Virginia . . . I seem to remember her. Gosh, she was old even when I was a kid."

Kim nodded. "Ninety-two years old when she died."

"She died? I didn't know."

"Yes. It was a couple of months before you returned to Ruby Lake." Kim's face took on a funny expression.

"What?"

"Well, it's kind of sad, really."

"This whole day has been sad." I wiggled my fingers at her. "Spill it."

"Virginia committed suicide."

"Suicide!" My arm shook and I spilled coffee all over the table. I jumped up and grabbed the dishcloth hanging over the edge of the sink. I wiped up the spill, then rinsed out the dishcloth, wrung it out, and hung it over the faucet.

"Why would a ninety-two-year-old woman commit suicide?" I asked, following Kim out to the living room, where she threw herself down on the sofa and stuffed a pillow behind her neck.

"I don't know." Kim's fluffy yellow slippers dangled over the side of the couch. "But the police found her hanging in her garage."

"Hanging?" My hands went involuntarily to my neck.

Kim nodded. "From the rafters."

I settled myself on a big chair near the cold fireplace. "Did she leave a note?"

"I have no idea." Kim's mouth stretched open in a yawn. The stressful day was starting to catch up with her. "Anyway, when Virginia died, a widow with no children—"

I leaned forward and pulled off my shoes. "What about a will?"

"I was just getting to that. With no immediate family of her own, she left everything to Tyrone's kids."

I let out a breath. "And the three of them were free to sell Kinley's Christmas House Village."

"Finch's Christmas House Village," Kim said with dismay. "And now I can never show my face in town again."

"You? I can only imagine how Mr. Belzer must be feeling. Christmas House Village was his listing, after all, right?"

"Yes. I spoke with him several times on the phone today. He says he was as completely blindsided by Finch's actions as I and everybody else was. He said several townspeople have already come to his office and his house to strongly express their opinions."

"I'll bet. I can picture the barbed comments he must have endured from the likes of Mrs. Fortuny and all the other disgruntled employees, soon to be former employees, of Christmas House Village."

Kim nodded her agreement. "And don't forget everybody else in town who sees Christmas House Village as a Ruby Lake institution. Once everybody hears it has been sold—"

"News does spread like wildfire around here."

"Yes, and when they also learn that the new owner is renaming Christmas House Village for himself"—Kim dragged her teeth over her lower lip—"things are bound to get worse."

I forced a smile I wasn't feeling. "I wouldn't worry about it. In a day or two the whole thing will have blown over."

"Do you really think so?"

"Of course." I slipped back into my shoes. "Get some rest. I have to go. We'll talk more tomorrow."

"Fine." Kim picked up the TV remote from the coffee table and hit the power button. The TV came to life.

"You are coming in tomorrow, right?" I asked. Kim was scheduled to work half the day at Birds & Bees.

Kim nodded.

I said goodbye and left through the kitchen, grabbing my coat and bundling up before exiting. I had not wanted to say it to Kim because she was distressed enough already, but she was probably right.

If the scene outside Christmas House Village and the sentiments of others like Mrs. Fortuny were any indication, the situation was bound to get worse.

4

"Did you know that Virginia Johnson took her own life, Mom?" I was driving my mom to the doctor's office and we were nearly there.

Mom turned suddenly, taking her eyes off the passing scenery. "Where did that question come from, Amy?"

I kept my eyes on the road and my hands on the wheel. We were on our way to Dr. Zann's office. Dr. Zann had been treating our family here in Ruby Lake for years. He'd given me all my childhood shots.

"I was just wondering. I was talking to Kim the other day. She told me what happened to her." I took a left turn and pulled into the parking lot of the tan brick office building. "So you knew?"

"Yes, of course." She made tsk-tsk noises. "Such a tragedy. Why on earth are you asking about Mrs. Johnson? To tell you the truth, I don't even like to think about such things. Too depressing."

I smiled. Mom was very sensitive about the subject of death. When we lost Dad, it had hit her hard. Now she was seeing Ben Harlan, Derek's dad, on a casual basis, but I felt there was something more than mere companionship developing between them.

I grabbed a parking space and helped Mom down from the minivan. She insisted she did not need my help. My mother suffers from muscular dystrophy; though, so far, it had expressed itself in a relatively mild form.

"I hate these annual checkups," Mom complained as we strolled arm in arm up past the row of late-blooming lavender azaleas that flanked the sidewalk leading to Dr. Zann's medical office.

"I know you do, but it's important." We went through this same discussion on every visit. I let go of my mother's arm and pulled the door open for her. "Let me help you with your coat."

A glass partition slid open and we stepped inside the office. "Hello, ladies," called the doctor's wife and receptionist, Nellie Zann. "Hello, Nellie." Mom unzipped her blue parka and handed it to me. I waved to Mrs. Zann, hooked Mom's bulky coat on the coatrack, then did the same with my own coat while Mom signed in at reception. Nellie Zann checked off her name and told her she could go on back to examination room two. That was one of the things I liked best about Dr. Zann's office. It was small and cozy, only two exam rooms. Dr. Zann was not part of some big corporate medical group filled with unknown faces. There were only eight chairs in the waiting room and seven of them were empty. An elderly gentleman in a thick coat snoozed, the back of his head pressed against the striped wallpaper.

I took a seat in the sun near the window and flipped idly through a recent history magazine—Dr. Zann was something of a history nut.

Mrs. Zann answered a phone call, then stuck her face through the reception window. "How's business, Amy? Is everything going well?" Mrs. Zann was a cheerful woman with a rosy complexion. Her coppery-red hair and chestnut-brown eyes brought the image of a pheasant to mind.

"Yes, thank you."

"I've been meaning to come check out your store," Mrs. Zann said. "I've been telling my husband how nice it would be to have a bird feeder outside the office. It would give me something to look at when things are slow. But Richard says that with winter coming on there's hardly any point."

I set down my magazine and walked over to the counter. "That's not the case at all," I replied, happy for a chance to talk birds. "It's equally important to provide a source of food for the birds in the winter as it is any other time. Sure, there are fewer birds around, but sunflower seeds alone can provide a high protein, high energy food source to help them get through when other types of food are scarce."

"I've made up my mind then," Mrs. Zann said with a twinkle in her eye. "I'm coming in no matter what the old grouch says."

I laughed.

"Tell me," began Mrs. Zann, "is Esther Pilaster still living with you?"

"Oh, yeah." When I'd bought the three-story house with the intention of turning the first floor into my bird lover's general store, Esther was already living there as a renter. She's still there. She is now working for me at Birds & Bees, too. Mom hired her. Mom, along with her sister, my aunt Betty, was a silent investor in my business. Somewhere along the line, the *silent* part of that expression had gotten lost. "Is Esther a patient of yours?"

Mrs. Zann nodded. "Practically everybody in town is. Especially if they are over sixty-five years old. What about you?"

"What about me?"

"When's the last time you had a checkup?"

The corners of my mouth turned down. "I refuse to answer on the grounds that it may incriminate me."

Mrs. Zann's hands went to the computer keyboard. "How's next Tuesday? I have a ten thirty open."

My mind went through a million reasons to decline, but I couldn't come up with a plausible excuse. "Fine." I sighed. "You got me." The doctor's wife wrote out a reminder card and handed it to me. I slipped it into a pocket of my purse. "Was Virginia Johnson a patient?"

Mrs. Zann pulled her lips tight. "Yes, the poor woman passed away. That was some time ago, as I remember. Why do you ask now, Amy?"

"I only heard about her passing from my friend Kim the other day. I had no idea."

"You had been away from home a long time." The phone at her desk rang and Mrs. Zann raised a finger to me while she answered it. After making an appointment for the caller and entering it on her computer, she turned back to me. "Now, what were we talking about?"

I leaned my arm on the counter. "You were telling me about Mrs. Johnson. Had she been depressed before . . . you know?"

Mrs. Zann's gaze darted to the waiting room. Satisfied that it was empty but for the napping gentleman, she said, "No, not so as I noticed. Maybe Richard would know better."

The doctor's wife bit her lip. "I probably shouldn't say, but she is dead so it can't hurt to tell you that for a ninety-two-year-old, Virginia Johnson was in reasonable health. I mean, she had the usual problems, a bit of a weak heart, osteoporosis, and her rheumatoid arthritis was quite bad, but it was under control."

"But not particularly depressed?"

Mrs. Zann shook her head. "No, yet who is to say what somebody else is really thinking or feeling? She was old, perhaps very lonely." She focused her eyes on me. "Maybe one day she simply decided she'd had enough. But as I recall, Richard was just as surprised as I was that she chose to end her life that way. As we all were."

I nodded. "I guess hearing about Mrs. Johnson just started me wondering about my mom."

"Your mom?"

"Don't get me wrong, she seems happy enough." My eyes drifted toward the examination room. "But what with losing Dad and the muscular dystrophy . . ."

Mrs. Zann smiled gently. "You worry that Barbara might suffer silently from depression and . . ."

I nodded once more. There was no reason to finish the sentence.

"I wouldn't worry about your mother." Mrs. Zann reached up to the window and patted my arm where it rested on the counter. "I think she's in good hands, especially with you back in town."

"I'm sure you're right."

"As for Virginia Johnson, bless her soul, and I know this might sound like a strange thing to say, but maybe her going when she did was for the best."

"How do you mean?"

"I'm not sure Virginia would be very happy to learn that Kinley's Christmas House Village has been sold to an outsider."

"You heard about that?"

"Who hasn't?" Mrs. Zann turned at the sound of my mother's approach from the back hall. "It's practically all the whole town's talking about."

"What's the whole town talking about?" Mom inquired, as she appeared from the hall and handed Mrs. Zann a printed form.

"Christmas House Village," I answered.

"I would think there are more important issues to think about than that," said Dr. Zann, walking up to stand beside my mother. Richard Zann stood just over six feet and, though in his early sixties, remained active. I often saw him biking around town. He still managed to have all his hair, too. "You, for instance, Barbara, need to see that you get more exercise. A good long walk several times a week should do the trick."

"Yes, Doctor," Mother said rather unenthusiastically.

"Good idea," I said. "You can accompany me on some bracing crack-of-dawn bird walks."

Mom raised one eyebrow. "If by crack of dawn, you mean nine a.m., and that walk includes coffee and bagels, I just might take you up on that, young lady."

We all laughed.

Dr. Zann wrote out a prescription and handed it to my mother. "Be sure to have Dr. Ajax send over the results of your exam when they're ready, Mrs. Simms."

"I will."

"What exam?" I asked as Mom came through to the waiting room. I grabbed our coats and helped my mother into hers before zipping up my own.

"Dr. Ajax is my neurologist. I have an appointment with him coming up." I narrowed my eyes at her as I held open the door. "Is everything okay, Mom?" "Of course." She patted my arm. "It's an annual thing. Nothing out of the ordinary. Dr. Ajax's specialty is MD. I see him once every year. Sometimes more, if necessary."

"The name doesn't sound familiar." We walked out to the parking lot and I unlocked the minivan and helped Mom up, then went around to the driver's side and climbed inside, starting up the engine to get the heat going.

"He's with Rheumatology and Neurology Associates over in Swan Ridge." Mom stuck her hands in front of the air vent, letting the warm air seep into her skin.

"What happened to that specialist you were seeing in Raleigh?" I backed up the minivan and turned toward the street entrance.

"I heard good things about Dr. Ajax, and his office is much closer. So far, I've been very happy with him."

"As long as you're happy with him, I'm all for saving a two-hundred-mile trip."

"Speaking of trips . . ."

"Yes?"

"Would you miss me if I was gone?"

"What kind of question is that?" I pressed my foot down on the brake. "Of course I'd miss you." I narrowed my eyes at her. "You're not thinking of doing anything crazy, are you?"

"What's so crazy about going to Florida?" Mom said, nonplussed. "It's warm there."

"Florida?" I checked the street and eased up on the brake. "I thought you were talking about . . ." I should have known better. All this death and depression had been getting into my head.

Mom turned in her seat to face me. "About what?"

"Lunch," I said. "I'm crazy hungry, aren't you?"

"Yes, and it's my treat."

"You'll get no argument from me." Was Mom really thinking of moving to Florida? I had just moved back to Ruby Lake to be with her. Was she actually considering leaving her lifelong home? "What are you in the mood for?"

"Diner food."

"Ruby's it is."

We returned home and went straight to the popular diner. Over burgers, we talked. "What's all this about Florida, Mom?"

Mom played with her French fries. I wasted no time with my onion rings. I ate three of them in a row and my hand dove back into the basket for number four like it had a mind of its own.

"It's warm there." Mom pinched her coat closer as if to make her point, although the diner was plenty warm. A cup of mint-green tea steamed away on the saucer beside her.

"If that's what you want." I nibbled at ring number four. "I'll miss you."

"It would only be for a couple of months in the winter."

"Oh!"

"What? Did you think I meant permanently?"

"You had me worried." I waved my onion ring at her. "But only for a second." I bent the ring in two and placed it in my mouth and chewed. "Florida, huh?" I washed the fried ring down with strawberry milkshake. It's important to get a dose of dairy every day. "What about . . ."

"What about what?"

"You know," I said, feeling a bit uncomfortable. Mom and I are close, but we have never really talked about her relationship with Ben Harlan.

"I'm not sure." Mom sipped her tea and looked out the window. "You know how I felt about your father, still do," she said, blinking several times as if to stem the flow of tears.

"I know." I reached across the table and patted her hand. Then I *borrowed* a handful of her French fries.

"Ben's lovely. We've become dear friends."

"Anything more than that?"

A smile crept over my mother's face. "Right now, a dear friend is the best for me." She picked up her burger and took a small bite. I followed suit. "It's what's best for you that I'm most concerned with, Amy."

I was taken aback. "Don't worry about me, Mom," I assured her. "I'm doing great. Business is slow, admittedly, but it's steady."

"I know, and I know you're going to make a big success of it. It's your personal life I'm talking about."

"What about my personal life?"

"You live with your mother. I don't want to be in the way."

I leaned back, pressing my hands against the edge of the table. "So, is that it? Is that what all this Florida talk is about?"

I tilted my glass and sucked at my thick milkshake through its fat paper straw, then wiped the strawberry ice cream from my upper lip. "Well?"

Mom studied the burger on her plate, lifting the top half of the bun and readjusting the lettuce leaf and tomato slice. "You and Derek are getting close and, don't get me wrong, I think that's wonderful but . . ."

"You're worried about being in the way." I snorted. "You'll never be in the way. I love living with you, Mom."

"Are you sure?"

"Have I ever give you any reason to doubt it?"

"No," my mother admitted.

"Who knows," I said, "maybe one day I'll have a grown daughter and she'll let me live with her."

"Will that include Derek?" Mom teased.

My answer was to eat a couple more onion rings, after which I answered, "Let's get through Christmas without any more problems before we worry about our futures. Deal?"

"Deal." Mom picked up her burger with both hands and took a solid bite. "From now on, let's focus on the holiday spirit."

"I'll eat to that," I said, attacking my burger.

5

"I don't know what everybody is complaining about," complained Esther. "Things change. Life goes on. Deal with it."

The subject, once again, was Kinley's Christmas House Village. The place was Birds & Bees. Nearly two weeks had gone by and little had changed regarding the town's latest resident and business owner, Franklin Finch. The demonstrations against him continued unabated. Some Ruby Lakers had long memories and held even longer grudges.

Esther was seated on the hardwood floor in the middle of the aisle, pulling new merchandise from a cardboard box beside her and placing item after item on the shelf. With Christmas around the corner, we had decided to stock up on packages of holiday- and bird-themed greeting cards.

Esther's a small, narrow-shouldered, elflike septuagenarian with a hawkish nose, sagging eyelids, and silvery hair. Gray-blue eyes hide under a pair of wispy white eyebrows. The woman has absolutely no filter when it comes to speaking her mind. A bluebird-blue Birds & Bees apron was tied around her waist and neck. A peach-colored, floor-length dress billowed out around it.

"I only wish everybody felt like you do, Esther," moaned Kim, who was busily stacking cellophane-wrapped packs of suet on the shelf above her.

"I don't understand why everybody is still mad at you," I said, moving to unlock the front door, though it was five minutes until the official opening time for the day. "You weren't responsible for the sale of the business. That was your boss's doing. Besides, Belzer Realty only handled the sale."

I twisted the thumb lock and turned the CLOSED sign to OPEN. "If folks around town are going to be mad at anyone, it's Kinley's children they should have a beef with." I crossed back to the register and checked to be sure there was enough cash in the till to make change. "Even then, the business is theirs to do with as they choose."

"*Was* theirs," Kim corrected. She straightened, went to the storeroom for a second box of suet cakes, and said as she passed me, "Everybody blames me and Mr. Belzer for not telling them about the potential sale before it happened."

"So they could stop it?"

Kim dropped the new box on the floor between the aisles. "Something like that."

Esther rose and scurried to the front door as two gray-haired women entered.

"You know," I began, rubbing my finger over my ear, "Birds and Bees has a contract for a two-gross of birdseed ornaments. Mom and I have already begun making them."

"I know," Kim said. "There must be hundreds of them piling up back there already."

She was talking about the storeroom. I had set up a long folding table I'd borrowed from a neighbor, on which we crafted our holiday ornaments. After some discussion, we had decided to use snowman and gingerbread-man molds.

The ornaments were easy to make. We combined safflower seed, two kinds of millet, and sunflower seed; the seeds combined with flour, water, agar, and corn syrup were pressed into molds. We cut plastic straws to create a hole through which we inserted red or green ribbon so the ornaments could be hung on Christmas trees. It was a slow, time-consuming but straightforward process. We had been crafting them in our spare time during store hours.

Christmas House Village had ordered nearly three hundred of the ornaments, a dozen dozen of each, and we were due to deliver the full order soon. We only had a few batches of snowmen left to go.

I untied my apron and fluffed my hair. "I think I'll go introduce myself to Mr. Finch. You and Esther can handle things here, can't you?"

Esther was hovering over her customers. She'd given them each a cookie and a cup of coffee and was now extolling the virtues of having a beehive of their own. "Nothing like honey that comes from your own yard," I heard her say.

The two women nodded, clearly intrigued.

"Go." Kim waved her hand at me.

I grabbed my coat and scarf from the storeroom. "Shall I say hello for you?"

Kim pulled a face. "Are you kidding? Mr. Finch is mad at me and Mr. Belzer because of the way the town is treating him, and the town is mad at me and Mr. Belzer because of Mr. Finch." She pulled at her hair. "It's enough to drive me crazy." She tilted her head. "Maybe I should go away for the holidays," she said with a sigh.

"Go away? Where would you go?"

"I could go to Florida," she said with a shrug. "Visit my mother."

"And miss your first Christmas with Dan?" Dan Sutton and Kim had recently begun dating, not long after Kim had broken up with her previous boyfriend.

Kim frowned. "Some Christmas this is turning out to be." She wrung her hands. "But things could be worse. At least I've got my job. I really do feel sorry for all those people that Mr. Finch is putting out of work."

"I know you do." I pulled on my gloves. "Who knows? Maybe Mr. Finch will have a change of heart."

"You mean change his mind?" Kim looked dubious. "I doubt it."

"Leave it to me," I said bravely. "I can be very persuasive."

* * * *

I drove uptown, past the town square that was home to the city offices and the farmer's market, and found a parking spot in the off-street public lot down the road from Christmas House Village. The parking situation at Christmas House Village had always been difficult. Between Thanksgiving and Christmas it was near impossible because they had no parking lot of their own.

I crossed the street to where a dozen or so people stood outside Christmas House Village, most of them elderly. They didn't look happy. A squad car was parked at the curb.

I spotted Dan Sutton bundled up inside the squad car with his leather jacket zipped up to his ears. I waved and walked over.

He rolled down the window. Steam rose from the paper cup of tea in his hand. As indicated by the imprint on the cup, the beverage had come from the Coffee and Tea House on the square. "Morning, Amy." Dan was a stocky fellow who knew his way around a weight room. He's Hawaiian on his father's side, with short brown hair and big brown eyes.

"Hi, Dan." I turned to the small crowd. "What's going on?"

He took a sip before answering. "Nothing. Chief Kennedy asked me to sit here for an hour. Then I can go."

"What's he afraid of? Does he really think there could be trouble? From these people?" They all looked like kindly old ladies and gentlemen.

"No, but that new guy, Mr. Finch, has been giving the chief all kinds of grief."

"Such as?"

"Such as complaining that these good folks here are disrupting his business and that he has every right to do with Christmas House Village whatever he has a mind to, seeing as how it belongs to him now."

"It's hard to argue with that." I draped my arms atop the squad car. "It's too bad everybody can't sit down and try to find a way to work things out though."

"Don't I wish. Kim is really upset." He cursed under his breath. "Then again, it seems like everybody in town is upset. It's awful. Townspeople are calling the chief telling him to arrest Finch—when the man's done nothing wrong. The chief has talked himself sick trying to explain that there's nothing he can do. So now they are all mad at him, too."

"That can't be doing much for Jerry's mood," I noted.

"You've got that right," Dan was quick to agree. "And Mr. Belzer is mad at the chief because he claims he's been getting all kinds of harassing calls and death threats because he was the real estate agent handling the sale." Dan let out a sigh that filled the squad car, then took another sip of his tea.

"Death threats?"

He shrugged. "So he claims." He set his cup between his legs. "What are you doing here?"

"Business. Over the summer, I made a deal with Kinley's Christmas House Village to supply them with several hundred birdseed ornaments for the holidays."

"Good for you. You really seem to be making a go of things with that store of yours."

The computer screen attached to his dashboard beeped. Dan glanced at it then turned to me. "A school bus has a flat tire and is partially blocking the road," he explained.

Officer Reynolds's voice erupted over the speaker, saying that he would handle the traffic situation. Dan turned down the volume of his radio. "Good," he said to me with a grin, "I can finish my tea." He sipped. "Yeah, when you first set up Birds and Bees, the chief was sure you wouldn't last till Christmas."

"Was he now?" Jerry and I—now Chief Jerry Kennedy—have a long history of mutual dislike. Our relationship hadn't been helped by a murdered man being found in my home prior to opening the store, or that I had been found standing over the dead man with the murder weapon.

But the past was the past, and today I had other things to deal with.

I took a deep breath and looked over the fence at the half dozen houses that comprised Christmas House Village. The entire scene looked so idyllic on the outside, if one avoided glancing at the surly, stubborn crowd on the sidewalk. "I guess I should be getting inside."

"Good luck." Dan rolled up the window as I walked toward the crowd. I got some ugly looks as I edged between them and started up the sidewalk. A big banner hung from two of the gas-burning streetlamps that lined the sidewalk, lighting the path from one Victorian house to the next for the evening shoppers. The ornate, cast-iron antique Corinthian column streetlights added to the small-town charm.

The banner's giant red letters spelled out: FINCH'S CHRISTMAS HOUSE VILLAGE.

"That's not going to win our Mr. Finch any new friends," I said under my breath as I passed beneath the banner.

A magnificent Fraser fir, taller than a small skyscraper and fatter than ten Santa Clauses, occupied most of the small circle of grass about ten steps from the entrance to the village. The Fraser fir was North Carolina's most popularly grown Christmas tree. It grows best in the higher elevations. On more than one occasion, my father had driven my mom and me up to the Carolina mountains where we got one fresh and carried it home tied to the roof of our car.

The Christmas House Village fir was said to be nearly as old as the enclave itself. The tree with its beautiful blue-green needles rose nearly sixty feet overhead, casting a shadow over me as I passed. Legend had it that Owen Kinley himself had planted the tree when he'd opened the original Christmas House store.

Each year over Thanksgiving weekend, the tree gets decorated with big, bright, red and green ornaments. At night, between Christmas and New Year's Day, it is illuminated with the light of a thousand bulbs. Carolers, a mix of adults and children, greet customers as they come into the village each evening.

The sidewalk split at the circle, going around the village on each side, then connected up again on the other side. Shaker-style wooden benches flanked the cobblestone walk. I went to the left.

I noticed a uniformed security guard leaning against one of the porch columns of the nearest house on the right, his eyes fixed on the crowd. Was he expecting trouble?

I stopped and waved to him. "Can you tell me where I might find Mr. Finch?"

He was a slim Japanese American, around fifty years old. He turned and pointed. "He's in his office, I expect. Do you know how to get there, miss?"

This was not the man I had seen with Mr. Finch the other morning. The other guard had been younger, huskier, more dangerous looking than the mild-mannered man before me.

"Yes, I remember." The office was in the last house on the left, up on the second floor. I had met there with Christmas House Village's manager, Eve Dunnellon, in her office when we'd inked our deal over the past summer. She was a sweet woman in her midforties, and I looked forward to seeing her again.

Above the office had been Tyrone Kinley's living quarters. I suspected it would be Franklin Finch's living quarters now.

He'd probably feel safer living there than anyplace else in town. At least until the townspeople calmed down. As I walked up the sidewalk, I noticed there were many shoppers moving in and out of the Christmas houses despite the small demonstration going on outside.

Along the way, a heavily bundled man in a dark blue parka and red knit beanie came walking toward me with his head down. A wiry black moustache clung to the underside of his nose like some exotic caterpillar trying to keep warm. His head bobbed up and down like a pigeon's with each step he took. It was Kim's boss, Ellery Belzer.

"Good morning, Mr. Belzer." I stopped in the center of the sidewalk.

He looked up and it was a moment before recognition crossed his face. "Hello, Amy. How are you?" Tufts of brown hair mixed with gray sprouted from the edges of his cap.

"Fine. You?"

Truth be told, the poor man didn't look so good. Mr. Belzer's face was drawn and there were puffy, deep brown circles under his dark blue eyes. "I've been better."

Ellery Belzer sounded like a defeated man.

"Were you meeting with Mr. Finch?" I asked.

"Yes. We had some details to discuss."

"He sure has a lot of ideas for Christmas House Village, doesn't he?"

Mr. Belzer smiled sourly. "If by ideas you mean changes, then that's exactly what he has." The real estate agent shook his head. "I had no idea what a hornet's nest of trouble the sale of Christmas House Village was going to be."

"Still," I said, "you must have made quite a commission."

Mr. Belzer's brow shot up. "Believe me, Amy, no commission is worth all this. Though, to tell you the truth . . ." He paused and looked over his shoulder toward the house containing Christmas House Village's office.

"What?" I asked curiously.

"Talking to Mr. Finch . . ." Maddeningly, he stopped once again.

"Yes? What is it?"

He stepped closer. "Now this is just between you and me, you understand?"

I nodded readily. "Of course."

"Well"—he looked over his shoulder once more, then looked at me—"talking to Finch, I get the idea that he's rather unhappy that he's bought Christmas House Village."

I tilted my head. "You mean, like buyer's remorse?"

"Big-time." Belzer shrugged. "At least, that was the impression I got. In fact, the man seemed depressed." He leaned in even farther and I felt his warm breath on my cheek. "The man has a history of depression, you know. That's part of the reason he left New York. Forced out of his own business. His wife divorced him." Mr. Belzer shook his head. "All in one year, mind you."

"That is rough."

"Mr. Finch wanted to make a new start. But now . . ."

Mr. Belzer had an annoying habit of letting his voice trail off. Kim might be used to it, but this particular trait of his personality was driving me crazy.

"He's not thinking of selling already, is he?"

Mr. Belzer merely shrugged as he stepped back and thrust his hands deep into his coat. "I'm afraid that would be a confidential matter." Nonetheless, he winked at me. "Good morning, Ms. Simms."

"Goodbye, Mr. Belzer." I resumed my walk, quickening my pace for warmth—it was cold standing in one place too long outdoors this time of year.

I climbed the festively decorated porch of Elf House, which was painted green with white gingerbread trim. Green garlands with red ribbons wound in and out of the porch railings. Each of the six houses was a unique color on the outside and contained an exclusive assortment of Christmas-related gifts and decorations on the inside.

The architectural layout of the houses themselves had remained untouched, giving the stores a very homey feeling as one wandered through each room. The kitchens remained as they would have been when these houses were occupied by families going about their daily lives. The kitchen counters, open cabinets, and even the refrigerators and stovetops in each house had been decorated with Christmas merchandise.

Even the bathrooms held Christmas-themed bath towels and shower curtains and more. In one house, as I remembered, Santa Claus sat soaking in the tub, hidden under a blanket of fake, foamy, snowflake-shaped bubbles.

From front to back, the houses of Christmas House Village were named Santa's House, Reindeer House, and Elf House on the left; Frosty's House,

Sugarplum House, and Nutcracker House were on the right side. Cobblestone paths connected houses on the same side of the walk to each other.

Elf House's theme included an abundance of toys in the rooms, from Christmas trains whirring forever and ever around artfully decorated artificial Christmas trees, to giant, foam-filled candy canes. Mechanized elves stayed busily working and whistling while they did so.

A woman in a green dress and green elf hat with white trim greeted me. "Good morning," she said with a cheery smile. "Happy holidays."

"Thank you." The living room smelled like it had been dipped overnight in pine oil and cinnamon-stick incense. Between the cacophony and the overpowering scent, one day in this house and I'd be batty.

"Are you looking for something special?" the middle-aged woman asked.

"Actually, it's someone special," I explained. "I'm here to see Mr. Finch."

Her smile faded and her finger pointed toward the ceiling. "He's in his office. You can go on up—if you dare."

"Excuse me?"

"Nothing, dear. Never mind me." She turned away.

I thanked her and headed for the narrow stairs. The old steps sagged under my weight as I climbed with trepidation to the second floor. Small windows to the outside had been cut into the stairwell. There was a short hallway to the right along which several doors were spaced. Each door was closed and held a sign clearly stating that the offices were private.

Unlike the rest of this house and every other house in the village, the second floor was unadorned and the contrast with the heavily decorated rooms below was jarring.

A smaller, steeper stairway along the left wall led upward to what must have been the living quarters.

I approached the nearest door. As I was about to knock, I heard voices. One was yelling, the other placating. I couldn't understand a word but I understood the tone.

Somebody was mad.

This was probably not the best time to talk to Franklin Finch, but I was here now, so there was really nothing to do but get it over with. Besides, this was business, and he would be glad to hear that our order would be ready for him on time. I was also determined to try and play peacemaker. There had to be some way to work things out between Mr. Finch and the townspeople.

"He can't be as bad as people make him out," I softly assured myself.

I took a deep breath to settle my nerves, played over again in my mind what I wanted to say, and knocked.

A security guard opened the door and peered at me. His thick brows pulled together over his forehead. His dark brown eyes examined me from head to toe. This was the guard I'd seen at Mr. Finch's side the morning of the first demonstration.

I squirmed uncomfortably.

"Can I help you, ma'am? This floor is off limits to shoppers."

"Yes, uh, Max," I said, reading his nametag. "I'm Amy Simms. I came to see Mr. Finch."

Max scratched the side of his nose. "What about?" He had short black hair and tiny silver studs in each earlobe. The green and red tattoo of a snake of some sort started at the back of his right hand and disappeared up his sleeve.

"Let the woman in, Max. Let her tell me herself why she's here." It sounded like the odd security guard had two strikes against him on Mr. Finch's scorecard already.

Max pushed the door open and stepped silently aside.

I poked my head through the open door. Franklin Finch sat behind a massive oak desk stacked high with papers and Christmas ornaments. "Mr. Finch?"

Finch made a face meant to indicate that I was wasting his valuable time. "Yes, yes. Come in. Come in."

The new owner sat in a high-back wooden chair. His three-piece suit was black wool and his tie black silk.

Two intricately carved antique oak accent chairs, upholstered in shiny yellow-and-gold-striped fabric, faced the desk. The chair on the left had been laden down with stacks of paper-filled folders atop which a black overcoat had been tossed.

"You say your name is Simms?"

"Yes." Up close, his brown eyes appeared even darker and his complexion more sallow, almost green. His hair was as black as a lump of coal. And was it my imagination, or did his nose look remarkably like the beak of one of his namesakes, the warbler finch, long, thin, and pointy? "You see, I—"

Mr. Finch held up a hand to stop me. "You can go, Max. Check on Leo." He scanned a report in front of him. "Make sure he's doing his job. I've had enough of all this mischief," he added rather angrily.

"Yessir." Max departed, leaving the door ajar.

Finch turned his attention back to me. "You'll have to excuse Max. He's young and he's new."

His lips curled as he eyed me curiously. "Are you here for a job? Have you ever worked sales?" Mr. Finch splayed his fingers out atop an olive-green blotter. "We're taking applications. It's the busy season, of course. Experience is preferred but not a requirement."

"Yes, I mean, no." Was he going to let me get a word in edgewise? His lips turned down with annoyance. "Which is it?"

"I own Birds and Bees."

Finch frowned. "I don't understand. You own birds and bees? What does that mean? Are you trying to say you own pets?" He turned his attention to the hodgepodge of papers spread across his desk. "If you are not here for a job, you'll have to excuse me. I'm really quite busy, miss."

"No, Birds and Bees. It's a store. It's at the end of Lake Shore Drive near the marina. You must have seen it."

He gave me a blank look.

"We don't sell pets; we sell bird-feeding and bird-watching supplies, plus some items for butterflies, bees . . ." I cleared my throat. "And other wildlife."

Mr. Finch looked across his desk at me, and he did not look impressed. "I fail to understand what that has to do with me. I'm selling Christmas."

My hand was shaking as I fumbled with my purse. The man was making me nervous. "I have a contract with Christmas House Village. We're providing birdseed Christmas ornaments for you. Eve Dunnellon and I worked out the arrangement this past summer."

The new owner frowned. "Birdseed? Why on earth would I want to sell birdseed?"

My mouth went dry. "I have a copy of the contract." I carefully removed the folded document from my purse and showed it to him.

Mr. Finch pulled a pair of reading glasses from his inside coat pocket and slipped them over his long nose. He took the contract from my trembling hand.

I watched his lips move as he silently read. After a moment, he removed his glasses and slipped them back in his pocket. He pushed the contract back toward me with his finger. "*That* is a contract with Kinley's Christmas House Village," he said matter-of-factly.

"Yes, I know," I said, unsure where he was going with that statement.

"*This*," he said, spreading his hands proudly, "as you may have noticed by the new signage, is *Finch's* Christmas House Village."

"I don't understand . . ."

He smiled, revealing a row of uneven lower teeth. "Your contract is not valid, Ms. Simms. Now, if you will excuse me, I have other business to attend to." He rose, crossed from behind his desk, and turned to leave.

I reached a hand out and held his arm. "But we had a deal."

Finch shook his head. "No, we did not and we do not have a deal. Your deal was with Eve Dunnellon. Ms. Dunnellon is no longer with us." He waved me out the office door. "And Kinley's Christmas House Village no longer exists."

I gathered my things and crossed to the door. I spotted Max, whom I thought long gone, leaning against the wall in the hallway. I stopped and turned resolutely. "Mr. Finch, I really wish you would reconsider—"

"I've made up my mind, Ms. Simms." Mr. Finch fluttered his hand at me. "Not about the ornaments, about Christmas House Village."

He furled his brow. "What about Christmas House Village?"

"Don't you think it would be nice to keep the original name, Kinley's, and to keep all the loyal employees who have been working here?"

"Max!" shouted Mr. Finch. "I know you're lurking out there!"

Max blushed and stuck his head in the doorway. "Sir?"

"Ms. Simms seems to be having some trouble leaving. Please see that she finds her way off the premises." Mr. Finch looked at me rather pointedly as he added, "*My* premises."

"It's nearly Christmas, surely that means something to you!" I insisted.

The corners of Mr. Finch's mouth turned down sharply. "It means profits, Ms. Simms. It means money in the bank. I invested heavily in Finch's Christmas House Village and I intend to see a return on that investment."

"Even at the expense of the people who helped make it what it is?"

His brow went up and he grinned an evil grin. "What it is, is *mine*. Mine to do with as I like." He folded his hands atop his desk. "Which is precisely what I intend to do."

Mr. Finch drilled the security guard with his eyes. Max tugged at his collar and stepped toward me.

I moved away. "Can I see your feet, Mr. Finch?" I snapped angrily.

"My feet? What do you want to see my feet for? What are you blathering about?" He pointed to his security guard. "Get her out of here, Max. I am losing my patience."

"Because I'm just wondering if your shoes are too tight!"

Max stuck out his hand and I brushed it away. "Keep your hands to yourself, buster."

The security guard shot Finch an odd look, then turned to me. "You heard the boss."

I frowned. "I heard him, all right." I stuffed the now useless contract in my purse and left.

6

"He really said that?" Derek removed a second slice of mushroom and artichoke pizza from the box and set it on his plate. I was still working on my first slice.

"Yes. Do you think I should sue?" It had been two days since Franklin Finch had practically thrown me out of his office, refusing to acknowledge our business arrangement. And I was still fuming.

"I don't think that would be in your own best interests, Amy." Derek grabbed the neck of his beer bottle and lifted it to his lips. "And lawyers can be expensive."

I scooted nearer him on the sofa. "What? I don't get the girlfriend discount?"

We were in Derek's apartment sharing a pizza I'd brought over for dinner. I'd picked it up at Brewer's Biergarten, which was located next door to Birds & Bees. The beer was an American blond ale called Bottled Blondie that had been created by Paul Anderson, one of the biergarten's owners.

Derek didn't have a kitchen table in his tiny apartment, so we ate our dinner on the sofa, using the coffee table to hold our food and drink.

Derek ran his hand along my thigh. "Of course you do. I just think the whole thing isn't going to be worth the trouble. Let it go. Get on with your life."

"I suppose," I answered, frowning as I said it.

"Trust me," he said, after taking a healthy bite of pizza. "You'll feel better if you just let it go."

"I suppose you're right. My bump-free future's getting bumpier by the minute." I looked toward the window overlooking the street. It was dark outside and the lights of Finch's Christmas House Village twinkled like magic fireflies. Unfortunately, something darker lurked beneath those lights.

"I only wish everybody in Ruby Lake could take your advice when it comes to Franklin Finch and Christmas House Village. The entire town would be better off forgetting all about Franklin Finch—as much as I dislike the rat—and getting on with their lives. Especially with Christmas just around the corner." I frowned. "I haven't seen any signs of tensions easing yet, though."

Derek chuckled. "Give it time, Amy. Folks will come around."

"I don't know. Some of them are pretty mad. Kim told me that some of the old employees have accepted Finch's offer and agreed to stay on for the thirty days to train their replacements, as much as they hated to, because they needed the money."

"I agree. That's low. But it's not illegal."

"It ought to be." I bit into my now-cold slice and chewed thoughtfully. "I feel bad for them, training their own replacements. I don't know what I would do in their places."

A sidewalk Santa near the entrance to Christmas House Village moved his arm up and down, slowly ringing his silver bell. A large basket sat at his feet. As people dropped in donations, he handed out candy canes.

"Be thankful you own your own business." Derek handed me a warm slice and I held out my plate.

"I am." I glanced at the television. Derek was indulging my love of musicals by watching *White Christmas* with me. Rosemary Clooney and Bing Crosby had launched into "Count Your Blessings (Instead of Sheep)," written by Irving Berlin. "You're right," I said.

"I am?"

"Not you," I said with a smile. "Him." I pointed to the flat-screen television. "I need to count my blessings." I leaned over and kissed his warm cheek. "Like you."

"I'll take that," Derek answered, pulling me closer.

"Mmm, you're nice and warm." I pressed my side into his and crossed my left foot over my right ankle.

"I'd light a fire, but without a fireplace that could cause some serious damage," Derek quipped.

"Very funny." I noticed his bottle was empty. "Can I get you another beer?" Derek started to rise. "No, I can get it."

"I offered. Stay. I'll be right back." I rose and crossed in my stockinged feet to the galley kitchen. It being pizza-and-beer night, I'd dressed casually for our very casual date: blue jeans and a blue sweater with snowflakes on the front and back.

In the refrigerator, I found a row of beer bottles on the second rack and pulled out two. The bottle opener was on the coffee table.

"Your purse is ringing," Derek said. He lifted it by its strap and handed it to me. I handed him the beers in exchange.

"I wonder who could be calling." Everybody that mattered knew I was on a date. I dug out my phone and looked at the screen. "It's Kim."

I stepped away from the TV so my conversation with her wouldn't disturb Derek—not that I was sure he cared. "Hi, Kim. What's up?" I raised a finger to let Derek know that I'd only be a minute.

"Amy," Kim whispered. "Where are you?"

Derek picked up the remote off the coffee table and hit the mute button. Next, he helped himself to another slice of pizza.

"That's why you called? To ask where I am? You know where I am. I'm on a date with Derek." I twirled a finger next to my ear and mouthed, "She's crazy," for Derek's benefit.

He grinned and settled back on the sofa.

"So you're at Derek's apartment?"

"Yes. I am. Why?"

"Good. That's good." Kim's voice was a shaky whisper.

"Why?" I asked. "Where are you?"

"Are you alone?"

"What? No, I'm not alone. I just told you. I am at Derek's apartment. *With* Derek." I rolled my eyes.

"Shh!" Kim admonished me. "I don't want Derek to hear. I mean, maybe we should just keep this to ourselves." There was a long pause.

"Kim?" I looked at my phone to see if we were still connected or if I'd lost her. "Are you still there?"

"Yes," she whispered. "I'm here." A short pause. "Oh, Amy," she sighed mysteriously, "I just don't know what to do."

"Kim," I said, my heart now pounding with worry. I moved to the kitchen. "Tell me where you are."

"I'm across the street."

"Across the street?"

"At Christmas House Village."

"Christmas House Village? Now?" I looked at the clock built into the stove. "It's nearly closing time." Christmas House Village closes at nine o'clock.

"I know that," Kim whispered.

"What are you doing there? Shopping?" I walked to the window with my mobile phone pressed to my ear. "I don't see you." Most of the shoppers had gone for the evening and only a few people moved along the sidewalks of the village. Even the car traffic on Lake Shore Drive was light.

"Amy, please, listen to me. I need you to come to Christmas House Village."

"What for?"

"Just come." I heard a small flutter, then she added, "Now. Please."

"Okay," I said slowly. "Derek and I will grab our coats and—"

"No." Kim cut me off. "Maybe you should come alone. Don't tell Derek anything—yet."

"I have to tell him something. He's right here!"

Derek and I exchanged a look. "What's going on?" he mouthed.

I threw my free hand in the air and shook my head helplessly.

"Tell him anything, Amy. Tell him your best friend is having a nervous breakdown and needs you!" Kim wailed.

"You mean tell him the truth."

"This is no time for jokes. Hurry up. This is really creeping me out."

Creeping her out? "Okay, sorry. I'll be right down. Bye." I started to end the call. "Wait!"

"Yes?"

"Where exactly are you?"

"Last house on the left. Elf House."

"On the porch?"

There was a short pause. "Upstairs."

"In the office?"

"No. I'm in Mr. Kinley's, I mean, Mr. Finch's apartment."

"You're with Finch? What's going on? He's not bothering you, is he?" The man was a jerk, but was he a cad?

"No. It's nothing like that."

"Are you sure? You're not in any danger? Is he listening? If he is, you tell him—"

"I'm not in any danger," Kim interrupted. "At least, I don't think so." Yet she sounded afraid.

I looked across the street once more at Christmas House Village. The landmark Fraser fir was lit for the night and stood like a shiny spaceship ready for takeoff. The flames flickered in the antique streetlamps running along the sidewalk of Christmas House Village.

Inside each house, various types of Christmas lights twinkled like stars. The exterior of each house was decorated and lit as well.

And now my best friend was calling me from the apartment of the new owner. And she sounded like she'd gone bonkers. What the devil was going on?

"I'll be right there." I hung up the phone and slid it into my back pocket.

"What's going on?" Derek sat at the edge of the sofa.

"I think Kim's having a nervous breakdown," I said, which wasn't a lie at all. I moved to the foyer and grabbed my winter coat. "I have to talk to her. I'm sorry. I'm sure I'll only be a few minutes."

Derek rose. "Should I come with you?"

"No, sit. Enjoy the movie. And your pizza." I walked over and gave him a kiss. "I'll be right back."

Derek nodded. "Did I understand right? Kim's at Christmas House Village?"

"Yeah." I shook my head. "She must have gone to talk to Mr. Finch. She's with him now."

"It sounds like she wants you to double-team him."

"You're probably right. She's been saying over and over that she wanted to have a word with him about keeping on the old staff at the very least. She feels just sick about what's happened."

Derek opened the door for me. "Good luck."

"Thanks."

* * * *

I hurried down the stairs, pulling my coat tight and tucking my scarf down inside for extra warmth. I pulled my gloves from the pockets of my coat and tugged them on.

I stopped at the corner of the alley, waved up to Derek, then turned and walked quickly up to Lake Shore Drive and crossed the road. The air was perfectly still and icy cold. The half-moon above held court over a handful of visible stars.

I glanced up at Derek's front window, noticed him watching me, and waved a final time. The carolers had called it a night. A sidewalk Santa's gaze followed me as I then made my way along the deserted sidewalk that bisected the village.

The sound of my footsteps echoed between the close-set houses. I had been to Christmas House Village in the evening, but the stores were brightly lit then and full of holiday shoppers. Even now, house lights were being flicked off and employees were leaving for the night.

Christmas House Village took on a spooky air with so few people about, all heading in the opposite direction. I felt like the only person on earth who didn't realize that I should turn around and flee with the others, from some unseen menace.

I quickened my step. Between Kim's unsettling call and the moving shadows, I was feeling more and more skittish and wished I had rejected Kim's suggestion that I leave Derek behind. I could have used some company.

Especially some big, strong, manly company.

I arrived at the last house on the left and couldn't help recalling my previous visit to Elf House, which had ended so badly. Mom had been disappointed when I had returned to Birds & Bees and given her the news that we had lost the Christmas House Village account.

After all our hard work, too, Mom had said at the time. Several of her friends and acquaintances had lost their jobs at Christmas House Village in the aftermath of Mr. Finch's purchase of the business. Losing our order with Christmas House Village had not been the first blow we'd suffered since Franklin Finch had come to town.

Mom's sister, my aunt Betty, had worked on and off at Kinley's Christmas House Village over the years. She hadn't done it so much because she needed the money as she did because she enjoyed the holiday atmosphere.

That atmosphere seemed somewhat blighted now.

I stepped up onto the porch. Rows of multicolored lights ran around the front windows. The porch light glowed green.

I went to the door and for the first time wondered how I was supposed to get inside. But I needn't have worried. The door was unlocked. I opened it, went inside, and closed it firmly behind me. I pulled out my scarf, already feeling the impact of the heated space, and got my bearings.

The mechanical elves had quieted for the night and sat frozen in place around the room. Most of the interior lights had been dimmed. A glowing three-foot-tall snowman on the landing stared at me with his big plastic-charcoal eyes and a long plastic-carrot nose.

I turned my head slowly. "Kim?" I pulled off my gloves and thrust them back in my coat pockets as I looked up the dimly lit stairs. "Great." I didn't relish going upstairs and facing the ever unpleasant Franklin Finch, but I didn't appear to have much choice.

Kim had said she was upstairs with him.

I moved upward slowly, the sound of the creaking steps the only sound I heard. I'd been expecting to hear voices yelling at one another.

On the second-floor landing, I stopped and listened again. Nothing. Not a peep. All the office doors were closed.

I took a settling breath and started up the remaining flight of thin-carpeted stairs to the top-floor attic apartment.

"Kim?" I called out softly from the top landing. "Are you in here?" The only door visible up here was ajar. I pushed it open with the palm of my hand. "Kim?"

A small globe ceiling-light above the door on the inside glowed yellow. The only other illumination came from the strings of lights twinkling on the outside of each window.

"Amy!" Kim scrambled to her feet from the braided rug she'd been seated on and rushed at me. "You're here!"

"Yes." I squeezed her. "I'm here. Now," I said, grabbing her by the shoulders, "tell me what is going on!" Kim's hair stuck out in several directions from her black knit cap. She was bundled up in a hip-length, houndstooth-wool duffle coat and black corduroy slacks with knee-high black leather boots.

"Don't you see him, Amy?" Kim was practically hysterical now, as if my coming had opened a tap of panic that she had heretofore been holding in check. "Don't you see him?"

"See who?" I replied, trying to hold her in place.

Kim pulled away and pointed. "Right there!" she shouted. "See? It's Mr. Finch!"

The living quarters had once been the home's attic. What I saw was a vaulted room with a convenient beam running lengthwise down the middle—convenient if one wanted to hang oneself, that is.

Because Franklin Finch was hanging from the center of the beam by a rope tied around his neck.

7

A brass floor lamp sat between two cozy, deep-red chairs. I stuck my shaking hand under the shade and fiddled with its innards until I found the light switch. I flicked the lamp on to get a better look.

Franklin Finch wore the same three-piece black wool suit that he'd worn the day I'd visited him in his office. Only the color of his tie had changed. This one was peacock blue.

A stool lay on its side several feet to his right. The window under the eave was ajar. There was nothing at all unusual about the room—discounting Franklin Finch hanging from the long rafter tie.

"And he was like that when you found him?" I whispered.

Kim was visibly shaking. "Just like that," she whispered back. "Swinging." She slumped to the floor, pressing her back against the wall as if wishing she could disappear within it.

"We have to call the police."

Kim nodded. "I already telephoned. I called Dan to report there had been a suicide before I called you."

"Good. I'm surprised he isn't here yet."

"He said they were all out on the highway assisting the state police. There's been a five-car pileup."

Ruby Lake's resources were thin at the best of times. "Don't worry. I'm sure they'll be here soon."

"Dan said the ambulance should be arriving as soon as they drop off some accident victims at the medical center."

I nodded. "That's good. What about the security guards?"

"I haven't seen any."

"That's funny. You'd think there would be at least one of them around."
I turned to the dangling body. Though I didn't think Franklin Finch needed
an ambulance as much as he needed a hearse, there was always a chance
he could be saved. "Come on. We should probably try to get him down."

"You're not serious?" Kim gasped and backed away. "Dan said not to
touch anything. He even made me promise not to call anyone. But I couldn't
stay here another minute alone."

I grabbed her wrists. "We have to, Kim. What if Finch is still alive?"
Kim's eyes grew. "Oh, my gosh! Do you really think that's possible, Amy?"

"No, not really. But we have to try, right?" I clamped my hands down
on Kim's shoulders.

"I-I suppose," Kim said, taking a look at Finch.

We hurried to the hanging body. It was a tall ceiling and there was no
way for me to reach his neck and loosen the noose. My eyes went to the
wooden stool he must have used to get himself up there. I picked it up and
set it beside him. "Hold it still for me."

Kim nodded and placed her hands on the side of the stool while I climbed
precariously, my hands clinging to Finch's trousers. I stretched to my tippy
toes and still could barely reach the rope. The knot was too tight.

I jumped back down. "It's no use. I can't budge him. Besides," I said,
glancing back at his still form and dead-looking face. "I think it is too late."

Kim broke into tears as several uniformed men burst onto the scene.

"Step back, ladies!" a burly man in a yellow paramedic's coat yelled.
He whipped out a knife and jumped up on the stool. "Joe, grab his feet!"

His curly-haired companion complied.

Kim and I moved aside.

"This is all my fault," Kim said through her tears.

I took her trembling hand. "Don't be silly. Of course, it's not."

"But it is, Amy. It is. Don't you see?"

"No, I don't."

"I called Mr. Finch and asked him to meet me. I never thought he would
agree, but he did."

"And this is how you found him?"

"No. We met at Ruby's Diner several hours ago. I told him what a terrible
thing he was doing to the town, to the people. I only wanted him to make
things right. I didn't mean for him to kill himself."

I looked at Franklin Finch as the paramedics carefully lowered him
to the ground. One of the paramedics checked for a pulse and shook his
head. "He's gone."

"This is all my fault," Kim repeated. "I killed him!" Kim groaned and mashed her face in her hands. "Mr. Belzer told me to leave it alone. Why didn't I listen to him?"

"Listen, Kim, everything is going to be okay."

"He got very upset in the diner."

"Who?" I asked.

"Mr. Finch," Kim explained. "Some of the locals started berating him, too. After Mr. Finch left, I felt terrible. So I decided to come back here and try to smooth things over. I never expected him to-to . . ." She broke down once again.

Chief Jerry Kennedy arrived with Officers Reynolds and Sutton in tow. All were bundled up in brown leather police jackets and caps. My former classmate, our chief of police, has a head of crew-cut blond hair, a boyish face with a squat nose, freckles that he's never outgrown, and dark jade eyes.

Jerry marched over to the body, which had now been placed on a stretcher. The thick rope had been cut and now hung loosely around Mr. Finch's neck. The rope's knot rested on Finch's right shoulder.

"Suicide, eh?" Jerry sighed. "And you found him, Ms. Christy?"

I peeked at the body over the chief's shoulder. Officers Sutton and Reynolds hovered on either side of their chief.

"Yes," Kim managed to say.

"If you don't mind my asking, what are you doing here this time of night? Christmas House Village is closed for the day."

Kim explained to the chief, like she had explained to me before his arrival, how she'd met with Mr. Finch at Ruby's Diner. "I felt terrible that our conversation ended the way it did. I knew he was living here. He told me so. I came to try to talk to him one last time."

"Oh, Kim." I sighed. "What were you thinking?"

"I was thinking that I would try one last time to convince him to let everybody keep their jobs and possibly take our birdseed decorations at cost, to cut our losses."

"Birdseed decorations?" the chief asked.

"I'll explain later, Jerry," I said.

Kim went on. "I was thinking that if only he would listen to reason, then everybody wouldn't hate me and Mr. Belzer." She dropped her voice. "I found him hanging there."

"Well," said Jerry, unzipping his jacket and pulling out a spiral notepad from his inner pocket, "I'm not surprised Mr. Finch killed himself. The man didn't exactly make himself any friends when he moved here. Half the town hated him already. That's not much of a start. It seems to me, the man simply couldn't take it anymore."

The chief tipped his hat back with his fingertip. "I've heard of people getting depressed around the holidays, but this is the first case I've ever come across where someone's actually killed themselves in a Christmas shop!"

"Must you, Jerry?" I said angrily. Couldn't he see he was only upsetting Kim all the more? I glanced at the body. Something didn't look right.

Kim groaned. "Mr. Finch had a history of depression, too," she added, clutching her hands. "I should have known better than to provoke him."

I pointed over Jerry's shoulder. "Did you notice how red, almost purple really, and blotchy Mr. Finch's neck is?"

Kim moaned behind me and I ignored her.

Jerry stared at me in disbelief. "The man just hung himself from that beam, Simms!" He jabbed his finger at the bit of rope still attached to the wooden rafter tie.

"Yes, but—"

The first paramedic bent, pulled Finch's shirt collar farther open, and tugged at the rope. He squinted. "She's right, Chief."

"Right about what?" Jerry looked down at him, a frown on his face.

The paramedic's finger hovered over Finch's sallow neck. "I think these might be finger marks."

Jerry sighed and dropped to his knees. "Yeah, maybe," he said, taking a closer look for himself. "And maybe Mr. Finch had second thoughts after jumping off that stool and hanging himself and was trying to save himself." Jerry's knees cracked as he stood. "That's sure as hell what I'd have been doing."

I moved around the loft, taking it all in for the first time. It was a large, open space with a simple kitchen tucked into the corner on the far right. The bed was on the far left wall with a nightstand beside it. An antique walnut rolltop desk sat several feet away from the bed, near the window.

An electric parabolic heater glowed yellow-orange near the desk chair. A silver computer screen sat on the corner of the desk in front of the cubbyholes. A keyboard lay near the edge of the desk. A bottle of brandy, two-thirds gone, and one glass with a trace of gold liquid at the bottom sat in the center. I sniffed. It was the brandy. Had Finch been drinking heavily before his death?

My hand hovered over the keyboard.

"Don't touch anything, Simms!" Jerry barked. He hurried over and pushed me gently aside. "Let's see if our Mr. Finch left us a note." Jerry hit the edge of the keyboard's spacebar with his knuckle and the computer screen came to life.

I glanced at the screen. "It looks like Mr. Finch was planning to go somewhere." The screen showed a motel website.

"Yeah." Jerry chewed his lip.

"Why would a man who is about to kill himself be making a motel reservation?"

"I guess we'll never know," Jerry replied.

"There's something else that's been bothering me. A couple of things really."

Jerry glared at me. "And what might those be?"

I grabbed his shoulder and turned him. "This space heater, for one thing."

"Lots of people use space heaters, Simms. We have two of them at the house ourselves. Not fancy ones like this, mind you."

"But the space heater is glowing, yet the window is ajar. It must be near freezing outside. Why would Mr. Finch do that?" I walked to the window in question and Jerry followed me. The window was open a good two inches.

"I have no idea, Simms," Jerry snapped, his hands on his hips. "And neither do you. Depressed people do strange things. Don't they, Reynolds?"

Officer Reynolds turned at the sound of his name. "I'm afraid I really wouldn't know, Chief." Larry blinked and turned his attention back to the dead man now strapped securely to the stretcher.

Larry's about six feet tall with thinning blond hair and a pinkish complexion. He's a quiet man in his midforties who's never been married. Somehow, his brown uniform always looks far more rumpled than those of his comrades.

I stood at the window and looked down at the street below. A narrow alley ran behind all the houses. Farther to the left, the bright light of streetlamps and cars moving along Lake Shore Drive lit the night. To the right, the alley dead-ended at a six-foot brick wall. On the other side was a dark woods that I knew led to a small creek.

I put my fingers in front of the window opening. "There's no breeze coming in through the window at all. Barely a whiff."

Jerry shook his head in exasperation. "So?"

"So Kim told me that when she came in the room Mr. Finch was swinging."

Jerry looked at Kim and she nodded. "Hey, Cliff!"

"Yeah?" called the first EMT on the scene. He seemed to be the leader of the team.

"How long would you say the man has been dead?"

Cliff tilted his head and studied the body. I wished they would cover it up. "Only a guess, but I'd say a couple of hours."

Jerry thanked him and stuck his hand in front of the open window. "Call Greeley and tell him to meet you at the hospital."

"Can we take him now?" the medic asked.

Jerry waved at Officer Reynolds. "Did you get pictures of everything?" Reynolds nodded and held his fancy camera aloft. "Pretty much, Chief."

I moved to close the window sash, then stopped. Some tiny bits of something were on the floor near the baseboard. "What is that?"

"What?" Jerry yelled from across the room.

I waved him back over. "Don't those look like threads of hemp?" I bent low to the ground.

Jerry hovered over me. "So?"

"So what are they doing here?" I twisted my neck and looked up at the chief. "Aren't those strands from the same hemp rope that Franklin Finch used to hang himself?"

Jerry's left eyelid twitched. He put his hand on my shoulder. "Out of the way, Simms." He pulled me up. "And don't touch anything."

Jerry pushed me aside and snapped his fingers. "Larry!"

Office Reynolds looked over. "Yes, Chief?"

"Get a photograph of this." Jerry chewed his lips a moment.

"What for, Chief? It's cut-and-dried, isn't it?"

"To shut Simms up," Jerry growled, and Officer Reynolds chuckled. The chief gave Kim a long, hard look. "Ms. Christy?"

"Yes?" For the first time in her life, I didn't hear Kim call him Jerry— which was usually done with a touch of disdain and loathing.

"I'll have to ask you to come down to the station and answer some questions."

She nodded.

"I'll take her." Dan stepped over and placed his arm gently across her back.

"No," Jerry countered. "Let's have Officer Pratt do it. You can relieve him downstairs."

With Dan and Kim dating, Jerry clearly wanted to maintain a certain professionalism. Not that there was any need to when it came to Kim in the current situation—even Jerry had to realize that she'd had nothing to do with Franklin Finch's demise. Whether that demise had been of his own doing or someone else's remained unclear to me, and I hoped it did to Jerry also.

Dan and Kim locked eyes. Dan opened his mouth, no doubt to protest, but Kim spoke. "It's okay, Dan." She extricated herself from his arm. "You go. I'll be fine." She forced a tiny smile. "I'll talk to you later."

Dan shrugged helplessly and headed out the door as Derek was coming in. "Derek!" I called to him and hurried over, dragging Kim with me. "What are you doing here? You must be freezing?" He wore a flannel shirt over a white T-shirt and blue jeans. "Where's your coat?"

"I was in such a hurry, I forgot it." Derek rubbed his arms. "I heard all the commotion. First it was the sirens and squealing tires. Then I looked out the window and saw all the lights—and I'm not talking Christmas, I'm talking police cars, a fire truck, and an ambulance!"

Derek ran a hand over the side of his head. "I figured it had to be you." I pulled a face but held my tongue.

"I've been waiting downstairs, trying to get past the officer down there." Derek looked past me and Kim to the now-shrouded body. "What the—?"

"It's Franklin Finch," I explained. Kim was squeezing my hand so hard I thought she'd break a bone or two, but I didn't have the heart to ask her to stop.

"The man hung himself," Jerry said, clearing us out of the path of the EMTs as they carted the dead man from the room.

"Maybe," I replied.

Derek's brow went up. "Maybe?"

"Maybe he did and maybe he didn't." I locked my eyes on Jerry. "There are some unusual circumstances."

"Such as?" Derek asked.

"Such as this is a police investigation and I'm asking you all to leave." Jerry shooed us toward the door and down the stairs.

We exited onto the cold front porch.

"Don't you go anywhere, Ms. Christy," the chief ordered. "Officer Pratt will give you a ride to the station. I'll be there shortly to take your statement."

"Come on, Jerry," I pleaded. "Can't you see how upset she is? Can't it wait until tomorrow?"

"That sounds like a good idea to me, Chief." Derek draped an arm over Kim's shoulder. "I promise my client will be in first thing tomorrow."

The chief opened his mouth—no doubt to protest—but Derek wasn't giving him the chance. "It will give you and your team more time to secure the scene and make a preliminary determination as to Mr. Finch's cause of death, right, Chief?"

I could practically see Jerry's mind turning. "Right, Counselor," Jerry agreed rather sourly.

As we moved along the sidewalk toward the street, I noticed a faint red glow coming from the far end of the porch of the Christmas house across the way.

If I wasn't mistaken, the lurking figure was Max, the young security guard, with a lit cigarette dangling from the fingers of his left hand.

8

Kim was in no shape to be alone and had spent the night at my house, sleeping on the sofa. After breakfast with my mom, we went downstairs to wait for Derek. He had promised to come by and drive her to the police station so she could make her written statement.

Because I had driven Kim to our house in my minivan, Derek would be driving Kim's car over from Christmas House Village and she would give him a ride back to his office when they were finished at the police station. We were waiting for him to arrive.

"Hello," I called, my hand sweeping along the stair rail. "Esther, are you here?"

"In the kitchen," I heard her reply.

The kitchen was a small kitchenette in the right-hand corner of the store where we kept coffee, tea, and snacks for the customers. It was a cozy nook where they could rest, eat, and read about birds and other wildlife from the small library of books and magazines provided.

It was a few minutes until the store opened. I looked out the front window. There was no sign of Derek, or Kim's car. A half dozen grackles, black with iridescent purple-blue heads, had settled on the lawn. A lone downy woodpecker nibbled at a suet cake hanging in a suet cage off the front eave.

"We have a few minutes," I said, taking Kim's hand. "How about another cup of coffee for the road?"

Kim nodded. Her face was drawn and she hadn't bothered with makeup. She'd slept in a pair of my pajamas and was now wearing the clothes she'd had on the previous night. She'd barely managed a word at the breakfast table and had eaten a mere half slice of wheat toast. I was worried about her.

Derek was going to drop her off at her place before they went down to the police station, so she could change into some fresh clothes.

We found Esther seated at one of the two rocking chairs near the bookshelves, a coffee mug on her lap and a fresh pot of coffee on the counter. Her store apron rested over the arm of her chair.

"Good morning, Esther," I said, moving to the counter and grabbing a couple of mugs from the cup tree.

Kim settled into the chair beside Esther.

"You two look terrible," Esther quipped, her eyes on Kim. "Who died?"

Kim began bawling and covered her face with her hands.

"Esther, look what you've done!" I said, handing Kim her coffee.

"What did I do?"

I put my arm around Kim. "I'm sorry, Esther. You didn't do anything."

"It's me," Kim moaned miserably. "I did something."

Esther's normally wrinkled brow wrinkled even further as she peered at Kim. "What did you do?"

"I-I killed Franklin Finch."

Esther leaned back and rocked faster. "That miserable man who bought Christmas House Village and put half the town out of work?"

Kim nodded.

"Good for you!" Esther slapped her knees. "Maybe there will be a Christmas after all," she added with a big, toothy smile on face. She leaned toward Kim. "How did you do it? Arsenic?"

"Esther!" I admonished her.

"What? I'm just asking."

"He hanged himself, if you must know," I said. "Maybe." The whole grisly scene still struck me as suspicious, and I'd barely slept a wink for thinking of it. I was dying to know what the police and coroner had to say.

Kim focused on her black coffee.

Esther drew in a breath and made the sign of the cross. She had applied far too much red blush and her cheeks glowed like Rudolph the reindeer's nose. I was pretty sure those delicate hairs scattered about her navy dress had come from a cat, but I decided now was not the time to bring the matter up.

Cats are a no-no at Birds & Bees. I have a severe cat allergy. Esther, I was certain, had a cat, though she refused to fess up to the fact. I had yet to catch her . . . but it was only a matter of time.

There was a rap at the front door.

"It sounds like we have a customer." Esther looked at her watch. "Time to open."

I set down my drink. "I'll come, too. That could be Derek."

Kim walked with us to the front door.

Derek waved from the other side of the glass and I let him in. I felt the cold tip of his nose on my cheek as he kissed me.

"How are all you lovely ladies this morning?" Derek asked with a grin. He was in his lawyering clothes, as I liked to call them, a sharp three-piece gray suit. Stylish black boots and a black peacoat completed the outfit.

Esther giggled as she attached her precious painted enamel cloisonné pin to the strap of her apron. It was shaped like a green parrot. Its gold lettering read: ESTHER PILASTER, ASST. MANAGER. The pin had been a gift to her from my mother—so had the assistant manager title.

The way she puffed out her chest like a male frigate bird in mating season every time she put it on, you'd think it was the Presidential Medal of Freedom.

"Do you have time for some coffee or tea?" I asked.

Derek shook his head. "We should get going. Especially if Kim wants to stop at her place first."

Kim pulled at her unruly hair. "Definitely. I am not going down to the police station looking like this."

I didn't blame her. Dan Sutton would likely be there, too. Kim couldn't be feeling too bad if she was concerned about her looks. That was a good sign.

"Okay," I said. "I don't suppose you've heard anything?"

"From the police?" Derek said. "Not a thing." He grabbed Kim's long coat from the rack and handed it to her. "Christmas House Village appeared to be open, though."

"It is? How is that possible? I mean, isn't it a crime scene?"

Derek shrugged. "If there's a crime scene at all, it's only the apartment where Franklin Finch died. You can't blame the owner of Christmas House Village for wanting to remain open. It is the height of the Christmas season."

"With this Finch fella dead, who is the owner?" Esther inquired.

We all looked at one another. None of us had any idea and said so.

"Ellery Belzer told me that Finch was divorced. I don't recall him mentioning if there were any children," I said.

"That's right," Kim said.

"Well, whatever the case, it's open and business is booming," said Derek. "Looking out my window this morning, I could see more people than ever wandering around."

"It's all the curiosity seekers," Esther speculated. "They're probably wanting to see where it happened."

"That's morbid," I countered. Esther merely shrugged. Kim had remained unnaturally quiet.

"If it's morbid," Derek said, as he pulled open the door for Kim, "then even our dear mayor has a sick streak."

"Mayor MacDonald was there?" I asked.

Derek nodded. "Yep. Him and Dave Arbon."

I turned the CLOSED sign to OPEN. "Dave Arbon?"

"He's the chairman of the Ruby Lake planning and zoning commission. I met him at a business luncheon some time back."

"What about the employees who've been protesting outside Christmas House Village?" Kim asked.

Derek cocked his head. "Now that you mention it, I don't recall seeing them. I guess they don't feel right protesting when the man they are protesting is dead."

Derek waved goodbye and promised to take care of Kim as they left Birds & Bees.

I had business of my own to attend to. Franklin Finch's death was troubling enough, but my best friend's pangs of guilt over her imagined part in it were all the more so.

Depression could drive people to do crazy things. I hoped that wouldn't happen to her, but if it did, I hoped it would be something that she *would* live to regret.

Anything else was too horrible to contemplate.

9

"Tell Mom I'll be back later to take her to her hair appointment with Rhonda," I instructed Esther.

"Where are you off to?"

"Christmas House Village," I explained.

"But I haven't even given you my Christmas wish-list yet," Esther said with a twinkle in her eye.

"Very funny. It's not buying that I have in mind. It's selling."

"Oh?"

"I'm going to do what I failed to do before." I grabbed my coat off the hook and threw it on. "I'm going to convince them to take those birdseed ornaments."

"They already said no."

"They haven't said no to taking them at cost."

"Are you crazy?"

I shrugged. "It's better than losing all the money we've put into them, right?"

"If you say so."

"I say so." I wriggled into my gloves. "Don't forget to tell Mom I'll be back in plenty of time. You're in charge!" I called, scooting out the back door.

"I know that!" Esther replied.

I frowned as I went to my minivan. If I wasn't careful, Birds & Bees would have a new manager—and it wouldn't be me.

* * * *

Derek was right. Business was brisk at Finch's Christmas House Village. Though how long it would remain Finch's, I had no idea.

I strode purposefully to Elf House and marched up to the second floor. A young man and woman, both dressed in matching elf outfits replete with green and red caps with gold bells, were focused on assisting customers and paid me no attention.

The office door stood open. The surprise on my face as I peered inside must have been evident because it was the former manager, Eve Dunnellon who spoke first.

"Hi, Amy. Come on in." She beckoned me with her hand. "Surprised to see me?"

"I'll say."

Eve chuckled. "Have a seat. I'll fill you in." Eve Dunnellon was a plump, large-bosomed woman with a shock of ash-blond hair that swept over her head from left to right. I knew it wasn't her natural color because Cousin Rhonda was her stylist-slash-colorist at Spring Beauty, a local hair salon.

I took the proffered chair. The second chair was still piled high with beige file folders. "Please do."

"Believe me, I'm as surprised to be here as you are to see me." She tugged at a single pearl hanging on a gold chain around her neck.

With her long, pointy nose and raspberry-red dress, she reminded me of a male purple finch. The confusing name, like so many others, is derived from the Latin *purpureus*, which essentially means crimson. When it came to naming and identifying birds, science and reality didn't always align, in my opinion.

"Congratulations. How did it happen?"

Eve placed her elbows on the desk and folded her hands together. "I'd barely gotten out of bed when I got the call."

"The call?"

"Yes, telling me about Franklin Finch's demise and asking that I fill in immediately."

I nodded toward her right arm, which was covered in a flesh-colored bandage. "What happened?"

"This? It's nothing." Eve Dunnellon raised her arm and turned it slowly. "It's merely a sprain. That's what I get for taking the trash out in three-inch heels. Trust me, I'll never do that again."

"So you got your old job back?"

Eve settled herself behind the big desk. Her hand went to a stack of papers. "Temporarily, at least. I have no idea what the new owner will do. Even if the job is only for a month or two, I couldn't afford to say no."

"Who is the new owner?"

Eve looked up at me. "Franklin's widow, I imagine. I haven't actually been told."

"If you don't mind my asking, who hired you back?"

Eve smiled. "I don't mind at all. I received a call from an attorney in New York, a Mr. Silbert. He said he'd handled the sale of Kinley's for his buyer, Franklin Finch. Apparently, Franklin left his estate to his ex-wife."

"That's odd."

Eve shrugged. "Tell me about it. My ex wouldn't leave me a single cent. I can tell you that. Of course, it could be that Franklin simply had not had time to change his will."

"Have you met his ex-wife?"

"Nope. Mr. Silbert said she was in New York, and as far as I'm concerned, she can stay there." Eve Dunnellon grinned at me. "Maybe that way, she'll let me keep my job."

"After everything that's happened, you still like it here?"

"What's not to like?" Eve replied. "It's Christmas every day."

I hated to quibble with her but couldn't help thinking about my conversation with Franklin Finch. Christmas had meant nothing more to him than a chance to make a buck or two. "You have worked here a long time, haven't you?"

"Nearly ten years. And I loved every minute of it—up until the sale, that is."

"I can understand that, considering how Finch fired you."

"Yeah, can you believe it? He wasn't here ten days when he canned me." Her gaze drifted off into space. "Franklin used me. I showed him the ropes, then he cut me loose."

My brow inched up. Had she meant the rope reference?

Eve waved a dismissing hand. "But that's enough about that. I admit, the sale came as a complete surprise. But Finch taking over was just the last in a long line of things going wrong around here."

"Going wrong? What do you mean?"

"It started about six months ago, I'd say. At first it was little things, a broken window, clogged toilets, a damaged display. Not much but more than usual. Then it escalated to things like graffiti and small fires. Somebody even lit a smoke bomb in Sugarplum House."

I whistled. "I had no idea."

"We try to keep such things hush-hush."

"Who do you think was responsible?"

"At first I thought it was kids. You know, their idea of pranks. But it caused a lot of damage. The Kinley kids were getting fed up with everything."

"Maybe that's what made them finally decide to sell."

"It didn't help. They've wanted to sell ever since their father died. I can tell you this, we never had half as many incidents in all the years Tyrone ran the business."

"How do you explain it?"

"I don't." The corners of her mouth turned down. "I hate to say it, but the troubles have escalated lately. Now I think it's disgruntled employees. Hardly anybody was happy when Franklin Finch took over from the Kinley family. All of us felt like we'd had the rug pulled out from under us. And, in a way, we had." Eve Dunnellon sighed. "Small towns don't like change."

"I believe you're right." I looked at the paneled wall behind the desk. A row of Kinley portraits had once hung there. Now there was only a cumbersome gilt-framed photograph of Franklin Finch. I had a feeling it wouldn't hang there much longer. "And you really think it was the employees committing sabotage?"

The newly reinstated manager nodded. "And the ex-employees. Don't forget, Finch had fired a lot of the longtime Christmas House Village staff. Half of them seem to parade around out front every day. Thank goodness that appears to be over. That's not good for our image or our business." She lifted her chin. "I'm hoping to hire many of them back."

"And has the sabotage ended then, now that Finch is out of the picture?"

"You would think so. I've just returned to the job, but I haven't been informed of any recent issues that would suggest vandalism."

"That's good. Franklin Finch's murder may have been the ultimate act of outrage against his ownership."

"Murder?" Eve shook her head. "Franklin hung himself."

"Maybe. I believe there are some suspicious circumstances."

Eve nodded. "That's right, you were there. You and your friend. What sort of suspicious circumstances?"

"I'm afraid I can't say. It is an active police investigation."

"I understand." She tapped a pencil against the desk.

The look on Eve's face told me I had struck a nerve. "What? What aren't you telling me, Eve?"

The manager bit her lower lip as she considered her words. "Look, I probably shouldn't be telling you this. I mean, the Kinley family always liked to keep unpleasantness out of the public eye."

"Unpleasantness?" Now she really had me interested.

"Things like vandalism, shrinkage."

"Shrinkage?"

"That's the polite way of saying employees stealing from us." She shrugged. "Believe me, it happens. Even in Santa's world. When it does, we handle it discreetly. It wouldn't be good for our public image to have such unpleasant activities and occurrences splashed in the news."

"I'm not sure what it is you're trying to say."

She sighed heavily. "Just between you and me"—she wiggled a finger between us—"occasionally we have to let someone go due to, uh . . . behavior issues. We recently had to fire someone."

"When was that?"

Eve thought a moment. "Right after Franklin arrived."

"For stealing?"

She shook her head. "For vandalism."

"One of your own employees?"

"That's right. He was seen damaging one of the boilers. We also think he was responsible for a recent computer virus. Our IT guy says the virus started on a computer this person had regular access to. Who knows what else he might have been responsible for? We've had a lot of computer glitches."

"Who was he? Have you told the police about him?"

"His name is Bobby Cherry. And to answer your question, no, I haven't told the police. I don't know if anyone else has."

Eve reached into her purse with her good hand and came out with a package of tissues. She pulled one free and wiped her nose. "I suppose I should. You have to remember, I wasn't an employee at the time of Franklin Finch's death."

"That's true. Where is Bobby now? Have you seen him since?"

"Nope."

"Do you know where I might find him?"

Eve's head jerked in surprise. "Why would you want to find him?"

"Not me personally," I said—a half-truth. "I'm sure Chief Kennedy would like a word with him, if he hasn't already."

"I suppose you're right. He had been living in a frog at Virginia Johnson's house until she passed away. I don't know where he's living now."

"In a—"

Eve stuck her hand up like a stop sign. "That's enough about Christmas House Village and its troubles. What brings you by, Amy?"

"Well, you see, I—" My brain was still on the *living in a frog* statement she'd dropped on me. Eve's cell phone at the corner of the desk blotter began chiming *ping! ping! ping!*

Eve picked it up and rolled her eyes. "Not important. Go ahead, Amy."

"Are you sure you don't need to get that?"

"They'll wait." She tilted back in her desk chair, folding her hands over her expansive waistline. "This is about the birdseed ornaments, right?"

"Yes," I said. Thankfully, the infernal pinging of her mobile phone finally ceased. I squirmed and clutched my purse. "As you know, you and I signed a contract for two gross and—"

Eve lifted a hand. "And when can I have them?"

The corners of my mouth lifted. "You mean, you want them?" Relief washed over me.

"Yes, of course. I ordered them, didn't I?"

"You did. But . . ."

"Yeah?"

"It might be dumb of me to say this, but when I came here the other day, Mr. Finch canceled the order."

"He did?"

"Yes. In fact, he practically tossed the contract in my face."

"Well, you don't see Franklin Finch here now, do you?"

I shook my head and chuckled. "You know, when I told him that my contract was with you, he pretty much said the same thing."

Now it was Eve Dunnellon's turn to laugh. "Ain't karma something?" She grabbed up a handful of file folders teetering on the edge of her desk. "Sorry to make this short, Amy. But I've got tons and tons to do."

"I understand." I stood.

Eve flashed a smile. "You get those ornaments to me ASAP. I've got some trees all ready to go in Santa's House. We're doing an entirely wildlife and nature theme there this year. Those ornaments of yours will be perfect."

Eve turned her attention to her papers and I turned to the door.

Downstairs on the sales floor, I watched a young boy gaze with fascination at the Christmas circus train running around two silvery artificial Christmas trees in a big figure eight. The half dozen mechanized elves clanged their approval while the live elves packaged up boxes for the customers lined up at the counter.

There had never been any doubt. Christmas was a big business. And at Kinley's, now Finch's, next whoever's, Christmas House Village, someone stood to make a mint.

The question remaining in my mind was who.

As the young man behind the counter finished and stepped back onto the sales floor, I nabbed him.

"Excuse me. May I speak with you a moment?"

"Hi." He looked me over. "Do you work here?"

"No, I'm a vendor, though."

"Cool." He had sharp brown eyes. The wreath attached to his green velvet vest identified him as Ryder. His breath identified him as a lover of gingerbread.

"I was just wondering, Ryder, if you were here when . . ." My eyes drifted upward.

"When?" Ryder spread his hands in a gesture to indicate he had no idea what the crazy lady was talking about. Crazy lady being me.

I pulled him behind one of the Christmas trees, not wanting to spoil the holiday mood of the shoppers filling the room. "When Mr. Finch . . ."

"Ohhh." Ryder nodded vigorously. "When the old guy tied the permanent knot around his neck." His candy-cane-colored leggings were less than flattering. I tried to imagine Derek in a pair and failed. Thank goodness.

"Well, I suppose that's one way of putting it."

"Yeah. Me and Deb . . ." He paused and pointed to the young woman behind the counter. "We were in all afternoon." He tugged off his elf hat, scratched the top of his head, then put it back on. "Right up until closing, as a matter of fact. Me, Deb, and Gladys."

"Gladys?"

"The old lady who's in charge of the house."

"I see. Did you see or hear anything unusual that day?"

He furrowed his brow. "You mean like Finch hanging himself?" He shook his head emphatically. "Nope. Not a peep." He suddenly grinned ear to ear. "Hey," he said, grabbing me by the shoulder, "get it? Finch? Didn't make a peep!" He snorted. "Funny, right?"

I tried to smile but couldn't muster one up. "Did you know a former employee here by the name of Bobby Cherry?"

Ryder frowned. "That jerk?" He shook his head. "That guy was nothing but trouble. He came in late and disappeared half the time he was here. Probably catching a nap or smoking when he wasn't supposed to. Good riddance, I say." He paused, a look of shock on his face. "I mean, you aren't related to him or anything, are you, lady?"

"No," I assured him. "Thank you," I said, pulling away. "I'll let you carry on." Talking to Ryder wasn't going to get me anywhere.

"Any time!" he called.

On my way out the door, I ran into the sales clerk I'd seen the last time I'd been to Elf House, the time I'd come to pay Franklin Finch a visit.

I stepped into her path. "Hi, remember me?" I stuck out my hand. "Amy Simms. I own Birds and Bees here in town."

"Hi," said the befuddled woman. "Can I help you?"

Her coat was unzipped to the waist. She wore a name badge shaped like a Christmas wreath, just like the rest of the employees. This one told me her name was Gladys and that she was from the North Pole.

I wasn't surprised. According to the nametags, every employee was from the North Pole. Christmas House Village went all-in to maintain the Christmas holiday spirit and setting.

"Hello, Gladys, right?" I nodded in the general direction of her name tag. Though my new friend Ryder had called her an old lady, she was probably no more than fifty years old.

"That's right." Gladys straightened the plastic wreath bearing her name. She looked past me to the door. "I need to get back to work."

I laid my hand on her sleeve. "Of course. I was just wondering if you noticed anything unusual about Mr. Finch before the terrible accident?"

Gladys turned wary. "Unusual how?"

"Was he acting funny? Did he seem depressed to you?"

"He wasn't friendly but"—she tilted her head a moment—"I wouldn't say particularly depressed." Gladys shrugged. "Who's to say, right?"

"When was the last time you saw him?"

Gladys frowned, deep in thought. "Maybe a few hours before closing."

"Did you notice anyone else going upstairs around that time?"

Gladys chuckled. "Yesterday was payday. We were all up there yesterday getting our paychecks. Let me tell you, I hope they get payroll worked out for next time. I had to go back twice to get my check. I saw Santa go back three times!" She held up three fingers. "Stupid computer system. I liked the old way. We used to get our checks handwritten. Not now—some dang computer has to spit them out. Eve was sure mad."

"Eve Dunnellon?"

Gladys ran her hand through her hair. "She came by to collect her severance pay and the accountant—"

"Gladys!" Eve called from the top of the stairs. "Where's that receipt log I asked you for an hour ago?"

"In a minute, Eve!" Gladys dodged to her right and was past me before I could formulate another question.

Why hadn't Eve mentioned being at Christmas House Village the day of Franklin Finch's demise?

Curious about Eve Dunnellon's plans for displaying and marketing our birdseed ornaments, I wandered down to Santa's House and went inside. Sure enough, stuffed animals climbed the tinsel that had been hung from the walls and the Christmas trees themselves. There were quite a few species of bird plush toys occupying the first floor as well. Eve was right, this would be a perfect complement to our Birds & Bees ornaments.

I rubbed my cold hands together. Hopefully, sales would be brisk and whoever took over Christmas House Village next would see the benefit of maintaining our relationship with them.

A security guard strolled past me. When he paused at the drinking fountain tucked under the stairwell, I patted him on the shoulder.

"Yes, miss?" It was the older of the two security guards I'd seen around Christmas House Village. This being the mild-mannered Japanese American, around fifty years old, a sharp contrast to the surly and menacing Max, who looked like he ate linebackers for breakfast.

"I wondered if I could talk to you about Mr. Finch." The security guard too wore a wreath for a name tag. His identified him as Leo.

"Mr. Finch died, miss."

"I know. I was the one who found him. Rather, not me, but my friend and then she called me and . . ." I stopped when I recognized by the look on his face that I was only confusing him. "I'm wondering if you'd heard anything. I mean, have the police told you anything?" I nudged my brow up. "Officer to officer?"

Leo chuckled. "They've not told me a thing, miss." He moved into the next room, his hands folded behind his back, and I followed. "Nor are they likely to."

"Were you here when it happened?"

Leo stopped, turned, and shook his head. "Nope. I come in when we open and leave at five. Max would have been here. He puts in long hours. He's a new hire. Worked last at some hotel in Black Mountain. I guess he wants to impress the boss. Not me. I've got a wife and kids. I like to get home. Know what I mean?"

I nodded to show I did. Besides, I had seen Max that night myself. Had the police questioned him? Probably. "A big place like Christmas House Village, you must have security cameras, right?"

The corners of Leo's mouth turned up. "The Kinleys never wanted them. They said it would detract from the holiday spirit." He waved his hand at the ornately decorated den we now occupied. "They like to keep things festive. Fun."

"I can appreciate that. Yet, if they'd had security cameras, they might have been able to avoid problems likes the ones Bobby Cherry caused."

Leo's face darkened. "That boy was bad news."

"At least he's gone now."

"Yeah," said Leo, "but the troubles aren't."

"They aren't?" That jibed with what Eve had told me.

"If you ask me, there are some people who would rather Christmas didn't happen."

"Like who?"

The security guard threw his hands in the air. "I don't have a clue. Now, if you will excuse me, I need to keep moving. I'm supposed to make my rounds once an hour."

"Of course."

He moved silently off to the next room.

Looking around, I could see how having security cameras might put a damper on that holiday spirit. Too bad though. The right security camera in the right place might have revealed what really happened the night Franklin Finch was found swinging from the rafter tie.

Because I had a hunch there was more to this Christmas story than met the eye.

10

Mom and I stepped into Spring Beauty for her three o'clock appointment. The salon was located on the east side of Ruby Lake in the middle of a low-slung brick building that also housed a laundromat on one side and a vintage clothing shop on the other.

"Hi, Aunt Barbara." Cousin Rhonda wiggled her brightly painted nails at us as we pushed through the door and hung up our coats. "Hello, Amy." She practically sang my name, making it sound like four or five syllables rather than the simple two it was designed to be. "I'll be with you in a jiff!"

We took seats in the rattan chairs lined up in front of the window. The chairs each held bubblegum-pink cushion seats. They were so bouncy, I felt like I was sitting on a big wad of bubblegum, too.

I tapped my mother's shoulder. "Mom, isn't that Mrs. Fortuny?"

"Where?" Mom whispered.

I pointed to a woman with a head full of baby-blue curlers stuck under a device that looked like something aliens might be using to scoop out human brains for later processing and critical examination back in a lab on their home planet. Though my cousin had tried to coax me under one of the scary machines on more than one occasion, so far I had resisted. I liked my hair—and my brain—the way it was and where it was.

"Yes, I believe it is." Mom folded her gloves neatly, laid them in her pocketbook, and clipped it shut.

Mrs. Fortuny's eyes flew open as if we'd just invoked a demon. "Barbara Simms, is that you?"

"Hello," Mom said with a wave. "How are you, Irma dear?"

"Dear?" I whispered in Mom's ear. "That woman clobbered Kim with her purse."

"I'm sure she didn't mean anything by it," Mom said, still smiling at Mrs. Fortuny.

"Getting my hair done. Perm!" The woman was shouting. I'd noticed over the years that being under the alien contraption had that effect on people. Well, that and the angry, loud noise it made—*it* being Irma Fortuny, not the device.

While I grabbed a magazine, Rhonda called my mother to come take a seat at her station, which was to the right of Irma Fortuny.

"I'm gonna leave you simmering for a spell, Irma." Rhonda patted Mrs. Fortuny's free hand. The elderly woman's other hand held a cup of hot spiced apple cider that I could smell from where I sat. "While I get started on Barbara."

Mom plopped herself down in the black leather salon chair. Mrs. Fortuny nodded her acceptance of the situation, and Rhonda wrapped an apron around my mom's neck. Rhonda is the fraternal twin sister to Riley. Both are the offspring of mom's sister, my aunt Betty. Barbara and Betty are twins, too.

Rhonda's thick brown hair, as per usual, was arranged in an over-the-top fifties-style bouffant. Her hazel eyes were weighted down with pink eye shadow, over which were two sharp and deadly looking eyebrows.

She pranced around my mom in a pair of white leather shoes, a red dress with a green sash, and a Santa Claus hat. That hat—now frayed around the edges—traditionally stayed on her head from Thanksgiving morning until New Year's Day. Rumor had it that she slept in it. But seeing as she slept alone, the rumor remained unverified.

Unable to focus on my magazine, I crossed to the brass refreshment cart and helped myself to a cup of eggnog and a snowball cookie the size of a baseball.

"I see you are getting your hair and nails done. What's the occasion, Irma?" Mom asked Mrs. Fortuny as a young manicurist stepped up to the plate and took one of the elderly woman's hands.

Irma swiveled in Mom's direction. "Going back to work tomorrow!"

"That's wonderful." Mom nodded, then closed her eyes as Rhonda reached across her forehead with a pair of scissors.

"Yes. With that horrible Mr. Finch gone, I shall look forward to returning." She yelped as the manicurist filed her flesh rather than her thumbnail. If she were smart, she'd stop squirming.

"Careful, dear." Mrs. Fortuny raised her thumb for a closer look, then set it back on the armrest. "Now, what was I saying?" She looked at my mother, whose eyes remained closed.

I moved nearer, taking a seat on a sturdy cushion next to the shelf holding the haircare products. "You were saying you're going back to work. Did you find a new position, or are you talking about Christmas House Village?"

"Of course I'm talking about Christmas House Village. I've worked there nearly thirty years." She frowned at me. "Where else would I work?"

I didn't know how to answer that question, so I ignored it. "Is it permanent?"

Mrs. Fortuny's free hand went to the side of her head, landing on a curler. "Yes, a permanent. I'm going back to work!"

I shook my head. "No. Are you going back to work, back to Christmas House Village permanently?" I found I was yelling despite myself. Every eye in the place looked at me.

"Amy," Rhonda said, coming over, scissors in hand and tapping my arm, "inside voices, please."

"Sorry." I rose carefully so as not to spill my beverage or drop my cookie, which had somehow shrunk by half already. "Well, good luck, Mrs. Fortuny. I'm very glad for you."

"Believe me," the elderly woman answered, "I'm very glad, too. Whoever killed Finch did us all a favor—a big favor!"

I froze. "Wait. What?"

"There's my William." Mrs. Fortuny's attention swung from me to the front of the shop. She snatched her hand from the manicurist and waved at the door. Sure enough, her acquaintance came through the front door bundled in a black leather cap, red parka and scarf, and sturdy boots.

Mrs. Fortuny looked at me once more. "The posse done strung him up. Heh-heh."

I moved aside as William took his place next to Mrs. Fortuny. The manicurist had given up, mumbling under her breath as she retired to the rear of the shop.

"Ready?" William asked, tapping his cane against the tile floor. As he flexed his fingers, I noticed that the handle had been expertly carved into the head of an eagle.

"Irma will be ready in five," Cousin Rhonda said, running her fingers along a curler, then lifting the top of the device. "I just need to remove your curlers and comb you out, dear." She turned to my mom. "Be right back, Aunt Barbara."

"Take your time, Rhonda." Mom's eyes were still shut. She may have been snoozing.

"What were you saying about Mr. Finch being murdered, Mrs. Fortuny?"

"I'm saying whoever did it, they ought to pin a medal on her." She rolled her neck. "Or him."

"But who told you it was murder?" I insisted.

"Karl." She tilted her chin up and thought a moment. "Yes, it was Karl."

"Karl Vogel?"

"That's right." Her voice had returned to a normal level now that Rhonda had turned off the alien device. Rhonda was slowly but deftly plucking plastic curlers from Mrs. Fortuny's springy silver hair.

"Now, Amy," Rhonda said, turning her eyes on me, "I'm either going to have to put you to work or give you a haircut if you want to keep chatting up our customers."

I hastily returned to my chair at the window. I knew a threat when I heard one.

William towered over me as Cousin Rhonda finished working her magic on Mrs. Fortuny. I'd never realized how big the man was. And I still knew next to nothing about him. "Don't mind Irma," he said, his voice barely above a whisper.

William leaned on his rubber-tipped cane. "She doesn't know what she's saying sometimes." He smiled, clearly for my benefit. "Irma gets confused."

"Confused?" Something odd was going on, but I couldn't figure out what it was.

William nodded ever so slightly. "Mr. Finch killed himself, Ms. Simms. Hung himself from the rafters." He thrust his free hand in his coat, his elbow sticking out like a chicken wing. "It's a shame, but that's all it was."

My heart raced and my ears pulsed. It might have been my imagination but every move, every word sounded like a threat. Still, I couldn't help saying, "And now Mrs. Fortuny's got her job back."

He smiled for real this time. "Yes, Irma has got her job back." His fingers tightened around the head of the cane.

I squirmed. The cushion under my butt suddenly didn't feel so bubblegummy. It felt more like granite. "I suppose you got your job back, too, Mister . . ."

William blinked but ignored my hanging question.

I stared at his hand. "That's quite a cane you've got there, William. I love the eagle."

His eyes went to his left hand. "Thanks." He ran the fingers of his right hand along the eagle's sharp beak. "I carved it myself. When it comes to handling a carving knife"—his eyes met mine—"I'm an expert."

I gulped. "You are?"

"If I do say so myself." He arched his brow. "You got something needs carving?"

An icy jolt flew up my spine as if the cold steel of a knife tip had touched me there. I cleared my throat. A flock of tundra swans had just unexpectedly landed there. "Not that I can think of at the moment."

"You let me know if you do." William smiled.

Rhonda walked over with a now bundled-up Mrs. Fortuny, breaking the spell between me and William. The elderly woman looked double her size in a lilac-colored down coat that draped past her knees.

"Here she is!" cooed Rhonda. She carefully wrapped the pale-blue silk scarf that Mrs. Fortuny handed her over the old woman's bouncy curls. "Don't you look lovely!" Rhonda took a step back to admire her handiwork.

I leaned past William. "Your hair does look lovely, Mrs. Fortuny."

"Thank you, dear." Mrs. Fortuny's hand went to her curls.

"Can I tell Kim you're not angry with her anymore?"

Mrs. Fortuny appeared befuddled.

"I mean, now that you've got your job back . . ."

"Why not? Life's too short." Mrs. Fortuny smiled. "At least for some of us."

William raced to the salon door and held it open against his back as Mrs. Fortuny dropped a five-dollar bill in Rhonda's palm and exited.

"See you in three weeks!" Rhonda called, waving the bill in the air.

I approached my cousin. "Who was that man, Rhonda?"

"That's Mrs. Fortuny's friend William." Rhonda went behind the register and placed a ticket in the drawer.

"William what?"

"Who knows?" My cousin shrugged. "Why?"

"No reason," I replied quickly.

Cousin Rhonda looked down her nose at me. "Amy, you're not letting your imagination get carried away again, are you?"

"What do you mean?"

"I mean you're always seeing mysteries and secrets behind every pair of eyes."

I took a step back. "The way you're waving those scissors in my face, I'm worried for my own eyes."

Rhonda looked at the long, sharp shears in her hand as if they had magically appeared. "Sorry." She thrust them in the front pocket of her apron. "But you should leave everything alone." She marched back to her station and returned her attention to Mom. "The town is back to normal. People are happy. It's Christmastime," she said, the brass bell on her Santa Claus hat jingling as she bobbed her head. "Why can't you be happy, too?"

That was a good question. Unfortunately, I did not have a good answer.

11

I called Karl Vogel and asked him to meet me at Ruby's Diner. The diner is on Lake Shore Drive, not far from the town's namesake, Ruby Lake, and directly across from Birds & Bees. A previous owner had converted the long-defunct gas station to its current existence as a casual eatery.

I walked across the street to the diner. Inside, I waved hello to Tiffany LaChance, a friend and waitress, who was delivering some open-faced sandwiches to a family of five. Moire, the current owner and hostess, was nowhere to be seen, and business appeared slow for the moment, so I helped myself to a capacious empty booth at the window.

From there, I had a great view of the tall sign in the parking lot with the big green dinosaur on it. Once the symbol of the station, the apatosaurus now shilled for the diner.

When the flashy, red, antique Chrysler 300B drove past, I knew Karl had arrived. Karl and Floyd, our mutual friend, had not long ago purchased the car from Robert LaChance, a local car dealer and Tiffany's ex-husband. Though we were only a few years apart, she had married, had a child, and divorced—three things I had never experienced.

Whether that was for the better or for the worse depended on my mood whenever I thought of it.

Karl and Floyd's automobile was a work in progress. As far as I was concerned, that pretty much summed up any car that Robert LaChance sold off his used car lot.

Still, Karl and Floyd loved the 1956 Chrysler dearly. Which was fitting, since so far it had cost them dearly—in time and money. And a whole heap of frustration.

Tiffany, a buxom blond beauty with green eyes, stepped over to my booth. "Hi, Amy. Eating alone today?"

"Karl's joining me," I explained. "Here he comes now," I added as the elderly man pushed through the door in a pair of baggy brown trousers and a weathered brown leather Town of Ruby Lake Police Department jacket.

Karl was the former chief of police. Having him for a friend was like having a mole inside the force, because Chief Kennedy was always calling him for advice.

A habit that I, and the rest of the town I'm sure, were grateful for.

I held up my arm. Karl hustled over, drooled a bit over Tiffany, then sat.

"How are you, Karl?" Tiffany leaned over and gave him a well-received kiss on his stubbly cheek.

"Better now," he said with a big grin. His old police cap balanced atop his head. White hair sprouted from the sides. A pair of heavy black-rimmed glasses teetered at the end of his nose.

"What can I get you to start?" Tiffany asked, pencil at the ready, hovering over her order book. Like all Ruby's Diner employees, her uniform consisted of khaki pants—of course, her outfit was a more flattering fit than most—and a Kelly-green button-down shirt with white name patch, stylishly reminiscent of those worn by old-school gas station attendants.

I half expected somebody to offer to clean my windshield for me while I ate.

We both ordered coffee because as much as Karl wanted a beer, Ruby's Diner did not have a license to sell alcohol.

"So what's this all about, Amy?" Karl said, finally able to get his old gray eyes off Tiffany's retreating figure and on me across the table. Karl considered himself quite the ladies' man, despite the fact he'd never managed to find the right lady.

"I ran into Irma Fortuny at Spring Beauty today."

Karl's left eye narrowed. "Your hair looks real smart, Amy."

"Thanks," I said, pushing a lock of untouched hair behind my ear. "But Rhonda didn't cut it."

"Even smarter." Karl chuckled. "If you were talking to Irma, you probably want to know about Franklin Finch's murder."

"You mean—" I leaned back as Tiffany settled our coffees on the table and slid the little stainless steel rack holding the cream and sugar packs between me and Karl. "Thanks, Tiff."

"Ready to order?"

We both were. I ordered the grilled cheese with broccoli slaw and Karl opted for a double cheeseburger. Tiffany left to put in our order.

I dumped some sugar into my coffee followed by a pack of cream. "It's true then that Mr. Finch was murdered? I had a hunch."

Karl nodded and sipped his coffee black. "Jerry told me Kim found the body and called you after she called the police." The retired police chief smiled over the rim of his mug. "He was madder than a rattlesnake that's had its tail stepped on, seeing you there."

"I wasn't so happy to be there myself."

"I can imagine. In all my years as chief of police, I never saw a single hanging victim. We had ourselves a suicide or two, but never by hanging. That's a rough one."

"You're lucky. Jerry's already seen two."

"Two?"

"Virginia Johnson," I explained. "I learned she committed suicide some months back."

"Yeah," Karl said, with unexpected softness. "Poor Virginia. I forgot about her." He rubbed his fleshy jowls. "Rest her weary soul."

I nodded and said a silent prayer. "So somebody really strangled Franklin Finch up in his loft and then hanged him?"

"Yep. Unless . . ."

"Unless what?"

"Unless he was strangled someplace else and then the killer took his body back to Christmas House Village to make it look like a suicide."

I tilted my head and pressed my fingers against my skull. "I hadn't thought of that."

Karl shrugged. "If you ask me, it's highly unlikely. It ain't easy dragging a dead body around."

"I suppose not." I was starting to feel woozy and it wasn't due to low blood sugar. "Unless there was more than one person involved."

"Meaning?"

"Irma Fortuny suggested it might have been a posse."

Karl leaned back with a chuckle, steam rising from his mug and washing over his wrinkle-lined face. "An angry mob taking the law into their own hands? Like in the movies?"

"Her words, not mine."

"Crazier things have happened, I suppose." He paused, then added with a wink, "Not usually in Ruby Lake, however. Not until you got here."

I sputtered, dribbling coffee down my chin and all over my paper place mat. "Not funny, Karl."

He apologized as I plucked a napkin from the canister and wiped my face in as ladylike a fashion as I could muster. "So those marks I saw on Finch's neck . . . ?"

"Were finger marks. Like you suspected. That was mighty smart of you."

"Can't the experts get some DNA then or something?"

"The killer was wearing gloves."

"And this time of year, everybody is wearing gloves." I sighed. When I had first suggested there might be more to Mr. Finch's demise than met the eye, I had hoped I'd be proven wrong. There were some things you didn't want to be true, no matter how unlikely that was. "How long had he been dead before . . . ?"

"A couple of hours or so," Karl answered without my needing to finish the sentence. "You okay, Amy?"

That jibed with what I'd been hearing. I wrapped my fingers around my mug for warmth. "Yeah. I just keep seeing Mr. Finch hanging there in my nightmares."

My eyes turned toward the window and Birds & Bees. The lights were on. I could see a few customers inside, Esther hovering in the aisle and Mom behind the sales counter. "Somebody really wanted Mr. Finch dead, didn't they, Karl?"

Karl nodded.

"But why?" I asked. "He had only recently moved to town. Sure, he made a lot of people angry, but who could have wanted him dead that badly?"

Before Karl could come up with a theory, Tiffany appeared at the edge of the table. She slid the grilled cheese my way, then handed Karl his burger and fries. "If you ask me, the whole thing is gruesome." Tiffany snatched the coffeepot from a passing waitress and topped off our mugs.

We turned and looked at her.

"We were just talking about Franklin Finch," I explained.

"I know. I couldn't help hearing." The waitress shook her head slowly. "Scoot over, Amy." Tiffany motioned for me to make room.

I slid across the red vinyl bench and Tiffany settled in across from Karl. She set the coffeepot on the table. "You should have been here the night he was killed. It was practically a mob. I was scared somebody might actually get hurt. Tiffany stopped suddenly, her green eyes growing wide. "Oh!" she said, bringing her dainty hand to her mouth. "Somebody did, didn't they?" She looked first at Karl, then at me.

"Are we still talking about Franklin Finch's murder?" I said.

"Then it *was* murder?" Tiffany said, her voice a whisper. "For real?"

"For real," Karl said. He extended his hands toward Tiffany. "The killer—"

"Or killers," I added.

"Or killers," agreed Karl, "strangled Franklin Finch with their bare hands then strung him up like a side of beef."

Tiffany gasped and recoiled.

"Karl!" I admonished. "Must you be so graphic?"

Karl dropped his hands and stuffed a French fry in his mouth. "Sorry, Tiffany."

She patted his hand. "That's okay, Karl." Nonetheless, she was rubbing her neck and looking troubled.

"Let me get this straight, Tiff. Are you talking about the night that Mr. Finch was murdered?" I pressed closer to Tiffany, my grilled cheese growing cold.

Color returned to Tiffany's face. "That's right," she said, playing with her pencil. "There was a whole group of Christmas House Village employees here. They had about half the tables."

"Employees or ex-employees?" I asked.

Tiffany merely shrugged. "I'm afraid I wouldn't know. Sorry."

"That's okay." I picked at my slaw with my fork. "Was Irma Fortuny here?"

Tiffany thought a moment. "Yes. Oh, and Eve Dunnellon. I know her because she comes in a lot." She shook her head in frustration. "And a whole bunch of folks whose names I don't know."

"What about William?"

"William?" Tiffany squeezed her brows together.

"He's a big-shouldered old man. He walks with a cane."

Karl chuckled. "There are a lot of old men walking around on canes in these parts, Amy. You've been out to Rolling Acres. The joint's full of 'em."

Karl was right, of course. Rolling Acres was the senior living facility where he owned a bungalow.

"He would have been with Mrs. Fortuny, probably," I clarified. "The cane has a bird's head handle."

Tiffany smiled in recognition. "Like an eagle?"

I nodded.

"Yes, he was here. Mr. Finch was here, too, with Kim. They were sitting right here in this booth." The waitress aimed her eyes directly at me. "As a matter of fact, Franklin Finch was sitting right where you are now."

I about jumped off the bench. There wasn't much less pleasant than sitting in a dead man's seat. Unfortunately, I was trapped between the plate-glass window and Tiff.

"Franklin Finch was here with his employees?" Karl appeared surprised.

"No, not with them." I explained how Kim had asked to meet with him to discuss retaining the employees and even keeping the original Kinley's name. "I'm sure she had no idea that a group of Finch's disgruntled employees would be meeting here at the same time."

"That was bad timing." Karl grabbed the catsup, lifted the top of his lukewarm burger, and gave it a dousing. He twisted the top of the bun back in place and took a huge bite.

"Was there any trouble?" I asked Tiff.

"There was a lot of hollering. For a minute or two, Moire was talking about calling the police to come break it up," Tiffany said. "Our customers were getting upset and looking uncomfortable."

"But nobody came to blows?" I pushed. "I mean, did anyone attack Mr. Finch?"

Karl smiled. "I see where you're going, Amy. You're wondering if those marks on his neck could have been caused earlier. But he was strangled, remember? Not beaten up."

I frowned. Karl was right.

"It's funny, now that I think about that night. There was a young guy in uniform with them," Tiffany added, "and he seemed as riled as the rest of them."

"What sort of uniform?" I asked.

"Green with a black leather jacket."

I narrowed my eyes. "Like a security guard uniform?"

"Exactly." That sounded like Max of the North Pole. The same Max who'd been in Finch's office when I'd had my initial meeting with him and whom I then saw lurking outside the office afterward. What was Max's story?

Whose side was he on? Had he been Finch's enemy or had he been his mole?

The line cook stuck his head out the order window and called Tiffany's name. She grabbed the coffeepot and stepped from the booth. "And like Karl said, nobody did any physical fighting. The only fighting here that night was verbal."

Tiffany headed up the aisle and looked back to say, "Once Mr. Finch and Kim left, folks quieted down."

Watching her leave, I said to Karl, "I can't help wondering if one of those people here that night might not have had some pent-up anger."

"And went back to Christmas House Village to finish the argument in private?" Karl said, before chomping down on his burger. "I suppose that would fit the timeline."

"Exactly. But which one of them was it?"

"There's no telling. Tiffany can't even say who all was here."

"I'll talk to Kim. Maybe she'll remember. Do you think you can find out anything about this acquaintance of Mrs. Fortuny, this William character?"

Karl rubbed his chin. "I'll see what I can do. The trick is to squeeze the information out of Jerry without him knowing. If he can't help, I've still got my sources."

"Thanks, Karl. While you're at it, how about checking out Irma Fortuny and Bobby Cherry?"

Karl looked amused at my mention of the first name and confused by my mention of the second. "If you say so, Amy. Do you know what you're looking for?"

"Not yet. But who knows? Maybe we'll find a killer."

Karl chuckled. "I wouldn't mind solving this one before Jerry does. Show him that an old dog can still hunt."

We finished eating our lukewarm meals. Karl promised to let me know if he learned any other inside information via Chief Kennedy.

"What are you going to do?" he asked, opening his wallet and forking over his share of the bill.

"After I talk to Kim, I think I'll pay another visit to Christmas House Village."

"Snooping?"

"Snooping? Of course not, Karl. 'Tis the season." I smiled disingenuously. "I'm going to do a little Christmas shopping. Pick up a few gifts. Maybe," I said, reaching across the booth and touching the tip of his nose, "I'll even get a gift for you."

And if that shopping included picking up a killer rather than a killer bargain, then so much the better.

12

The next morning, Esther and I worked the morning shift at Birds & Bees. Kim had been scheduled but was a no-show. I had been unable to reach her last night, and I was growing more and more concerned about her.

After trying several times over the course of the morning, I'd called Dan Sutton on his personal cell phone to see what he could tell me. Dan explained that he had spent some time with Kim the previous evening. He assured me she was okay, if a bit gloomy. Dan did not know if she would be going to work that day, either at Belzer's Realty or Birds & Bees.

She hadn't been working much at all lately and seemed to be coming apart at the seams.

Dan also told me there hadn't been any real progress made in Franklin Finch's murder except to confirm the strangling and that the police were conducting interviews. He may have known more than he was telling, but that was all I could get out of him—on or off the record.

Customers trickled in and the morning dragged on. I wasn't concerned; I knew things would pick up after lunch. Happily, Derek called before noon and we made plans for dinner that night.

In a cleared space near the center of the store, I was giving a scheduled early-afternoon demonstration on crafting roosting pockets when Cash Calderon came in the door. He took a look around, noticed me surrounded by a handful of customers, and waved. He mouthed that he was going down to the basement.

I nodded an acknowledgment and continued the demonstration.

Seated on a stubby, wooden three-legged stool, I held the roost between my knees and was weaving a long strand of grass in and out.

Woven from raffia grass, an easily workable, light brown, dried palm frond, such as you might see a traditional hula skirt made from, the teardrop-shaped roosts were the perfect spot for birds to escape the cold, the wet, and the wind. The roosting pouches were particularly attractive to chickadees and wrens, which typically roost alone.

The demonstration wrapped up about a half hour later. Then I spent a few minutes chatting and answering questions from the small audience.

"Can you handle it from here?" I asked Esther.

"Sure thing."

I carried the roosting pocket I'd woven during the demonstration over to the ten-foot Christmas tree along the wall between the seed bins and the sales counter. Cutting a strip of narrow red ribbon from a spool, I ran the ribbon through the loop I'd created at the top of the grass pocket, then attached the pocket over a slender branch, joining the dozen or so that were already hanging there.

Cousin Riley had brought the Christmas tree to the store earlier that week. He then affixed silver and gold tinsel along the sales counter and strung more across the ceiling. He promised to get to the outdoor holiday lights soon.

Riley's a bit of a jack-of-all-trades and helps out in and around the property, in addition to working for anyone else in town who needs a hand now and then. He also helps out at the Theater on the Square, our town's community theater, where he mostly builds scenery but keeps hoping for his big acting break.

I asked Esther to tend to the shoppers and hand out the sheets I had printed up listing the necessary items and basic building instructions for the roosting pockets to everyone who wanted one.

Some customers were buying materials to have a go at building their own roosts. Others opted to buy from the supply of premade pockets we kept on hand. While we carry the roosts all year, I had arranged a larger, more prominent display of them now with winter around the corner.

In addition to the woven pockets, we sold wood roosting boxes. I was thinking of having Aaron Maddley, a local farmer and craftsman who supplied us with birdhouses, come in one day and give a workshop on building those if there was enough interest. I'd put a sign-up sheet on the bulletin board and see how many signatures we collected from our customers.

I picked up my stool and set it out of the way near the window, then crossed to the basement door. I was about to head downstairs when Cash Calderon appeared from around the corner as he came up the steps.

"Hi, Mr. Calderon," I said, unable to hide the surprise in my voice. "This is a pleasant surprise."

"Hi, Amy." Cash Calderon, a local general contractor, clomped up the wooden steps, swiping a cobweb from his red-and-black-checked flannel shirt. "I finally had some time to check out the furnace for you."

"And?" I'd been complaining about the lack of hot water and, now with the colder weather, the lack of sufficient heat. I had called Mr. Calderon's company, CC Construction, several weeks ago and his wife had promised he'd come out first chance he got. I'd told her there was no hurry and wasn't expecting him until after the holidays. I was glad to see him sooner rather than later.

No news is good news, isn't that what they say?

"And it's not good, I'm sorry to say."

While I'd heard Mr. Calderon was approaching sixty, working construction kept him as fit as a man twenty years younger. His eyes were dark blue and he had a distinctive mole just below his left earlobe.

My face fell. "Not good as in what?" The contractor had made a number of repairs on my house since I'd moved in. He'd also scolded me for not having had a home inspection performed before buying.

I was still paying for that mistake. I had bought three stories, an attic, and a basement full of trouble.

Mr. Calderon pulled a notebook from his leather jacket, licked his finger, and began flipping through the pages—the sheer number of which was scaring me. He looked up at me. "You might want to sit down for this."

I drew my teeth across my lower lip. "Come on. I'll buy you a cup of coffee." I led him to the kitchenette in the corner of the store. "Have a seat." I lifted the coffeepot. "Help yourself to the cupcakes." Mom and Esther had made a morning trip to C Is For Cupcakes and brought back a couple dozen for our customers. There were plenty remaining.

"Thanks. I don't mind if I do." The contractor's hand hovered over the open box a moment before selecting a chocolate cupcake with strawberry frosting.

I set our coffee mugs on the table between our two rocking chairs. "Go ahead," I said, gripping my knees. "Let me have it."

He licked a bit of frosting off his thumb and set his papers across his thigh. "First off, the water heater is shot."

I groaned and lifted my knees to my chest.

"Second, your plumbing is shot."

I stood and reached for a cupcake. I didn't care what flavor it was, I wanted the one with the tallest pile of frosting. I plucked the foil paper from its edges, tipped it over, and ripped off the bottom.

Cash Calderon watched, his brow slightly raised, but made no comment. I plopped down in my chair and urged him to continue.

"You've got cast-iron pipes running throughout. They've rusted and rotted and will have to be replaced with PVC. " He looked over at me for a moment. "That means tearing up the basement floor."

"PVC, right." I chewed, swallowed, and went for the top half, the half with all the vanilla buttercream on the banana-flavored cupcake.

"That is code." He paused and cleared his throat. "On further inspection, I noticed you have asbestos in the ceiling. Because we're going to be cutting into the walls, that will need to be ameliorated."

"Ameliorated, right." I nodded and considered a second cupcake. The only thing preventing me was that he had yet to finish his first. I opted for my coffee instead and took a slow drink.

"And then there is the electrical . . ." He looked at me.

Was that pity I was seeing in his eyes?

"Electrical?" I dropped my feet to the floor. "I have noticed some occasional problems."

"Like appliances shorting out, popped fuses, and the smell of burning toast?"

I smiled. "Yes, like that. Glitches."

His brow arched. "Those glitches could burn down your house."

"Oh." I reached for a second cupcake. Sugar is a known cure for anxiety. Sugar and fat. "So," I said, peeling back the second wrapper and breaking my cupcake in two. "How much is this going to cost me, Mr. Calderon?"

He flipped through his papers some more, to the accompanying clicking of his tongue. "I'll work up some numbers back at the office and get back to you."

"Ballpark?"

"It will cost less than a ballpark," he said with a smile, "but not by much."

My jaw fell.

"Sorry!" Mr. Calderon said, snatching in midair the cupcake that fell from my open hand. "Bad joke."

The cupcake was now a pile of yellow mush in his palm. "Let me get that for you!" I jumped to my feet, grabbed the washcloth, and turned on the tap.

"No bother." Mr. Calderon stood and stuck his hand under the running water, then wiped it dry with the towel. "Good as new."

I pulled a face. "I wish my house was."

"Sorry, Amy. But when you buy a house built in the eighteen hundreds, you're going to have a few problems."

"Yeah," I agreed. "Like eighteen hundred of them." Over the contractor's laugh, I asked, "Speaking of old houses, have you ever done any work over at Christmas House Village?"

"Of course," said Mr. Calderon, picking up his now-empty mug and rinsing it in the sink. "In fact, I have a maintenance contract with them. At least, I did."

"Did? Did Franklin Finch drop you, too?"

The contractor nodded. "Our firm had an annual agreement with Christmas House Village. The Kinleys renewed it each year." The corners of Mr. Calderon's mouth turned down. "Franklin Finch called me up and declared it null and void."

"And now he's null and void," I quipped.

Surprise showed on the contractor's face. "You're not thinking I had anything to do with his death?"

"No," I said, quickly patting his sleeve. "Not at all. I just wondered if you'd noticed anything going on over there."

"Or knew who might have wanted him dead?"

I pouted. "Something like that."

"Sorry, Amy." I noticed a hesitation in his eyes. "Although . . ."

"Yes?"

"Now that you mention it, I have had several persons asking me questions about Christmas House Village."

"What sort of questions?"

He shrugged. "Nothing particular. They were curious as to what condition the property was in."

"Who wanted to know?"

The contractor thought a moment, then tugged at his collar. "Sorry, Amy. I don't think it's my place to say." He turned and headed toward the back door. "Like I said, I'll get back to you soon with some numbers."

"Take your time," I replied, as he stepped out into the cold. I had a feeling those numbers were going to be large.

He waved and pulled open the driver's-side door of his big, black 4x4. As he put one long leg inside, he turned and said, "As for who was asking questions about Christmas House Village, I can tell you this, they are always happy to kiss a baby or two!"

What on earth did that mean?

13

And that was exactly the question I asked Derek when we met at his place, then walked over to Jessamine's Kitchen for dinner that night. The homey, Southern-style restaurant was a recent addition to the Town of Ruby Lake.

The pleasant owner, Jessamine Jeffries, is a retired accountant from Greensboro now following her passion for cooking. She has a real flair for it, too. She's a zaftig woman of sixty-some years with shoulder-length brown locks and matching brown eyes. Divorced and unattached, she receives the attention of many of the older and even some of the younger men in town.

The restaurant's décor, with its simple Shaker style tables and chairs, was as cozy as the food. Soft blue-and-white-checkered tablecloths covered the tables. The floor was reclaimed wide-board pine.

A beeswax candle on the tabletop in a small cut-glass bowl shaped like a tulip flickered between us. We had a table near the black cast-iron woodstove glowing in the center of the room.

"Cash Calderon came by Birds and Bees today. He told me someone had been asking him questions about Christmas House Village." I wasn't going to bother Derek with my own house's troubles. He had enough going on in his life without having the extra burden of worrying over my financial situation.

"He's a contractor. What sort of questions?"

I could only shrug. "Contractor-type questions, I suppose. He really wouldn't tell me."

"Did he say who was asking the questions?"

"Nope, only that they liked to kiss babies."

"Huh?"

"That's what he said. That, whoever they were, they were happy to kiss a baby or two."

"Cash actually said 'kiss a baby or two'?" Derek had ordered a bottle of merlot that our waiter now poured.

"His words exactly."

Derek leaned back, glass in hand. He shook his head and took a drink. "A pediatrician, maybe?"

I nodded. "That could be. But why would a pediatrician be asking about Christmas House Village?"

Derek didn't have a clue and neither did I.

"While I was having lunch with Karl at Ruby's Diner, Tiffany mentioned that there were a number of disgruntled Christmas House Village employees and ex-employees at the diner the evening that Kim was there with Mr. Finch."

I sipped my wine and ran my tongue over my upper lip. "Apparently it was practically a mob, right there and then."

Derek sighed. "It's a nasty business, all right. I don't like to imagine that anybody in this town murdered him. Especially the way they did it."

"I know, it's weird, but it would be nice if it turned out to be a stranger."

"Yeah," Derek agreed, "but I don't think Franklin Finch's being strangled and strung up in his own loft was the act of a stranger. That sort of crime strikes me as being very personal."

"I agree."

We paused in our conversation to place our dinner order. After the waiter left, I picked up where we'd left off. "I asked Karl to see what he could find out about Mrs. Fortuny and her friend William."

"What?" Derek teased. "You think because the woman hit Kim in the head with her purse that she might have strung up Franklin Finch? I don't think she has the muscle power. In fact," he added, "I don't recall Kim complaining of the blow leaving so much as a bruise, let alone a concussion."

"Very funny." I pointed my fork at him. "But I do believe William—whatever-his-last-name is—could provide that muscle."

"I've seen him, remember? He was with Mrs. Fortuny at C Is For Cupcakes. The gentleman walks with a cane."

"Maybe it's made his arms stronger."

Derek chuckled. "So," he said, rubbing his hands, "let me see if I have this right. We have a seventy-something-year-old woman and an equally old man with a cane as our chief suspects in the strangulation and subsequent hanging of one Franklin Finch."

Two servers arrived with food-laden trays, saving Derek from my shrewd yet pithy reply—and saving me from having to think up one.

After a meal of family-style skillet-fried chicken, green beans, cheese grits, and biscuits, I suggested that we take a stroll around town.

"Sure," Derek agreed amiably. "The downtown looks great this time of year."

"I agree. Just enough Christmas lighting and decoration to make it pretty." I knotted my scarf and placed a knit cap on my head. "But not so much as to be gaudy."

The town does a really good job of setting up the town square, too, with a thirty-foot Christmas tree, a giant wooden sleigh, Santa's throne for the kiddies, and a petting corral wherein the ponies wore fuzzy brown antlers.

Derek settled the bill and we walked to the door.

"Let me guess," Derek said, bundling up his black peacoat. "This little stroll of ours is going to take us right past Christmas House Village, isn't it?"

I tilted my head and smiled. "Why, now that you mention it, we will be walking right past it. Would you care to do some holiday shopping?"

Derek laughed.

"What? I did promise Karl I would buy him something."

Derek shook his head as we stepped out into the chill night air. "Amy Simms, I've heard a lot of stories from clients, but yours is one line I'm not buying."

"Hey!" I protested.

"Don't worry," he said, throwing up his hands. "I'm not vetoing the idea."

"Good." I locked my arm with his.

"Besides, with me along, you just might stay out of trouble."

"Ha-ha." I gave him a hip bump. "You are quite the comedian tonight, Counselor."

"I try."

We strolled companionably across the town square, and up Lake Shore Drive. The lure of Christmas House Village's lights was like the draw of a moth to a flame. Shoppers swarmed the well-lit houses and many carried bags and gaily wrapped packages.

We walked up the main path, our eyes climbing to the big yellow star atop the outdoor Christmas fir. The streetlamps cast a pleasant glow that lit the path.

"Do you know what you want for Christmas?"

Derek squeezed my hand. "I've got all I need."

"Okay," I said, "but all you want?"

"What about you?" he asked, turning the tables. "Anything special that you'd like?"

"No way, mister. You answer my question, then I'll answer yours."

Derek's eyes twinkled. "I'll give it some thought. You do the same." He kissed me in front of the Christmas tree and I blushed.

"It's a deal," I said after he'd kissed me again. I'm easy that way. "Hey, you don't even have a Christmas tree for your apartment," I said, running my hands through the fir needles. "We have to get you one!"

"Whoa!" Derek held up his hand. "First a bird feeder and now a Christmas tree? I don't know . . ." He shook his head.

"Come on," I nudged, "what's Maeve going to think if her own father doesn't have a Christmas tree?"

Derek pulled a face. "You're right. Okay, you win. We can pick one out together at one of the tree lots."

"Oh, no," I said, "you need to go Christmas-tree shopping with Maeve. Think what fun she'll have. You can't leave her out."

"You're right." Derek nodded.

"Of course I am."

"But only if you'll come with us."

"Are you sure?"

"Sure, I'm sure. It will be fun."

I took a deep breath. "Okay. What about—"

"Amy?"

The Amy in question wasn't me. It was the other Amy—Amy Harlan. Amy-the-ex, as I liked to call her. She was Maeve's mother and Derek's ex. She was no friend of mine, not that I hadn't tried to be civil to the woman. I had a hunch she wanted Derek back.

Maeve, their eight-year-old daughter, lived mostly with Amy-the-ex at her place out at the Apple Mountain Country Club.

"Yes," I said. "I don't think she's going to want me shopping for a Christmas tree with you and Maeve."

"You misjudge her," he said, as we strolled the path around the Christmas tree. "Amy's not a witch."

"No, but she's something that rhymes with it," I muttered. "Sorry," I added quickly. "That was a cheap shot." We rounded the far side of the circle. "Hey, look who's here," I said softly.

"Who?" Derek stopped.

"Gertie Hammer. She's sitting on the bench on the right." I nodded ever so slightly. "I wonder what she's doing here."

The elderly woman sat bundled up at the far bench, her lips pulled tight. As usual this time of year, she had wrapped herself up in her puffy, lime-green, three-quarter-length down jacket that appeared two sizes too big for her.

Her plus-size green coat made her look like a big green holly shrub. With the near-freezing temperature, she had an appropriately berry-red face. The coat's floppy, cocoon-brimmed hood draped over her forehead, hiding the gray-black hair that lurked beneath. Her sharp blue eyes followed the shoppers as if she was stalking each and every one. Her hands were stuffed into puffy black mittens.

"Shopping?" Derek said.

I frowned. "I don't know. She could be, I suppose. I just always thought of her as more the Grinch type than the gift-giving type." If every small town had its curmudgeon, Gertie was ours. "And I don't see any packages." As we watched, she clumsily pulled a stubby pen from one pocket and a notepad from the other and scratched something down.

"Do you want to say hello?"

"No, let's not." I wasn't in the mood for a sparring match with Gertie. "There's somebody I'd like to say hi to, though." I tugged Derek's sleeve.

"Oh? Who?"

"Him. That's Max. He's one of the security guards."

Derek turned and studied the uniformed young man in question. "So I see. What do you want to talk to him for?"

"When I first met him, I got the impression he was Finch's flunky. Then Tiffany mentioned that Max was at Ruby's Diner with the rest of the disgruntled Christmas House Village employees." I bit my lower lip. "I wonder what he's up to."

"Maybe Finch sent him to the meeting at the diner."

"Like as a spy, you think?"

"Maybe."

"I've been wondering the same thing."

The security guard seemed to take note of us. He then turned and entered Sugarplum House. Ignoring Gertie and whatever she was up to—and, knowing Gertie, she was always up to something—I pulled Derek along toward the front entrance, not wanting to lose sight of Max.

Sugarplum House was chock-full of Christmas ornaments. Each room of the house was devoted to ornaments of a particular European country or sometimes subdivided into several countries. These nations ranged from ones you'd expect, like Great Britain, Germany, and France to smaller nations like Denmark and Switzerland.

Inside, we weaved through the crowded rooms. I caught a glimpse of the back of Max's head, a dark jacket and green trousers, as he squeezed between a family of four and headed up the narrow stairs to the second floor. "Come on," I urged.

By the time we got upstairs, there was no sign of Max. "I don't get it," I complained. "You saw him come up here." I looked across the hall to the room we'd just left. "Where did he go?"

Derek shrugged. "He's probably back downstairs. We must have missed him. There are, what, four display rooms up here? And we're practically shoulder to shoulder. I can't believe how busy this place gets. Christmas House Village really is a gold mine, isn't it?"

"It has always been very popular. More so than ever, I'd say."

"Look at this." Derek's hand fell on a glass snow globe with a porcelain base. He picked it up and gave it a shake. The scene represented a quaint farmhouse. A boy and girl dressed for winter teeter-tottered on the front lawn as the snow fell silently around them.

"It's very pretty."

"Do you think Maeve would like it?"

"Definitely."

"I think I'll take one." Derek set down the snow globe and picked up one already wrapped in a red and green gift box with gold ribbon.

"Come on." Derek took my hand. "Maybe Max went next door to Nutcracker House. He's probably making his rounds. I'll pay for this downstairs. You can go over if you want to, and I'll meet you there."

"Good idea."

While Derek went to pay, I went out the door through the kitchen. I knew from having come to Christmas House Village many times as a girl that this led out to the cobblestone path that connected Sugarplum House with Nutcracker House. There was a small porch and a wooden stairway leading down to the path. Firewood was stacked high against the wall. I paused and searched the shadows for movement but saw no one.

As I stepped onto the path from the stairs, I heard a horrible crack, followed quickly by a booming crash. I glanced over my right shoulder. A wall of firewood was tumbling toward me. I hollered and ran.

"Amy!" Derek shouted over the rumble of the falling wood.

Several pieces of firewood slammed into my feet and I felt myself falling. I threw out my hands.

As quickly as the thunder had started, it subsided.

I was on my hands and knees. Firewood was scattered around me and all over the yard between the two houses. The strand of white holiday lights lining the narrow path had been smashed by the rolling wood. Several shoppers stopped to ask if I was okay as Derek helped me to my feet.

A clerk stepped out on the porch and hurried down to assist us. "My goodness," exclaimed the young woman. "Are you all right?"

I nodded. "Just a little shaken."

"What happened?" Her eyes took in the scene of destruction.

Another employee appeared and inspected the wood bin. "It looks like one of the supports gave way." He pointed to a splintered old two-by-four. He sighed. "We'd better call someone." He turned to his coworker. "Who's in charge of maintenance around here, anyway?"

The young woman shrugged. "I have no idea. I just started less than a week ago."

"Me, too," the young man replied. "I guess I should call Ms. Dunnellon." He kicked at the nearest log, then went inside, presumably to make the phone call.

"Are you sure you're okay, Amy?" Derek eyed me solicitously. His package was on the ground beside him.

I looked at my hands. "I'm glad I was wearing gloves." I glanced at my corduroys. "And slacks." Though there were fresh holes in the knees, and it wasn't a fashion statement. I stuck my finger in one of the jagged holes. "I'll be fine." I had a feeling my bump-free future was a thing of the past.

The young woman wrung her hands. "Do you need a doctor, ma'am?"

I shook my head. "No, thanks. Really, I'm fine."

"I'm terribly sorry," the young woman went on. "If you'd like, I can get the manager over and—"

I raised a hand to cut her off. "That won't be necessary." I turned to Derek. "I think I'd like to call it a night."

"I'll take you home." Derek picked up his present for Maeve.

Several Christmas House Village employees stepped out in winter coats and gloves and began clearing the firewood from the path and restacking it loosely at the side of the house.

Derek held my arm and led me back to the front path. My hands and knees throbbed but I was sure no permanent harm had been done.

Gertie was sitting on the bench, same as earlier.

There was no sign of Max the security guard, but I had a hunch he'd been trying to tell me something.

14

Feeling only a little worse for wear the next morning, I took a steaming hot shower—or at least tried to. The hot water sputtered out after a mere thirty seconds.

Cash Calderon was right. I was going to have to do something about all the long-overdue repairs on my house. Without them, the house would be unlivable and my business would suffer. It's hard to run a store when the electricity goes out, which it occasionally did.

Robbed of the wickedly hot shower I'd dreamed of, I consoled myself with a cup of coffee hot enough to scorch my tongue and strong enough to burn a hole in my stomach.

Max of the North Pole had eluded me and Derek the night before, but in the light of day I wasn't going to give him the chance to do it again.

Derek had driven me home and tried to convince me that the episode had been nothing more than an accident. Call me suspicious, but I wasn't so sure about that. The wood crib might have been old and it might have broken . . . but it might have had some help in the form of a pair of strong arms, or perhaps a foot, that had caused the wood pile to come crashing down just as I was passing.

Mom and Esther were working the floor at Birds & Bees and Cousin Riley had shown up to hang the outdoor holiday lights. I knew he'd be available to help inside if the two needed him.

That left me free to take care of other business. I loaded up the minivan with a cardboard box of individually wrapped birdseed ornaments. I had selected six each of the snowmen and gingerbread men. I wanted a second look at the scene of my "accident." I also wanted a word with Max.

I climbed into the Kia, started the motor, and cranked up the heater. The birdseed ornaments in the back of the van gave me the excuse I needed. I would take them to Christmas House Village for Eve Dunnellon to get a look at.

I drove downtown and turned down the long, narrow alley that led behind Christmas House Village. The alleyway served as the delivery entrance.

I pulled up directly behind Elf House. To my surprise, Max was coming down the back steps. I cut the engine and went around to the back of the van.

"Sorry, ma'am, but you can't park here," he said. "It's for employees and—" He stopped and smiled sheepishly. "Oh, it's you. You're the bird lady, right?"

I smiled back. "I've been called worse." I yanked open the back door of the minivan. "I'm dropping off some merchandise. I've got the first box of birdseed ornaments for Christmas House Village."

I reached inside and dragged the box closer. "I thought I'd show it to Ms. Dunnellon for her approval." I lifted the cardboard box and held it against my chest.

He pulled off his cap and scratched his head. "I'm afraid she isn't here. She was in late last night. We had some trouble. Don't spread it around, but a customer practically got herself killed when a stack of firewood gave way."

I narrowed my eyes at the guard. Was he trying to tell me something? "I know. I was here last evening."

"Oh?" I couldn't tell if he was playing dumb or really hadn't seen me.

I nodded. "In fact, I was the one who got hurt." I set the box back down in the rear of the van. "Sort of." My feet still hurt from the firewood running over them, and my hands ached from rubbing along the cobblestones.

"Sorry to hear that." I couldn't tell from his tone of voice whether he'd meant it or not.

I reached for the box once again. "If you don't mind, I'll just run these upstairs to Ms. Dunnellon's office."

Max placed his hand atop the box. "I'll handle it for you."

I looked at him a moment, unsure what to say, but I was getting the feeling I didn't have much choice in the matter. "Thanks," I said after a beat. "You'll be sure that she gets these?"

"You can count on it."

I handed Max the box. "So," I began as nonchalantly as possible as I shut the rear door to the van, "any rumors on what will happen with Christmas House Village next?"

Max balanced the box in his arms. "How do you mean?"

"Have you heard anything about it being sold again?"

Max eyed me with unhidden suspicion. "What makes you ask that?"

I struggled for a reasonable response. "Well, as a business owner with a relationship with Christmas House Village, I'm hoping that everything continues to run smoothly."

"Why wouldn't it?" His frown deepened.

"No reason," I said quickly. "In fact, last night Christmas House Village was as busy as anytime I've ever seen. That's a good sign, right?" I smiled at him.

"Yeah." He looked back at the house. "I'll get this inside."

I touched his sleeve. "Before you go, I was wondering if you know Bobby Cherry."

"Nope, never heard of him."

"That's funny, he works here, at least he did until fairly recently. And from what I've heard about the young man, I would think that you of all people would know him."

Max pinched his brows together. "What's that supposed to mean?"

"You are a security guard. I've heard from several sources that he was something of a troublemaker." The two of them appeared to be close in age, too.

"Like you?" He smirked. "There are a lot of people working here. Plenty of them seem like troublemakers, if you ask me."

"What about Mr. Finch? Did you consider him a troublemaker?"

"I'm not saying anything about a dead man."

"Were you working the night he was killed?"

"Nope. I was on the day shift."

"Oh? I was sure I saw you."

"My stepsister was here working that night. I came by to give her a ride home. That's when I saw the police and stuff."

"And you didn't think to come see what was going on?"

"I asked the cop on the porch. He told me to stay clear." Max didn't sound like he'd been happy about that though. "She never said anything about hearing anything out of the ordinary."

"Wait. Your stepsister works at Christmas House Village, too?"

"Yeah. You met her."

"I did?"

"You *were* the lady that got tangled up in the firewood?"

I nodded.

"My stepsister told me she was the one who went outside to see if you were okay."

My eyes grew wide. "That was your stepsister?"

"Lizzie Poulshot."

"I see." And maybe I did see—more than Max realized he'd given away. Was that what had happened? Were brother and stepsister in collusion? Had he waited outside, hoping for my arrival, and then his stepsister gave him the word and he broke the wood support holding back the firewood? Had he been trying to kill me or merely intimidate me?

"It's possible that Mr. Finch was strangled elsewhere and then his body was brought back to Elf House, where it was staged to look like he had hanged himself."

Max snorted. "Yeah, and it's possible that Santa Claus is going to come down one of these chimneys."

"What were you doing at Ruby's Diner the night that Mr. Finch was killed?"

"Eating dinner."

"Mr. Finch didn't mind you consorting with the very same employees who had been demonstrating against him?"

Max smiled, showing his teeth. "I don't hear him complaining, do you?"

I shivered. I was alone in the alley with a possible murderer. It was time to get in the van and drive away. "Thanks for your help."

I hopped back inside and locked the door behind me. Max watched me from the back step of Elf House, cardboard box in hand, as I rumbled farther up the alley and rounded the corner with the intent of following the alley the long way around and coming out on the other end of Lake Shore Drive.

I kept an eye on the rearview mirror in case he tried to follow me.

Around the bend, I was forced to stop. A pickup truck pulling a trailer covered with yard maintenance equipment was blocking the way. A large shed with double doors hanging open took up the remaining width. The sign over the shed read: Santa's Reindeer Barn.

There was a lone man inside. He wore green pants and a green army jacket. A beanie was pulled down over his ears.

He must have heard my approach because he stepped out of the shed, a long plank in his left hand. He held up his finger to indicate that he'd only be a minute.

I rolled down my window. "No problem. Take your time."

Ignoring my assurance that I was in no hurry, the man tossed the plank next to a couple of others in the trailer, then sauntered over to me.

"Are you looking for something, miss?" His name badge identified him as Tito. While, like everyone else, he was supposed to be from the North Pole, his accent was all Latin America.

"No. I was dropping off some merchandise."

"Okay, I'll be out of your way in a minute. I needed to pick up some lumber. I need only to grab the hammer and nails."

"Are you the maintenance man?"

"Not usually." His breath came out in clouds. The day was getting colder rather than warmer. "I do the landscape. But a wood crib broke last night and the manager asked me to repair it."

I nodded and shut off the engine to save gas. I didn't bother explaining my involvement in the matter.

He sighed. "It's always something around here. After Mr. Tyrone died and then Mrs. Johnson . . ."

"Mr. Tyrone?"

Tito smiled. "Tyrone Kinley. I called him Mr. Tyrone. Things started to fall apart." He held his thumb and forefinger within a hairsbreadth of each other. "Only a little at first, but it was getting worse. The Kinley kids lived far away."

"And then Franklin Finch bought the place."

"Yes." Tito made the sign of the cross over his chest. "I was here the night he died." He looked in the general direction of Elf House, whose gable was visible.

"You were here working at night?"

Tito nodded. "Mr. Finch asked me to replace a couple of the Christmas trees inside the houses. They were losing a lot of needles."

"Which houses would that be?"

"Elf House and Santa's House. Why?"

"Elf House? The office?"

Tito nodded.

"Did you notice anything odd?"

He shook his head sadly. "Sorry, no. The police have already asked me. I heard a noise in the alley. But it was only one of the cats. We've got a couple of black-and-white strays that like to go ratting back here."

"A cat? Are you sure?"

"I saw it myself."

"I know this might sound strange, but in the short time that Mr. Finch was here, did you see or hear him arguing with anyone in particular? Was there somebody who wanted him dead?"

The landscaper smiled at my question. "Nobody argued with Mr. Finch. Not if you wanted to keep your job."

I tried another tack. "What about the rope?"

His brow furrowed. "Rope, miss?"

"The rope that the killer used to hang him from the rafter tie. Did it come from Christmas House Village, you think?"

"Ah." He tilted his head back in understanding. "Come." He turned and motioned for me to follow.

I climbed down from the van and accompanied him to the big shed. He pulled a string attached to an overhead light, bringing the musty contents into sight. Inside was a veritable hodgepodge of yard and building supplies.

The landscaper skirted between a stack of empty pallets and a trash bin to reach the far side of the shed. When he got to the wall, he frowned. "Hmm."

He did a slow turn and crossed to the other side of the shed. "Ah. Yes, see?" Tito laid his hand on a coil of rope hanging from a sturdy hook on the wall. "We have plenty of rope."

I moved closer. The rope did appear to be the same type of rope that I had seen knotted around Finch's neck. Tito was right. There was plenty of it, too. Maybe fifty yards' worth.

Was this where the killer had gotten the rope used to hang Franklin Finch? If so, that fact pointed even more to the killer being a Christmas House Village insider. After all, who else would have known about a source of rope being out here in the shed?

The nearest end of the rope had been cleanly cut. I ran my finger along the edge. Something still didn't make sense. Kim said that when she entered the loft, the body of Franklin Finch was swaying. The police had determined that he'd been killed two hours earlier. Why was he swinging when she found him?

I felt like I was missing something crucial and I didn't have a clue what it might be.

I turned and took careful inventory of the cluttered shed. The largest single object was the pine workbench against the back wall. Its top was about the size of a standard door. A heavy red vise was attached to one end. An electric power strip was screwed into the right side just under the tabletop.

Various tools of the trade, from saws and screwdrivers to hammers and wrenches covered the pegboard fastened to the wall above the workbench. What fascinated me most was a pair of machetes that hung side by side above a jagged-toothed circular saw blade.

"Okay?" Tito asked.

I nodded and we stepped outside. I thanked the landscaper for his time and returned to my minivan as he latched the shed doors. I noticed there was no lock.

I also noticed Max Poulshot looking down at me out of a second-story window of Reindeer House as I exited the alley.

15

Belzer Realty sits at the edge of town out past the Ruby Lake Motor Inn. It is the first structure that tourists see as they come into town, winding through the mountains from the interstate and then onto Lake Shore Drive. I was sure it was no coincidence. While Belzer's wasn't the only real estate agency in town, he wanted people to think of Belzer Realty first.

Like many businesses, including mine, the building that was home to Belzer Realty had started out as a modest family dwelling. After its last owner passed away, the house sat vacant for a number of years until Ellery Belzer had purchased the property some thirty-odd years ago with the intent of operating his then fledgling real estate business from it.

The sign out front had been repainted a number of times, as had the white clapboard-sided house itself, and a few trees had risen and fallen, but the tall sign at the road still read: BELZER REALTY—COME HOME TO THE TOWN OF RUBY LAKE, WHERE EVERY HOUSE IS A JEWEL.

Mr. Belzer was not one for brevity. It was a sign no one could miss, though we, the townspeople, often tried.

The small two-story Colonial house sits on two acres of lightly wooded land. It is a prime piece of real estate, but Mr. Belzer has held on to it, without parceling it off or expanding. There was a quaint charm to the property that I found calm inducing. Even now, a fire burned in the hearth, as evidenced by the picturesque gray-white smoke trickling lethargically from the chimney and disappearing into the clear blue sky.

I took pleasure in the sound of my tires crunching over the crushed quartz driveway that curved up the small incline to the house.

Mr. Belzer's gray sedan was parked near the front door. A light green minivan sat beside it.

I parked close to the small, uncovered porch and climbed out. There was no reason to lock the van's door out here, so I didn't. If a squirrel or raccoon wanted to take the Kia for a joyride, so be it.

I banged my boots against the front steps and pulled open the office door. I was immediately struck by the scent of pine and the soft and pleasing sounds of Christmas carols coming from the small black speakers hanging in two of the room's upper corners.

The front room, which had once been a living room, now served as the main office. The windows were filled with pictures of the properties currently on the market in the greater Ruby Lake area.

Three identical wood desks occupied the front of the room, spaced perpendicularly along the main window. A silver-haired agent in a gray tweed blazer sat at the first of the three desks. With her were a man and woman with their backs to me. Ellery Belzer sat at his desk in the far corner, which faced the window.

A stone fireplace, fire aglow, all but filled the far wall. Christmas stockings hung from the rustic wood mantel. A trio of brass reindeer sat in front of the hearth, as if gathered there for warmth. An immaculate Christmas tree stood to the right. The skirt around the tree was piled high and deep with gift-wrapped packages in all shapes and sizes.

"Mr. Belzer."

The agent looked up from the papers before him as I stepped inside. "Amy," he said with surprise. "Come in."

"Thanks." I wiped my feet, popped open the top button of my wool coat, and crossed to his antique desk. "How are you, Mr. Belzer?"

"Ellery, please." The roundish man circled from behind his desk and gave me a bear hug.

I pointed to the Christmas tree. "It looks like somebody's going to have a nice Christmas. A very nice Christmas."

Mr. Belzer smiled as he looked at the presents. "It's from our annual toy drive. Every year we host a party here for the less fortunate children."

"That's really generous of you."

The real estate agent shrugged off my compliment. "I only do it because I get to dress up and play Santa Claus," he said with a mischievous wink.

He folded his hands over his round belly. "It's the people of Ruby Lake who have been generous this year. As always."

Mr. Belzer motioned for me to sit in one of the upholstered chairs facing his desk, then returned to his own leather chair. I settled into the seat nearest the fire, letting the dry heat seep into me.

"I'm sorry. If I'd known about the toy drive, I would have brought something. I don't remember Kim mentioning it to me."

"Don't give it a second thought," Ellery said. "As you can see, we've collected plenty. I expect every child will have a wonderful Christmas."

I nodded but made a mental note to pick up a couple of gifts from the toy store and send them over with Kim the next time she came to the realty office.

"I heard about your accident last night, Amy. I'm happy to see you're all right."

"You heard?" My hand went to my sore knees.

"Small town." He leaned closer. "I only hope it *was* an accident. There have been a number of unfortunate incidents at Christmas House Village."

"So I heard."

"Oh?"

"Eve Dunnellon told me that Christmas House Village has been having trouble ever since Tyrone passed away and that it has only increased exponentially once Franklin Finch bought the place."

Ellery nodded. "I wouldn't know firsthand, but I have no reason to doubt her. I warned Franklin myself that he would be facing opposition if he proposed too many changes. Folks around here like their Christmas House Village."

"That's the point, isn't it?" I agreed. "The people of Ruby Lake do think of it as *their* Christmas House Village."

"Yes, I see what you mean. It's a shame those same people didn't back up their attitudes with their wallets."

"Are you saying Christmas House Village wasn't making any money?"

"Not like it used to. There's a lot of competition, discount stores, the internet."

"I suppose." Christmas House Village always looked so busy whenever I went in or passed by. "You think it was Christmas House Village employees who were behind all the incidents?"

"I wouldn't want to say anything negative about my fellow Ruby Lakers. But it is common knowledge that certain employees and other townspeople were unhappy with the situation."

"I hate to think of Christmas getting so ugly."

"It will pass."

"I hope you are right."

"Speaking of which, how's Kim holding up, Amy?" Ellery brushed his hands together. "Back to work soon, I hope?"

"You and me both."

"Would you care for some mulled apple cider?"

"How can I resist?" The smell of allspice, cloves, cinnamon, and apple rising from his own mug was making my mouth water.

Ellery rose once again, moving to a cherrywood side table overlaid with a blue tablecloth sprinkled with fake snow, which stood near the fireplace. He grabbed a mug in the shape of Santa and stuck it under the spigot of the large stainless steel urn. A wood tray filled with unshelled nuts sat beside the urn.

I wrapped my fingers around the body of the ceramic mug as he handed it to me. "Thanks." I inhaled, then took a sip. "It's delicious"

"You're welcome, but I can't take any credit. Patricia made it." He pointed to the agent at the front desk. "She brews it herself. It was her mother's recipe. I look forward to it every year."

"The secret's in the brown sugar!" Patricia called.

"It's wonderful, Patricia," I said.

Mr. Belzer folded his hands on his desk. "Was there something else that I can do for you, Amy? You're not considering selling, are you?" He waved to the window. "I have some lovely properties on the market if you're looking to move farther out of town."

I shook my head. "Nothing like that. This is really a personal visit." I opened my coat the rest of the way and rested my purse in my lap and my mug on my leg for extra warmth. "I'm worried about Kim. She seems to be taking this whole Franklin Finch murder very hard."

Mr. Belzer nodded.

"And it isn't just the murder, it is the whole Christmas House Village fiasco. I mean, the sudden sale, the changing of the name from Kinley's Christmas House Village to Finch's."

Ellery Belzer held up his hand. "Trust me, no one feels the pain more than me. However, the sale of Christmas House Village wasn't sudden." He smiled. "Even though I'm sure to an outsider it appears so. The Kinley family contacted me to sell the property quite some time ago. And the deal with Franklin Finch was a long and complicated process."

I nodded my understanding. "It's just that it came as a surprise to me and the rest of the town. I think that was what was hardest about it—that is, about the sale itself and the name change."

Mr. Belzer nodded in acknowledgment. "My hands were tied. Believe me, I wish I could have told everyone what was going on, but it wasn't my place to tell."

"Nor Kim's," I said. I blew on my cider and took another drink.

"With you two being so close, I was afraid she might let something slip along the way." He smiled. "She never once mentioned it to you?"

"Not even remotely."

"Good for her." He let out a long, slow breath. "I wish the entire thing had never happened. And I'm sorry that Kim had to be involved. I actually thought it would be good for her to participate in a bigger deal than the usual house or condo. It also meant a share of a bigger commission than normal. I thought I was doing her a favor. As it turns out, I didn't do her any favor at all. It's bad enough that the town hates me—now they're mad at her, too."

"Mrs. Fortuny actually smacked Kim with her purse when she learned of the sale."

"Oh, dear." Ellery Belzer's hand went to his lips.

"Mrs. Fortuny says she's willing to forgive and forget now that Mr. Finch is dead and she got her job back."

"Glad to hear it."

"I heard you personally have been taking a ton of heat over the sale."

"And then some." Belzer blew out a breath. "I was getting anonymous phone calls in the middle of the night. Angry messages left on the machine here."

He pointed to the phone answering machine. "If you want to know the truth, I was afraid somebody might take out their frustration and anger in a more dangerous fashion. I mean, some people around here own twelve-gauge shotguns!"

"Did it really get that bad?"

"Believe you me, I'd been walking around with one eye looking over my shoulder ever since news of the sale became public knowledge." He paused and sighed. "I guess I should have known better. I'll say it again, this is a small town. We don't like change."

"I suppose there's a certain truth to that."

"It's over now, at least I hope so. Kim's young and she's tough. She'll put this behind her and get back to business soon enough. Give her another couple of days. Trust me."

"I hope you're right, Ellery. I've never seen her like this before."

Behind me, I heard Patricia preparing to leave with her clients. Before she did, she called out to her boss, "I'm going to show the Todds the Johnson and Deidrich properties, Ellery." Patricia plucked a set of car keys from her purse. "Back in an hour."

"Those are two great homes, folks," Belzer called out with a big smile. "If you like either one, I wouldn't wait too long to make your offer!"

The couple muttered that they'd keep that in mind and left with the silver-haired real estate agent.

"The Johnson house?" I asked, after Patricia and her clients had stepped out. "Are you talking about the Virginia Johnson house?"

Ellery Belzer nodded solemnly, his eyes on the three people moving toward Patricia's minivan. "Yes, it's Patricia's listing." The corners of his mouth turned down. "To tell you the truth, I'm having a hard time selling the place. Too many bad memories, you know."

"I can imagine." I rubbed my arms, feeling a sudden chill spread over me despite the heat of the fire. Instead of visions of sugarplums, I was having visions of Virginia Johnson dancing from the end of a rope.

"Speaking of bad memories," I began, "what do you think will happen with Christmas House Village now?"

Mr. Belzer shrugged in clear confusion. "It's too soon to tell, I suppose. Franklin Finch is barely cold in his grave. Besides," he said, reaching for a mug of cider on a heated coaster at the edge of his desk, "no one has approached me regarding a sale, if that's what you mean."

"You haven't heard from Mr. Finch's ex-wife?"

Ellery Belzer seemed surprised. "No, should I have?" He drank slowly, then carefully set his mug back on the warm coaster.

"Not necessarily. I was talking to Eve Dunnellon. She told me that she heard from a lawyer up north that his ex was the new owner."

"Eve is back?" Ellery threw up his hands. "That's news to me." He thought a moment before adding, "Whatever happens, I hope it's best for the town. I hate to sound mercenary, but when you're in the real estate business, like I am . . ."

"I know," I finished for him. "It's all about maintaining property values. Believe me, I'm going through some issues of my own. If I could do it all over again, I would have bought a property through you rather than buying direct from the seller."

Belzer chuckled. "You aren't the first person to try to save on a real estate commission and you won't be the last. But that Gertie Hammer you bought your house from is one tough old cookie." The corners of his mouth turned down. "I was afraid that house of yours would be trouble."

He waved a pencil at me and I felt like I was back in school. "I told Kim to tell you that, when I learned through her you were considering the property."

I pulled a face. "I know you did, and it's my fault for not listening. Gertie's deal sounded too good to be true."

"And it was, wasn't it?"

I sensed a touch of amusement but also compassion in his tone. "Yes, and now Cash Calderon has a list of repairs a mile long that he says I need to make if I don't want the entire house either falling down on me, burning to the ground, or slowly poisoning me to death."

Ellery arched his brow at me and pushed a three-ring binder toward me. The cover read: *Current Local Listings.* "Are you sure you aren't in the market, Amy?"

"Trust me," I quipped. "If you saw my bank account you'd know the answer to that question without even having to ask." I stiffened. "Something has just occurred to me."

"What's that?"

"I wonder how Franklin Finch could afford to purchase Christmas House Village. It couldn't have been cheap."

Ellery smiled. "It wasn't. I made a hefty commission on that sale and I'd give it all back now if it would change things."

"Don't chide yourself. If you hadn't brokered the deal, someone else would have."

"True. That's the only reason I accepted the listing. As for how Finch got his money, I honestly couldn't say. My impression was that he'd sold his previous business for a substantial sum. He put down a considerable down payment and financed the rest with a commercial lender up north."

I finished my drink and rose. "Thanks for your time and the cider."

"Anytime." He rose and walked me to the door. "And if you're ever in the market . . ."

"I know who to call."

"That's right, Belzer Realty." He pulled a business card from his jacket pocket and handed it to me. "And Kim will be more than happy to show you some listings." He paused as we stood at the door. "If you hear anything from Kim, you'll let me know?"

I took the card and promised I would. "And if you hear anything about Christmas House Village, you'll let me know?"

"Absolutely. But I've washed my hands of Christmas House Village."

I buttoned my coat and put on my gloves. "Can you imagine who might have wanted to kill Franklin Finch?"

Mr. Belzer twisted his mouth. "I didn't know him long or well. Considering how mad everybody was at me and Kim, and we were only the brokers for the sale of Christmas House Village, I can only imagine how angry some of those same people might have been at Mr. Finch for buying it *and* changing the name. Before the ink had even dried on the contract, I might add." He furrowed his brow. "Mad enough to kill, maybe."

"What about Irma Fortuny?"

"Are you asking me if she might have been mad enough to kill Franklin Finch?"

I nodded yes.

"I doubt it." He chuckled at the thought. "I've known her a long time. She attends my church."

"And William?"

"William?"

I gave Ellery Belzer a description of the man.

Ellery smiled in recognition. "William Sever. He takes care of Irma."

"Interesting." Maybe he took care of her dirty work, too—like murder. "Do you know a Max Poulshot?"

"No." He shook his head slowly. "I knew a Eustace Poulshot. I sold her a house some years ago. Three bed, two bath, as I recall. Why?"

"I met Max. He's a security guard at Christmas House Village. I can't figure him out." Was he Finch's henchman or his killer?

"I remember him now. A young fellow?" I nodded and Ellery Belzer continued. "Franklin hired the fellow himself. I remember him saying they needed extra security." He frowned. "Not that it ended up doing him any good."

"Did he say why he needed extra security?"

"I think Franklin realized he wouldn't be making any friends when he rebranded Christmas House Village and laid off a lot of the older workers. He did mention that he was afraid of vandalism. I told him such things may happen in New York but not in Ruby Lake."

As it turned out, it hadn't been vandalism that Franklin Finch should have been worrying about. "Are you sure you can't think of anybody in particular who had been threatening you?" It stood to reason that whoever had been harassing Ellery Belzer and Kim would also have had a strong motive for murdering Franklin Finch.

"You mean can I name names?" I nodded and the broker shook his head. "Sorry, Amy. People like that don't leave their names or their calling cards."

He was right, of course. Unless their calling card was murder.

16

Another day went by with no word from Kim.

"I'm really worried about her, Mom." I was driving my mother to the nearby city of Swan Ridge for her appointment with her neurologist. Now that I was living back in Ruby Lake, I intended to accompany her as often as possible to her medical appointments. I wanted to make sure she was getting the best of care. I also wanted to be sure she followed the doctor's advice.

"I have to say," Mom said, her hands in her lap, "I'm worried for her, too. Have you gone by her house?"

"Not lately. I haven't had a chance. I'll stop by later today."

"Yes, do that, dear." She swiveled the air vent away from her legs. "Has Dan talked to her?"

"He hasn't returned my calls," I replied. "I think he's been busy with the Franklin Finch murder case."

Mom nodded. "People seem quite agitated over the whole thing." Her hand went to her throat. "Such a nasty business. Are the police any closer to finding his killer?"

"Not that I know of. I've been meaning to talk to Jerry. Not that either of us ever enjoy our conversations."

Mom chuckled. "Jerry's doing his best."

"Yeah, that's the scary part."

Following my mother's directions, we arrived at a sleek two-story tan brick building in the heart of Swan Ridge. There was a large, vacant corner lot on one side of the office building and a white cottage on the other side that housed a bail bondsman.

I parked the minivan in the nearest empty space and helped Mom down. We went inside and Mom led me down the hall on the left to the offices of Rheumatology and Neurology Associates of Swan Ridge.

I helped Mom with her coat as she checked in for her appointment with Dr. Ajax. I found us a couple of chairs looking toward the wall of windows facing the empty corner lot and sat. Mom joined me but was soon called for her appointment.

"I'm coming with you." I started to rise.

"Nonsense," said Mom. "You stay here. I'm not a child. I promise to tell you exactly what the doctor tells me."

"Fine." I fell back into my chair, pulled out my cell phone and checked my messages. Still nothing from Kim. I sent her yet another text: *Call me.* A thought struck me and I texted once more: *U have 1 hour or sending police to check on u.*

I was sure that would get Kim's attention. She wouldn't want Chief Kennedy or one of his officers—Dan, in particular—showing up, lights flashing, sirens blaring, at her doorstep.

I stuck my phone in the pocket of my butterscotch corduroys where I could get to it quickly and searched the stack of magazines—an assortment of health and nutrition rags. Why not a decent magazine on birding?

"What's with all the protesters?" I asked the receptionist, to pass the time. A small crowd stood gathered around a small folding table near the edge of the road on the weedy acreage.

The receptionist leaned forward. "They're protesting a new development. I guess they figure a lot full of weeds should stay a lot full of weeds." From her tone, I didn't think she agreed with the protesters.

"Ruby Lake has had its share of protesters lately, too."

"Oh?"

"Some employees were protesting the new owner of Christmas House Village."

"Kinley's Christmas House Village has a new owner? I hadn't heard." The receptionist was clearly surprised. "Wait till folks hear."

"It's Finch's Christmas House Village now." How long it would remain so, I had no idea. "The protests seem to be over now."

"Why did they stop? Maybe we can try the same thing on that lot. I'm tired of looking at them every day."

"Mr. Finch, that was the new owner, died."

"That will do it, all right." She frowned as she angled her head to see out the window to the vacant land. "Unfortunately, that's not a supportable option in this case."

"I take it you are in favor of this development?"

She nodded. "Rumor has it a big hotel chain is considering building on the lot next door. I say, let them come. This town could use the taxes, the jobs, and, dare I say it, even a decent hotel to stay in."

"There's a lack of accommodations here in Swan Ridge?" I moved closer to the reception window.

"There's nothing but a forty-year-old roadside motel up at the other end of town. There are only a dozen or so rooms, and I doubt if the owner has updated those tiny guest rooms once in all those years. It goes by the name of Smoky Comfort. I ask you, what kind of name is that?" The receptionist's nose wrinkled up. "Smoky Comfort? It doesn't sound comfortable, does it?"

"No." I had clearly hit one of the receptionist's nerves. "Fortunately, we have the Ruby Lake Motor Inn and a handful of nice B and Bs."

"Lucky you. I live in a one-bedroom apartment. I'm embarrassed to have to ask my friends to stay at Smoky Comfort"—her nose wrinkled again as if it couldn't help itself as she repeated the motel's name—"when they visit."

The receptionist looked pensive for a moment and then her words jumped to another topic. "Hey, Finch, that was the man who hanged himself, wasn't it?"

"He was found hanging, but the police have determined that he was hanged after he was strangled."

"Wow. Crazy world, isn't it?"

I agreed that it was.

The receptionist was silent a minute. "Must be contagious," she quipped. "We had a patient some time back who hung herself."

She bounced her pencil off her teeth several times. "What was her name?" She snapped her fingers. "Virginia Johnson." She nodded. "Yep, that was it. She was nice. I was real sorry to hear she went like that."

"Yes, I only recently heard about her passing myself."

"She suffered terribly, so I suppose it shouldn't have come as a surprise."

"She had MD like my mom?"

"No, I don't recall so."

"Then you must mean depression?"

"Depression?" The receptionist's look told me she hadn't meant that at all. "No, all the old-age stuff. Aches and pains. We all get it. Trust me." She tugged at her lower lip.

"Apparently so, since she committed suicide."

"I suppose poor health might have made her depressed." The receptionist gripped the edges of her seat. "But it was the rheumatism that was the worst. The poor woman could barely use her hands. She was one of Dr. Santiago's patients."

"Really?" I'd seen Dr. Santiago's name on the door. Her specialty was rheumatology.

The receptionist nodded. "Mrs. Johnson had trouble opening packages and couldn't do half the things she used to. Couldn't open her pill bottles. She couldn't even drive. A taxi brought her here once every three months for her checkups."

Mom appeared at the back counter. "Ready, dear? Dr. Ajax says I'm good to go."

The doctor laid some papers on the desk behind the counter. "That's right, your mother's good for another fifty years or fifty thousand miles, whichever comes first."

Mom and I laughed at his little joke.

But I wasn't laughing when I thought about what the receptionist had told me. If Virginia Johnson's hands were so bad, how had she managed to tie a noose around her neck and hang herself?

17

I looked at my watch and frowned. It had been over two hours. Kim had called my bluff.

I drove straight to the police station. But it wasn't to have the police check on Kim. I wanted to check on the police.

The Town of Ruby Lake Police Department is on Barwick Street, far from city hall, which is located in the center of the town square. The building housing our small police force sits close to the street with nothing more than a narrow strip of patchy grass and a sidewalk between the quaint headquarters and the curb. Tree roots have worked their way beneath the sidewalk and the concrete slabs tilt dangerously in all directions.

I parked at the curb and went inside. It was a small office, no more than a couple hundred square feet with several desks scattered about, and with absolutely no sense of style at all.

The only windows were on the front of the building and dusty beige metal blinds covered them most of the time. Not that it mattered, because the view of Barwick was blocked by a row of dented and rust-pitted filing cabinets. Drawers hung open and papers bulged from within them. Overflowing documents, no doubt dating from the Roosevelt administration, balanced in precarious piles atop the cabinets.

There were a couple of drooping potted plants perched on the file cabinets, too. What they were supposed to be, I could only guess. If anybody ever decided to water them, I feared they would die of shock.

Officers Sutton and Reynolds had desks to the right of the front door. Jerry's office was on the back wall toward the left. Anita Brown, their dispatcher, had a desk near the back on the right.

I noticed that a third desk had been added to accommodate Officer Pratt, a recent hire. His desk had been squeezed in on the left near the gun rack. Next to the locked gun rack hung the pictures of all of the town's previous, and current, chiefs of police. One portrait showed a twenty-year-younger Karl Vogel, looking quite handsome and rather dashing in his brown uniform.

Officer Reynolds's desk was empty. So was Dan's, but I spotted him conferring with Chief Kennedy in back. Officer Pratt, a big African American man in his forties, had moved to Ruby Lake from New Orleans. He'd once handcuffed me, but I had since forgiven him, so I waved a friendly hello as I walked to Jerry's desk at the rear.

Jerry looked up as I approached and stopped talking. In a flash, his demeanor went from professional to peeved.

Dan, who was seated in a chair across from the chief, turned to see what had caused the change in his boss.

"Hi, Officer Sutton, Jerry."

I could practically see the blood begin to boil and rise in Jerry's cheeks as I realized my mistake. "I mean, Chief Kennedy." I smiled to relieve the tension.

"That will be all, Dan." Jerry tapped out a beat on his desk with the pencil in his left hand. "Let me know what you find out."

Dan pushed himself up from the wood chair. "Yes, sir." He nodded at me, moved to his desk to retrieve his hat and coat, then departed.

As soon as Jerry caught me eyeballing the papers spread out on his desk, he scooped them up, stuffed them in a tan folder, and dropped the creased folder in desk drawer. "What do you want, Simms?" He slammed the drawer shut with his knee.

I claimed the seat Officer Sutton had surrendered. "Listen, Jerry, I mean, Chief Kennedy—"

He leaned forward and held up his hand. "Forget it. Whatever you want to know about Franklin Finch, I'm not telling you a thing. This is an ongoing murder investigation and you are not part of it!"

"I'm not here to talk about Franklin Finch." I dismissed his concern with a wave of my hand.

"You're not?" Jerry leaned back with a squeak of his leather-backed chair and pinched his brows together. Not a pretty sight. They looked like they were mating.

"No, I'm not." I unbuttoned my coat and clasped my purse on my lap. "I'm here to talk to you about Virginia Johnson."

Jerry gave his head a shake. "The woman is dead and buried. If you'd like, I can tell you where to find her tombstone out at the cemetery. I'd say the time for that discussion has long passed."

I leaned forward and rested a wrist on the edge of his desk. "And I'd say the time for that discussion is long overdue, *Chief*," I added with a smile. A little flattery could go a long way with Jerry.

Jerry's mouth turned down. "I know I am going to regret asking this," he said, sounding terribly put out, "but why would that be?"

"Because," I said, taking a quick breath. "Franklin Finch was—"

There went that stupid hand of his up in the air once again. "I am not talking about Mr. Finch."

"Fine. Hear me out. I drove my mother over to Swan Ridge for her appointment with her neurologist, Dr. Ajax."

Jerry dropped his head to his chest and closed his eyes. I chose to ignore the melodramatics and continued. "The receptionist there told me that Virginia Johnson suffered from rheumatoid arthritis."

Jerry popped his eyes open and stared at me. "Let me get this straight—the receptionist at a doctor's office told you that an old woman had arthritis."

"Yes," I said with an accompanying nod.

"Well, thanks for that news bulletin." Jerry began gathering up papers on his desk. "Now, if you don't mind, I have rather a lot on my plate at the moment."

He rose, planted his fists atop his desk, and loomed over me. "Like resolving an ongoing murder investigation." His cheeks bulged out like a chipmunk's.

I ignored him. "Franklin Finch was—"

The hand shot up again. "Uh-uh!"

I stood and looked Jerry in the eye. "Franklin Finch was found hanging in his loft!" I blurted before he could *uh-uh* me again. "Virginia Johnson was found hanging in her garage!"

I plopped back down in my chair and locked my arms over my chest.

Jerry leaned forward once more and narrowed his eyes at me. His voice was low but firm. "Franklin Finch was strangled first and then strung up for some reason. I intend to find out what that reason was."

He huffed out a breath to let me know how annoyed he was with me. "Virginia Johnson committed suicide. She hung herself from the rafter tie in her garage!" He pointed at the ceiling.

"But what if Virginia Johnson was strangled?"

"Virginia Johnson was not strangled." Jerry was adamant. "She hanged herself."

"But what if she was strangled first?"

"You mean like Finch, don't you?"

"Yes. Isn't it possible?"

"Yes, I admit it's possible." Jerry slammed the folder down on his desk. "But in this particular case, it just isn't so. Virginia Johnson hanged herself, plain and simple."

"How can you be sure? Maybe you should ask the court to exhume the body. See if there is any physical evidence that might have been missed the first time."

The chief of police fondled the handle of the weapon on his hip as he debated with himself. "Fine. Follow me."

He led me to the filing cabinets, and after some searching he threw open a thin folder and stabbed at the close-up shot of Mrs. Johnson's neck. "There are no signs of strangulation. No fingerprints. No nothing. And the autopsy didn't find any evidence to suggest anything other than what it was." He pushed the folder shut, mangling it as he did so. "Suicide. By. Hanging."

Steam practically poured from his nostrils as he shoved the file back in the cabinet—in a space not even close to the one he'd removed it from.

"That's some filing system you have here. I'm surprised you boys can find your own lunches each day."

I heard a chuckle from Officer Pratt. Unfortunately, his boss had heard it, too. Jerry sent the officer a withering glare. Maybe that was the true reason for the droopy potted plants—Jerry might have given them his patented withering look.

"Don't you have some patrolling to do, Officer?" The tone of Jerry's voice made it clear that the question was not a question.

Officer Pratt apparently interpreted it that way, too. He leapt to his feet and grabbed his hat. "Yes, sir." In a flash, he was out the back door and on his way to a squad car.

"Goodbye, Simms." Jerry turned and headed for his desk.

I followed. "Okay, so Mrs. Johnson wasn't strangled."

Jerry stopped midstep and turned. "She wasn't."

"I agree," I said, tagging along once more as he flopped into his chair. "She was hanged. No strangling, I get it." I stood at the edge of his desk. "What I don't get is how."

Jerry lifted his brows. At least they had stopped mating. I was waiting for the appearance of a baby brow anytime now. "How what? Let me paint a picture for you. A woman is depressed. She's sad. She's lonely. She's *old*."

"Yes, but—"

Jerry held up his hand. It was all I could do to keep myself from reaching out and giving it a slap. "She gets a piece of rope from the garage, slides over an old piano bench, ties one end of the rope over a big old beam and the other end around her neck. Then . . ." He splayed his hands. "End of story."

I pulled a face. "Can I talk now?"

Jerry mashed his hands into his face. "Can I stop you?"

"How did she do it, Jerry?" His mouth opened and I put up both my hands to put a stop to it. "How did Virginia Johnson drag a piano bench across her garage, tie one end of a rope over a high beam and the other end around her neck"—I stopped and angled my head to one side, never taking my eyes off of his—"when her hands were so bad that she couldn't drive, couldn't open packages, couldn't even open her own pill bottles?"

Jerry's mouth hung open but no words came out.

"How did she do it, Jerry?"

Jerry leapt to his feet and began pacing, his heavy black leather boots stomping out his frustration. Finally, he turned and looked at me from the other side of the room. We were the only two people in the place. "Are you trying to suggest Virginia Johnson had help?"

"She didn't hang herself, Chief. She couldn't."

Jerry's hand went behind his neck and he rubbed it vigorously. "If she didn't hang herself—"

"Then she wasn't depressed and somebody hung her up there. They murdered her, Jerry."

"But why?" Jerry rolled his neck. "Why kill an old lady?"

I shrugged helplessly. "I don't know. But it's the same M.O., isn't it? Isn't that what you say?"

"You mean modus operandi?"

I nodded. "Virginia Johnson was hanged. So was Franklin Finch."

"Yeah, except that it wasn't the same M.O." Jerry parked his butt on the edge of Officer Reynolds's desk. "Virginia Johnson was hanged by someone, *maybe*," he hedged, "but Finch was definitely strangled first."

"But it was made to look like a hanging."

Jerry's eyes narrowed. "The fact is, it did seem like somebody went to a lot of trouble to make it look like Finch hanged himself."

"Think about it, two hangings!" I held up two fingers. "What are the odds that they aren't related?"

"Not high," admitted the police chief.

"What are the odds that the person who murdered Virginia Johnson is the same person who murdered Franklin Finch?"

Jerry bit his lower lip. "Pretty high, I'd say."

I couldn't help smiling.

Because for once we agreed.

I moved in for the kill. "And what is it that Virginia Johnson and Franklin Finch have in common?"

Jerry furrowed his brow. "What do you mean? Like we've been talking about. It now appears the two of them were murdered."

"And?"

"And they were both found with noose neckties?"

I flinched. "Yeah, there's that, but what else?" I was excited now because the truth was, the *what else* had only come to me a moment ago.

Jerry shook his head. "I am not in the mood for your guessing games, Simms." He slid off the desk and crossed to the water cooler. He grabbed a paper cup and filled it, drinking quickly.

I came up behind him. "Christmas House Village?"

Jerry frowned. "What?"

"Christmas House Village, Jerry, Chief Kennedy. Franklin Finch owned Christmas House Village."

He pulled a face. "I know that, Simms." He crumpled his cup and tossed it in the receptacle beside the water cooler. The man wasn't much for reuse, recycle.

"Jerry." I grabbed his elbow, then removed my hand quickly as he flashed a look at me and headed over to his desk. If I wasn't careful, I'd end up with a withered arm.

I followed like a faithful puppy. "Virginia Johnson was part owner of Christmas House Village."

Jerry leaned back in his chair and stared at the ceiling.

"Virginia Johnson is found hanged in her garage and everybody assumes it was suicide. A few months go by, then Franklin Finch, who is by now the new owner of Christmas House Village, is strangled and found hanging in his apartment in an attempt to make his death look like suicide, too."

The ensuing silence was, as they say, deafening.

"Well?" I asked. "What do you think?" I gulped and waited. Had he fallen asleep? Was he thinking of ways he might strangle me and hide the body?

Jerry's feet fell to the floor as he leaned forward. He draped his arms over his desk. "I think," he sighed, "I have some thinking to do."

18

I left Jerry with his thoughts, buttoned up my coat, and marched outside. Officer Sutton stood on the grass, his shoulder resting against the trunk of a bare oak.

"Dan, I didn't expect to see you here."

Dan straightened as he nodded toward the door. "I thought I'd make sure you got out of there alive."

"Very funny."

"How's Kim doing?"

I fished in my purse for my key ring. "I was hoping you could tell me."

Dan frowned. "I talked to her for a minute or two yesterday. It was the middle of the day and she was moping around in her pajamas. I told her that folks around here aren't as volatile as they were before the murder."

"The best thing she can do is get out and go about her life."

"I agree," said Dan. "But how do we get her to do that?"

I tapped my foot on the sidewalk. "Good question." I smiled. "And I think I have the answer. Where are you off to? Is Jerry sending you on some top secret mission, like fresh cupcakes?"

Dan chuckled. "No, not this time, anyway. We've had a call about some vandalism over at Christmas House Village."

"Again?"

"What do you mean, again?"

"I've heard rumors," I said, deciding to remain vague. Eve Dunnellon had told me that Christmas House Village preferred to keep such things quiet. "What is it this time?"

"A shopper called to report that someone had dumped a gallon of red paint and a dead squirrel in the men's room at Mrs. Claus's Kitchen."

"Christmas House Village?"

"Yep."

"That's disgusting." Mrs. Claus's Kitchen was located in Frosty's House and served light Christmassy drinks and snacks year-round.

"The chief wants me to check it out. At least I won't be the one having to clean it up." He glanced at his watch. "I'd better get going. Let me know if you hear from Kim."

"I will."

Dan climbed into his squad car idling at the curb. I approached the passenger-side window and motioned for him to roll the window down.

"Yeah?"

"Do you know a Bobby Cherry?"

Dan thought a moment, one eye on the monitor on the dash. "No, should I?"

"Ask Eve Dunnellon about him."

"The manager at Christmas House Village?"

Dan agreed and drove off.

Back at the store, I found Riley and Mom finishing up the birdseed ornament order in the first floor stockroom. Esther was running things out front.

Mom looked up from the gingerbread man mold on the table in front of her. "Hello, dear. We've a dozen each to go, and then we're done."

"That's nice to hear. I dropped some samples off earlier for the manager."

"I know," Mom said. "Ms. Dunnellon called and said they were perfect."

"She's real anxious to get the rest," Riley put in. He had the snowman mold filled with seed and was now adding some unshelled black-oil sunflower-seed buttons to its belly. "If you want, I can drive them over in my pickup later." He wore a hideous green and red Christmas sweater featuring a drunken reindeer.

"That would be great, Riley." I patted him on the back. "Speaking of your pickup, would you mind if I borrow it to pick up a Christmas tree?"

Riley turned to face her. "No, I don't mind at all. But you've already got a tree."

"I know, but that's for the store. It has been pointed out to me that we don't have a tree in our apartment."

Mom smiled. "What a good idea. A Christmas tree in the living room will really liven things up."

"I'll check with Derek and see what works for him," I told Riley.

"Derek?" Mom's antenna went up.

"Derek needs a tree, too. For his bachelor pad."

Riley cleared his throat.

"What about you, Riley?" I inquired, picking up on his signal for attention. "Have you got a Christmas tree?"

"Of course I do. You know I do. I always do." Riley plucked bits of birdseed from his palm. "You haven't come by to see it yet," he added, under his breath.

"And is the John Deere tractor ornament on it?"

"It's my tree topper." He beamed. "Same as every year."

"I promise I'll come by soon. Mom and I both will."

Mom readily agreed. "I'll bring my raspberry poinsettia blossom cookies." All my life, my mother's been baking her raspberry blossom cookies for the holidays. I'd miss them if she really did move away for the winters.

"Can anybody join this party?"

We all turned.

"Derek!" I pushed a lock of hair behind my ear and gave him a kiss. "We were just talking about you."

"All good, I hope?" He said hello to my mother and Riley.

"Of course," I said.

Riley snorted.

"Ignore him. What brings you here?"

Derek was dressed casually in jeans, a black sweater, and a hooded parka. "I had the rest of the day off and thought I'd stop by and see if you wanted to go get that Christmas tree now."

"Now? What about Maeve?"

"She's out of school. She's hanging out with her Mom at the dress shop. We can stop and pick her up, if that works for you?"

"Okay," I said, "but there are a couple of other stops I'd like to make first." I squeezed his hand. "If that works for you?"

"Your wish is my command." Derek bowed in my direction.

Mom giggled. "Have fun, kids."

"Thanks. Come on." I grabbed Derek's hand and pulled. "Let me get my coat and hat out front and we can go."

"Aren't you forgetting something?" Riley hollered.

"Like what?" I stuck my head back around the corner.

Riley raised his right hand and jiggled the set of keys in his fingers.

"Right!" I hurried over and snatched them from him. I kissed his cheek. "We'll get it back to you soon as we can!"

"No hurry."

Cousin Riley's red Chevy pickup was parked behind the shop. I handed the keys to Derek. The early eighties pickup had belonged to Riley's father,

Aunt Betty's first husband, who had passed some years ago. The truck, and a truckful of memories, as Riley liked to say, were all his father had left behind. Riley loved the truck as if it were his only child.

We climbed in and Derek turned the key in the ignition. "Where to first?"

"Kim's house," I replied, dropping my purse on the floor.

"Okay. What's up?" Derek pulled out into traffic.

"We're going house hunting."

Derek turned quickly in my direction. "You're looking for a house?"

"No." I shook my head. "You are."

"I am?"

"Remember the other day in your apartment?" Derek grunted his confusion and I continued. "You told me you didn't expect to live there forever."

"I believe we were talking about bricks and mortar," he said with a grin. "I'm not in the market for a new house right now, Amy. I've barely gotten settled into the place."

"Don't be silly." I patted his arm. "Of course you are in the market for a new house. A new, old house, to be precise."

"That brings me back to my first question: I am?"

I explained as Derek drove past the lake in the direction of Kim's bungalow. In a matter of minutes we were at Kim's door. Derek pulled the pickup into the driveway behind Kim's sedan.

"You want me to wait here?" he asked, as he eyed the house.

"Nope. I want you to come inside. If I go in alone, she'll just weasel out of coming, make up some sorry excuse or another."

Derek pushed open his door and stepped down. "And if I come in with you?"

"She will still make up some sorry excuse or another," I explained, climbing down from the passenger side, leaving my purse in the truck. "But with you there for muscle, we can kidnap her if we have to."

Derek's laugh followed me to the back door. I had decided against knocking. I went straight for the spare key hidden under the flowerpot off the back porch, blew the dirt off it and stuck it in the kitchen door.

"And we're in," I said with a grin.

"As a lawyer," Derek mumbled a step behind me, "I'm not sure I am entirely comfortable with this."

"Nonsense, I do it all the time."

"It's called unlawful entry." Derek's eyes took in the small, dimly lit kitchen.

"It's called being a friend." I flipped on the kitchen light and peeked in the living room, expecting to find her sprawled out on the sofa in her underwear with the TV droning. "Huh."

Derek came up behind me and laid his hand on my shoulder. "Huh, what?"

"She's not here."

Derek looked over my shoulder. "So I see. She does appear to have been nesting there though." He pointed to the two blankets, pillow, balled up tissues, and open box of sugary cereal spread over the sofa cushions.

"Is that you, A—" Stepping out of her bedroom into the hallway, Kim froze. Blond hair flew in every direction. A large, fluffy white robe swaddled her like a giant diaper. Her face was free of makeup. Her feet were bare of shoes or even a decent pair of slippers.

"Derek!" Kim's hand flew to her hair and she did her able best to smoosh her unruly mop into shape.

She was clearly appalled to be seen in such disarray. I took that for a good sign. Caring about her personal appearance was a sign of good mental health.

"Hello, Kim. Sorry to barge in on you like this." Derek's cheeks glowed pink. Ever the gentleman, he averted his eyes, shooting me a look that said he was extremely uncomfortable with the situation I had thrust him into.

"What are you two doing here?" Though the words were directed at both me and Derek, the tone and the angry eyes were for me alone.

I took a step in Kim's direction. "You didn't answer your phone."

"Because I didn't want to talk to anybody, Amy."

Derek grabbed the sleeve of my coat. "I think I'll wait outside."

"Maybe you—"

"No," Kim interrupted. "There's beer in the fridge. Help yourself, Derek." She leveled her gaze at me. "Amy, can I see you for a minute?"

I pulled a face.

"In my bedroom?"

Derek and I exchanged glances.

"A drink sounds perfect." He stepped into the kitchen and I heard the rattle of the refrigerator door being yanked open.

I followed Kim to her bedroom. She had never been the neatest housekeeper in the world, but her room looked like some giant, angry ogre had come in and turned it violently upside down.

"Maid forget to show up?" I quipped in an attempt to lighten the mood.

Kim threw herself down on her bed. "How could you bring Derek here? Without any warning?"

I spread my hands, kicked a couple pairs of jeans out of my path on the rug, and joined her at the bedside. "How could I give you any warning when you won't answer your phone?"

Kim frowned at me. I frowned right back. It's a friend thing.

She kicked her feet in frustration. "I just need a couple of days of alone time."

"No," I said, reaching for a clean outfit in her closet. "What you need is some friends-and-family time. And since I'm the closest thing you've got around here, you're stuck with me." I tossed the blue turtleneck sweater dress at her. "Put this on." She always looked good in it, even at her worst. Like now.

She glanced at the dress. "Where are we going?"

"House hunting."

Kim wrinkled her nose at me. "Who's looking to buy a house?"

I nodded in the general direction of the kitchen. "Derek."

Her forehead creased up. "Derek's looking to buy a house?"

"That's right. And he needs a hotshot agent." I nudged her foot with my toe. "That's you. So get washed, get dressed, and let's go house shopping."

Kim rested her elbows on the bed and narrowed her eyes at me. "Why do I get the feeling that you're up to something?"

"Because you have an unnaturally suspicious nature." I grabbed her hand and pulled her to her feet. "Now hurry up and get dressed before you lose a customer with an excellent credit score."

Kim mumbled and grumbled some more but picked up the dress I'd selected, grabbed a nice pair of knee-high leather boots from her closet to go with it, and scooted off to the bathroom.

About a half hour later we were all lined up in a row on the cushy bench seat of Cousin Riley's pickup truck. Derek drove, Kim had the passenger side, and I was scrunched up in the middle.

Derek backed carefully down the drive. "Where to first?"

"Let's stop at the office," suggested Kim. "I'll grab my tablet and we can take a look at the current listings before starting out."

"Okay," Derek said rather uneasily.

I patted his leg.

Kim lowered the sun visor and was disappointed to find no mirror. She pulled a hand mirror from a black leather case in her purse and applied a line of cranberry-colored lip gloss.

I cleared my throat. "Actually, I was telling Derek about one house in particular that he and I thought he might be interested in."

"What house is that?" Kim asked, checking her work in her pocket mirror before slipping it back into its case.

"The Virginia Johnson house," I answered. "Isn't that right, Derek?" I gave his leg another pat.

"Yes, that's right," Derek said, rather woodenly, I thought. "It sounds exactly like what I'm looking for."

Kim shrugged. "If you say so. The place is a bit of a fixer-upper, you do realize? Mrs. Johnson really let the place go in her later years."

"I'm always up for a challenge," Derek replied gamely. Later, when we were alone, I'd ask him why he was looking hard at me when he was answering Kim that he was always up for a challenge.

Was he implying that *I* was challenging?

19

"Okay," agreed Kim. "We won't have to stop at the office then. There's a lockbox on the door." She focused her eyes on Derek. "Just remember I warned you."

Derek nodded and Kim gave him turn-by-turn directions. In a matter of minutes, we were on Mrs. Johnson's street.

Virginia Johnson's house was in one of the town's older neighborhoods, filled with large trees, equally large yards, and quaint homes. Most had Christmas decorations on their front lawns and attached to their houses.

Derek slowed as we approached a modest pale green house with dark green trim, set back from the curb.

A Belzer Realty sign bearing Ellery Belzer's picture stood in the yard; another had been attached with plastic ties to the front porch rail.

"This must be the place." Derek parked and looked at the house. The yard was overgrown with weeds. In the middle of the front lawn, a pin oak, now devoid of leaves, towered above the pitched, double-gabled roof. Several shingles were missing and needles from the tall pines nearby clung to the edges of the roof and overflowed the gutters. There was a detached, single-gable garage to the left, with a couple of windows near the roofline.

"Yes, this is it. I warned you, remember?" Kim said, opening her door and sliding out. "Three beds, one-and-a-half baths. Plus the FROG."

I tumbled out after her. "Frog? Eve Dunnellon said something about Bobby Cherry living in Mrs. Johnson's frog. What the heck are you talking about?"

Kim headed around the side of the truck and pointed at the garage, which had been painted in the same color scheme as the house. "Furnished room over garage." Kim climbed the porch steps and twisted the dials on the lockbox. Inside were two keys.

"Oh." I looked at the windows in the single-car garage, then followed after her and Derek. "Kim, why don't you show Derek around inside? I think I'll start with that guest room."

Inspecting Virginia Johnson's house up close, I could see that the paint was chipped, faded, and peeling. There were signs of wood rot, whether due to water damage or termites, I couldn't tell. Maybe both.

Whoever ultimately bought this place could make my contractor Cash Calderon's boat payments for him for a year for all the work this place needed.

Kim shrugged and handed me one of the two keys in the lockbox. It was cold to the touch.

"Suit yourself, Amy. Come on, Derek." She unlocked the front door and motioned for him to follow her.

Derek opened his mouth, but I wasn't giving him a chance to talk. "Yes, Derek. See what you think," I said. "I'll join you in a minute."

His look told me there was going to be a price to pay later for his uneasy cooperation with my machinations. I'd deal with that later.

I left him with Kim and walked up the driveway to the garage. Narrow wooden stairs to the right led up to the garage apartment. The treads were splintered and sagging. I held on to the rail as I climbed the steps. I stopped at the top landing and turned the key in the lock. The door opened with a grunt.

A business card that someone had stuck in the edge of the door advertising car insurance fluttered to my feet. I picked it up.

A waft of stale, moldy air commingled with tobacco hit me first. The room was cold and dark. I tried the light switch just inside the door. Nothing. Either the electricity was turned off or the bulb in the cheap plastic ceiling fixture had burned out.

I tossed the business card into a trash can advertising a popular brand of beer, which sat to the right of the door. The rusted and dented can was nearly full with empty food containers, beer cans, and cigarette butts.

I crossed to the window and pulled the thin yellow curtains open. Several desiccated wasps and a lone, dead house fly lay on the unpainted sill. I then turned to examine the FROG. Not surprising, the room was longer than it was wide. The ceiling rose to a point some twelve feet or so high.

Calling it a furnished room was something of an exaggeration. A bed was stuffed in the far corner, nothing more than a mattress on a sagging box spring on a flimsy-looking, laminated particle-board frame. There was a mismatched six-drawer bureau along the back wall, a portable radio from another era on the floor beneath the windows.

A dorm-sized refrigerator beside the bed also seemed to have served as a nightstand as it held a beeswax candle and a couple issues of a motorcycle magazine.

The room's cheaply paneled walls were pocked with small holes and protruding nails. Strips of plastic tape hung to the walls, indicating where things may have once been. There wasn't a single picture or bit of art on the walls now.

A rickety-looking rectangular table and two mismatched pine chairs occupied the center of the room. Atop the table, an ashtray, a jar of generic instant coffee, several napkins, and an empty white paper sack from a fast-food joint out at the main highway created a tableau that only added to the bleakness of the room and its one-time occupant.

A greasy black sweatshirt with frayed sleeves rested on the bedsheets, which themselves were stained and dusty. The room was in need of a good top-to-bottom clean. Junk mail lay scattered in loose piles, along with an old newspaper or two and a handful of takeout-food flyers.

There was no formal kitchen, not even an informal one. The bathroom, which I discovered behind a narrow door, was closet-sized.

The FROG wasn't much. Real frogs living in the Louisiana bayous had it better. But from what I'd heard from others about Bobby Cherry, he wasn't much either.

There were two very interesting things about Bobby Cherry, however. Number one, he was living upstairs here in the FROG at the same time that Virginia Johnson was quote-unquote hanging herself in the garage below.

The second curious thing about him was that he'd been, according to Eve Dunnellon, causing trouble at Christmas House Village.

Why?

Was he the person responsible for the latest incident that Dan had told me about?

I walked slowly around the room, careful to avoid banging my head on the lower portions of the sloped ceiling.

I heard a sudden banging close by and stuck my head out the door. A Northern flicker was attacking the decaying corner of the garage roof. As it did, bits of wood fell to the barren ground below. The riddled wooden siding was probably chock-full of insects.

There was nothing in the room to give me a clue as to who Bobby Cherry was as a person or what he might have been up to. There was no clue as to what part, if any, he might have played in Virginia Johnson's death.

Frustrated, I locked up, put the key in my coat pocket, and went back down the wobbly stairs. I wanted to get a look in the garage before Kim and Derek finished up in the house. There was no point in Kim knowing what I was up to. She was fragile enough as things were. No good could come of more talk of hanging and murder around her.

The side door leading into the garage was locked and my key wouldn't fit in the lock. I went to the overhead garage door and gave the handle a tug. The old wood-paneled door was heavy, but I was able to lift it with effort.

Winter sunlight spilled inside the cluttered space. My eyes went immediately upward to the unfinished ceiling. Long beams ran parallel with the door. There was no sign of the rope that Mrs. Johnson or, more likely now, somebody else had used to string her up.

The walls of the garage were unfinished bare wood. Several metal trash cans stood near the front of the garage on the left. Old yard implements leaned against the walls. Mouse traps layered in inches of dust lined the walls. Racks of faded, threadbare clothing lay in heaps on the stained concrete floor. Stacks of sagging cardboard boxes, black with mold, dust, and bug droppings created a wall behind which I found an antique white spinet piano.

I didn't see a piano bench. Jerry had mentioned that Virginia Johnson had supposedly used the bench to climb up and attach the rope from which she was found hanging. Somebody must have taken it away.

As much as I knew I was going to regret touching one of those disgusting boxes, I opened one of the least grungy and peeked inside. It was filled with old housewares, cups and plates, tattered dishtowels. It would appear that Virginia Johnson was something of a pack rat.

I bit my lip and sighed. I took a second look at the thick beams. They were high, but with a piano bench, I was sure I could reach one. As for Virginia Johnson, I had no idea of her height but expected that the police would have accounted for that.

Just to make extra sure, I picked up the smallest of the trash cans and carried it over to the center of the garage. Moving slowly and carefully, I lifted first one knee then the other up on the lid. The thin lid caved in a bit, but held. Satisfied that I wasn't about to fall on my face, I gripped the sides of the can for balance and tried to get one foot under me.

"Amy!" shouted Kim.

I twisted. It was Kim, and Derek was with her. She stamped her foot. "What are you doing?"

20

"What?" I felt my balance slipping and the can teetering as I tilted my head toward them. Suddenly the world turned on its head. Or rather I did. I let go of the trash can as I fell helplessly to the floor. The garbage can crashed against the ground and rolled to my right, spilling garbage as it went.

Derek ran over, held out a hand, and helped me to regain my footing. "Are you okay?"

"Yes, more startled than bruised," I answered as I brushed myself off.

"Glad to hear it." Kim's hands were planted on her hips. Anger and confusion were planted on her face. "But I repeat, Amy, what are you doing?"

My face was red and it wasn't from the fall. "If you must know, I was checking something."

Derek picked up the trash can, placed it with the others, and then went to work replacing all the garbage that had spilled out.

Kim moved into my personal space. "Like what?"

I glanced toward the beam. I hadn't meant to. I couldn't help it.

Kim slanted a look at me. "You're not here because he wants to look for a house!" She pointed a finger at Derek, who was suddenly finding the trash extremely interesting. "You wanted to take a look at where Virginia Johnson hanged herself!"

Kim steamed out a breath. "That's gross!" Her eyes bulged. "Amy, that's, that's morbid!"

"All right, it's true." I had already explained my theory and my reasoning to Derek. It was time to do the same with my best friend.

"I learned that Virginia Johnson had rheumatoid arthritis. Her hands were so bad," I said, "that I don't think she could possibly have managed to tie a rope and hang herself from there." I pointed to the support beams.

Kim's mouth fell open. She looked at the nearest beam then back at me. Derek was still on trash pickup duty. "Really?"

"Really," I said. "I was just about to climb up for a better look. Mrs. Johnson apparently used a piano bench, but all I could find was a trash can."

"Who would want to murder Mrs. Johnson?" Kim asked. "She was a sweet old lady."

"She was also a Kinley and, as such, a ten percent owner of Christmas House Village. At least, she used to be." I bent and began helping Derek pick up the spilled garbage.

"You think somebody killed her to get her share of Christmas House Village?" Kim pitched in.

"It seems a likely possibility," Derek said. "I think you're on to something, Amy." He held out the trash can and I dropped in a handful of the junk I'd gathered up.

"Thanks," I said. "The question is: Who? Franklin Finch ended up with Christmas House Village and—"

"And now he's dead, too," Kim finished.

"Yes," Derek said. "And now Tyrone Kinley's children are free to spend all the money they got from the sale of their father's business."

I had told Derek what Kim had explained to me about the Tyrone Kinley family and their desire to rid themselves of Christmas House Village, and Mrs. Johnson's desire to keep it in the family. "That is a very good point, Counselor."

"Thanks. I try." Derek pushed the trash can toward Kim and she dropped in a handful of debris. "There's a pile of old business cards in here." He nosed inside the can. "Christmas House Village, an insurance company, pest control, a motorcycle dealer, several real estate cards, even a couple of Belzer Realty business cards in here," he said, riffling through the pile. "You want them?"

Kim took a peek. "Eeew, no thanks. Mr. Belzer prints them up by the millions. I left several on the kitchen counter myself. In fact"—she dug in her purse, pulled out a leather business card case, and handed Derek two of them—"I forgot to give you one."

Derek looked at the cards. "You know I'm not really in the market, right?"

Kim grinned. "In case you change your mind."

Derek took them and put them in his wallet. "Thanks." He recovered the lid of the trash can and set the closed can next to the others.

"Kim, you said before that Tyrone's children live out of the area. How far out did you mean?"

"Do you mean like not so far that one of them couldn't have come to Ruby Lake and given Mrs. Johnson some help with the rope?"

"Something like that."

Kim twisted up her lips. "It seems to me they were all out of state. But I'll check with Mr. Belzer."

"Thanks. What about Bobby Cherry? Did you know him?" I asked.

"No, not really. I met him briefly when I came by with Mr. Belzer after Virginia Johnson's death. We had to break the news to him that he was going to have to move out."

"Didn't her nephews and niece come by?"

"Not initially, though I imagine they were here for the funeral."

"What about the sale of Christmas House Village?"

"How do you mean?" asked Kim.

"Weren't the Kinley kids here for that?"

Kim shook her head. "All the contracts were handled by mail and fax."

"How did Bobby take it when you and Ellery told him he was going to have to move out of this house?"

Kim planted her finger over her lips as she thought back. "Okay, I guess. To tell the truth, he didn't say much of anything. He was kind of quiet." She visibly shivered. "If it was me and somebody had hanged themselves downstairs of my room, I'd be more than happy to leave. In fact, you couldn't keep me here."

"Just what I was thinking," added Derek.

"Do you know where Bobby Cherry is living now?" I asked.

"I don't have a clue," Kim said. "I could ask Mr. Belzer that, too. Maybe he knows or can find out. Belzer Realty does manage several commercial properties."

"Now that you mention it, so does Randy," I said hesitantly. Randy Vincent was Kim's previous boyfriend. He and his wife run Vincent Properties and own a number of rentals around town.

Randy had been separated from his wife, Lynda, for over a year when Kim and he started dating. Lynda had always appeared okay with it.

However, Randy and Lynda had unexpectedly reconciled a short time ago. I wasn't sure that Kim was completely over the trauma the breakup had caused.

To make matters worse, living in a small town made avoiding the source of your pain difficult. I could only hope the same thing didn't happen to me and Derek.

"Not on your life," was Kim's quick reply. "But feel free to ask Randy yourself."

I said I might. "What about Bobby? Do you remember anything else about him?"

Kim shrugged. "Only that he was young—must have been in his early twenties—had dark hair and pretty bad acne scars on his face. That's about it, why?"

"I heard some unflattering things about him from Eve Dunnellon."

"Unflattering how?" asked Kim.

"Unflattering as in mucking things up, disrupting the business with computer viruses, and other acts of vandalism."

"That's criminal mischief." Derek whistled.

"This Bobby Cherry sounds nasty." Kim pulled a face. "Why would Mrs. Johnson put up with him?"

I bent and picked up a couple more scraps of paper, one of which was a black and silver LaChance Motors business card. "Bobby worked at Christmas House Village." I opened the trash can lid an inch and dropped the papers inside. "Until he was fired."

"That might explain why he was living here at Virginia Johnson's house," suggested Derek.

Kim nodded. "Mr. Belzer told me that she occasionally took in boarders who worked at Christmas House Village. In fact, he said that employees were the only boarders she would take in."

"The house is in bad shape," I noted. "Do you think Mrs. Johnson was hurting for money?"

"I wouldn't think so," answered Kim. "She didn't work, as far as I know, but I imagine she did collect her share of Christmas House Village profits."

"According to your boss, Christmas House Village wasn't all that profitable."

"Really?" Kim's surprise showed on her face. "I always assumed."

"Don't look now but we've got company," Derek said softly.

Kim and I turned to see a police car pull into the driveway. Chief Kennedy was at the wheel and Officer Dan Sutton was in the passenger seat.

"Uh-oh," I said.

Chief Kennedy stepped from the squad car, zipped up his leather jacket, then thrust his hands in the pockets as he swaggered up to us. Dan came around the other side. "What are you folks doing here?"

The three of us walked out of the garage.

"Hello, Chief. Hi, Dan." Kim wiggled her fingers at the officer. He nodded a reply. "I was showing Derek the Johnson house. He's in the market. Isn't that right, Derek?"

Derek stepped to the forefront. "That's right. I can't live upstairs in that tiny apartment of mine forever."

Jerry wriggled his jaw. "Is that so?"

"What are you doing here, Jerry?" I asked.

"We were on our way to Swan—" Dan started.

Jerry gave him a look that told him that he would do the talking. "It so happens that we *are* on our way to Swan Ridge," the chief admitted. "I thought it would be worth driving by the Johnson house again."

"Are you going to interview Virginia Johnson's rheumatologist, Dr. Santiago?"

I left my question to Dan Sutton, regarding the most recent purported vandalism at Christmas House Village, unasked because I didn't want to get Dan in trouble with his boss. Jerry wouldn't like Dan sharing information with me. What Jerry didn't know wouldn't hurt him. I'd ask Dan about it later.

Jerry squirmed, his hands still buried in his pockets. "If what you say is true, Mrs. Johnson's death may bear some further looking into."

I took his words for what they were worth. I knew he'd never tell me I'd had a good idea, let alone helped him in any fashion.

The police chief walked into the garage and gazed up at the beams. "We found her right there."

Chief Kennedy turned back to the three of us. "There was no reason to suspect anything other than a suicide." He sighed and his breath came out in a small cloud. "It happens more than you might think."

Jerry grabbed the inside handle of the garage door and gave it a pull. The heavy door rattled on its tracks and slammed into the ground. "Let's go, Dan." He turned to Derek. "Good luck with the house hunting, Mr. Harlan."

"Thanks, Chief."

"Bye, Dan!" waved Kim. "Call me later?"

Dan blushed and nodded once more before climbing back into the passenger seat of the squad car.

I found myself grinning. I couldn't help thinking that Kim had turned the corner on her depression. "Come on," I said, heading down to Riley's truck at the curb, "let's go get us some Christmas trees!"

"Christmas trees?" Kim held out her hand. "Give me the apartment key."

I handed her the key to the FROG. She returned both it and the house key to the lockbox, jiggled the front door knob to be sure she had locked up, then scurried to join us. I took the middle seat and she squeezed in beside me.

"What's all this about Christmas trees?" she asked.

"Derek does not have a Christmas tree—"

"Nor do you," interrupted our handsome driver.

"Nor do I," I agreed. "We're on our way to pick up Maeve and hit the tree lot. You want to come? I noticed you don't have a tree either. We'll get you one, my treat."

"Thanks," replied Kim. "But if you don't mind, I think I'll ask Dan to take me."

"Better yet," I conceded. "When you see him, ask him what happened at Mrs. Claus's Kitchen."

"What happened at the café?" Kim asked.

"When I saw Dan earlier outside the police station, he mentioned there had been a report of vandalism. He was on his way to check it out."

Kim promised she would. She also boasted that her Christmas tree would be bigger and more fantastic than mine.

"I'm not even going to dignify that remark with a reply," I said, pushing a strand of hair behind my ear while silently vowing to settle for nothing less than a fifty footer even if it meant cutting a hole in my ceiling to contain it.

21

We dropped Kim off at her place, then went to pick up Derek's daughter.

"There's a tree seller a few doors down from my office," Derek said as we passed Birds & Bees. "Next door to my barber's."

"Okay. Riley got our store tree at the lumber yard. But a tree's a tree."

Derek turned to me with a grin. "As long as it's twice the size of Kim's?"

"It wouldn't hurt," I agreed, to the sound of his laughter filling the cab.

We parked in front of Derek's law office. Ben waved from his desk in the front. I waved back and waited in the truck while Derek went next door to Dream Gowns to pick up Maeve. From there, the three of us walked to the tree lot.

The usually empty lot sat between two downtown buildings, a bank on one side and a barber shop on the other. Stacks of Fraser firs leaned against the walls of the neighboring buildings and more trees stood in temporary stands, their limbs open for display. Several were decorated with ornaments and tinsel.

Festive Christmas carols played from speakers nailed to long two-by-four pine boards pounded into the earth. Wires connected the speakers to each other, then joined up at the compact teardrop-shaped trailer near the street. The trailer had a large red bow atop it. A real fir Christmas wreath hung from the trailer's open door. Two three-foot-tall plastic candles flickered on either side of the entrance. Atop the trailer, Santa rode his sleigh and seven reindeer provided the muscle power.

There were tables of wreaths for sale. Bundled-up tree shoppers strolled the aisles between the trees, cups of free eggnog, hot apple cider, or hot chocolate in their glove- and mitten-covered hands.

I couldn't help but smile as we walked up together. Maeve held hands with her father. So did I. "Smells like Christmas," I remarked.

Maeve and Derek agreed.

My smile disappeared when I saw the man in the Santa Claus hat step down from the sales trailer.

Despite the Santa-like appearance, the man was a real scrooge. This man was Robert LaChance, a local businessman.

I groaned.

Derek paused at the entrance, where a young man in a knit cap and dirty jeans was bundling up a tree in thin red netting in preparation for tying it to the roof of the silver SUV idling at the curb. "What's wrong?" asked Derek.

I couldn't get the frown off my face. "It's Robert." Robert LaChance had exchanged his usual pinstripe suit for a tailored Santa Claus costume. There was nothing fat and jolly about this Santa stand-in, however. He wasn't wearing a beard, white or otherwise.

Robert was wearing black leather boots, but the pair on his feet looked more like they'd been designed and crafted by expert Italian cordwainers rather than shoemaker elves.

"Good afternoon, folks." He looked us over. I noticed his smile fade ever so slightly when he recognized me as the woman with the father and daughter duo.

"Oh, it's you. Hello, Amy."

"Merry Christmas, Robert."

Robert turned to Derek. "Derek, good to see you again." He pulled off his black leather glove and extended his hand to Derek.

"You, too, Robert," Derek said as the two men shook.

"Is everything going well?" Robert asked.

"The holidays are always a difficult time to get any work done," Derek replied. "As you can see, people have other priorities." He tousled his daughter's hair. "But we're plodding along."

Robert nodded and rubbed his chin. "And who is this lovely lady?" He bent at the waist to address Maeve.

"This is my daughter, Maeve."

"Pleased to meet you also," Robert said with a smile. His teeth were too white and Santa had never had a tan, let alone one as deep as Robert's.

"Hello, Mr. Santa, sir."

Robert laughed. "Wait, Maeve. I believe Jimmy has mentioned a Maeve. It is such a beautiful and unique name. I'll bet that's you." Jimmy was Robert and Tiffany's eleven-year-old son.

Maeve nodded. "We're both in the Christmas choir."

"That's wonderful. I'm looking forward to the concert." The dealer shook her little hand as well. "Help yourself to a cup of hot chocolate, Maeve. I believe you will find Jimmy assisting the customers, if you'd like to say hello." He slipped his glove back over his bare hand.

Maeve said she would. "Okay, Daddy?"

Derek told her to have a good time and not go far. I watched her fill a Styrofoam cup from one of several stainless steel urns that had been set up on a rustic picnic table near the entrance. Semitransparent plastic lids protected rows of Christmas cookies from the elements.

"Since when are you selling Christmas trees instead of cars?" I asked as Maeve took her drink and a cookie and disappeared between the trees.

Robert shrugged. "Since I haven't been able to sell this empty lot. I made a deal with a local tree farm." He rubbed his hands together. "What are you two interested in? We're mostly carrying Fraser firs, but I have a few Scotch pine, Douglas fir, even some cypresses."

"We're not looking for anything fancy," Derek replied. "As long as it's green."

"Follow me."

Derek and I shared an amused look.

As we walked, I motioned for Derek to lower his head. "What was that all about?"

"What?" Derek appeared confused.

"Your conversation with Robert."

"Nothing. Just making small talk. Isn't that what people in small towns are supposed to do?"

"Fine," I answered, not fully believing him. "But there is no way I am buying a Christmas tree from this man," I whispered breathily in his ear.

"Okay by me." Derek patted my arm. "Let's just humor him. We can always go to one of the other tree lots, if you like."

"I like," I whispered firmly. We quickened our steps to catch up with Robert as he rounded a waist-high wooden bin overloaded with plastic tree stands of various shapes and sizes.

"Back here is where I keep the big ones," explained Robert.

Derek winked at me. "That's just what we're looking for, isn't it, Amy."

I nudged him in the ribs with my elbow and walked on.

In the middle of the sea of trees, Robert paused and turned to us. "And if you buy today, I'll even toss in a free Christmas wreath for your front door." He started walking again. "Or car. They make great hood ornaments," he said, looking back over his shoulder.

"What, no free undercoating or rust-proofing?" I quipped.

Derek laughed. Robert ignored me. That was fine by me.

"What do you think about these babies?" Robert stopped and ran his hand along the limbs of a tree that stood about twice as tall as Derek and was as big around as a small car.

I gazed up at the magnificent fir. "I'll take it."

Derek looked at me in surprise. "You will?"

I nodded. "Wrap it up, Robert."

Robert's grin, impossibly, grew bigger than his face. "I'll get one of the boys over." He looked around the sea of people and trees, spotted one of his staff bundled up in a black wool high school football letterman's jacket with tan leather sleeves, and waved him over.

"What about you, Derek? See anything you like?"

"Well, I—" Derek turned. His daughter was tugging at his coat with her free hand. "Hey!" He ruffled the top of her head again. "Where did you come from?"

His daughter ignored the question. "I like this one, Daddy." She placed her hand in the middle of the fat tree at her side.

Derek nodded his approval. "Okay, looks good to me." He turned to the used-car salesman turned Christmas tree dealer and said, "We'll take it."

"Can't we take two?" Maeve looked up hopefully.

Derek drew his brows together. "Two?"

I could practically see what he was thinking. There would barely be room for one monster Christmas tree in his tiny apartment, let alone a pair of them. He might have to move the big flat-screen TV out to make room.

"Yes," Maeve said, bobbing her head excitedly. "One for you and one for Mommy."

"Oh, ah . . ." Derek stuttered.

I laid my hand on Maeve's shoulder. "I think that's a wonderful idea."

"You do?" mouthed Derek.

"I do." I turned to the young man who had come at Robert's behest. "We'll take that one," I said, pointing to my tree—it was definitely going to be bigger than Kim's—"and this one, and?" I looked at Maeve for the answer.

"And this one!" She pointed to a tall fir.

I nodded appreciatively. "Good choice. That branch at the top is perfectly straight. Just the right spot for a tree topper."

Maeve beamed.

"Great." Robert clapped his hands and told his employee to round up the trees. "Follow me to the trailer and we'll write you up." He reached into his cashmere pocket and pulled out a handful of tiny candy canes. "Anybody care for one?"

Maeve and I helped ourselves while Derek abstained.

"Can I interest either of you in a tree stand?" Robert looked questioningly at us as we passed the crate of stands.

I said no. We had our family stand tucked away in the attic. Derek bought two identical stands, one for his tree and one for the tree they'd be setting up at Amy-the-ex's house.

We settled up inside the trailer. Derek and Maeve then walked down to get Cousin Riley's pickup truck so we could load up our trees.

As I stood at the curb awaiting their return, a question suddenly occurred to me. "Did you know Virginia Johnson, Robert?"

The question seemed to take him by surprise. He leveled his dark eyes at me. "Not really," he said after a moment. "Why?"

"Because I found one of your business cards in her trash can."

As I said the words, his look of surprise turned to one of wonder and disgust. "You were digging through her trash can?" His brows pinched together. I'd never seen Santa appear so confused. "Isn't she dead?" He scratched his head through his Santa hat. "In fact, didn't she die some time ago?"

"Yes, she is." I gave him the story about Derek being in the market for a house. "While we were at Mrs. Johnson's house, I accidentally knocked over a trash can and your business card spilled out."

"So? We must give out a dozen a day."

Robert paused and stepped back as the young man hauling our trees brought one of them to the prep station, where a second young man wielding a chainsaw deftly attacked the base of its trunk. He then set the tree to one side and wrapped it in plastic netting for the ride home.

"Come to think of it, Virginia Johnson didn't even drive. She came into the lot maybe ten years back wanting to sell me her old Buick. It wasn't worth much, but I gave her a grand for it."

"Nice of you."

He nodded, though I hadn't exactly meant it as a compliment. Knowing Robert LaChance, it had probably been worth twice that.

Derek and Maeve pulled up in the pickup but had to double-park while a couple of vehicles ahead of us waited to have trees loaded on their rooftops.

Robert stuffed his hands deep in his faux-fur-lined pockets. "If Virginia Johnson hadn't died, Finch never would have got hold of Christmas House Village."

I sensed anger and frustration in his tone. What was that all about? "You care what happens to Christmas House Village?"

He blinked at me. "Don't you?"

22

I didn't get the opportunity to follow up on that curious remark of Robert LaChance's because it was time to load up our trees. Derek drove me and my tall, green beauty back to Birds & Bees, where Cousin Riley and I managed to lug it upstairs without leaving too big a trail of fir needles.

Esther, bless her heart, followed behind with a broom and a dustpan, sweeping furiously at the needles we did drop.

And cussing furiously as she did.

I was grateful there were no customers in the store at the time. Some of her words were even making me blush.

Derek and Maeve were planning to take his tree upstairs to his apartment with his father's help. I knew they would do the same with the tree that Maeve had asked they buy for her mom, too. When he was done, Derek brought back Riley's pickup.

We met Derek in the lot behind the store—we being me, Riley, and Esther. Riley and Esther seemed to have a poor understanding of my desire for privacy, especially with regard to Derek.

"Thanks for everything, Derek." I gave him a kiss despite the onlookers. "Where's Maeve?"

"Back at my apartment with her grandpa. I promised I'd be right back to help her decorate."

I smiled. "Have fun. See you tomorrow?"

"Only if you promise there will be mistletoe."

"I'll do my best."

Derek handed my cousin the keys to his treasured truck. "Thanks, Riley." "No problem."

Derek climbed in his car and drove off.

Riley was delighted to see that Derek had swept out the bed of the truck for him.

"That Derek's a keeper," Riley said, standing in the middle of the truck bed, having walked twice around the truck to ensure that we hadn't scratched it—not that I was at all sure he could have noticed, considering the nicks, scratches, and scrapes that already gave the old truck its character.

"He even topped off the gas tank," Riley said after glancing at the gauges on the dash.

"Maybe you ought to ask him to borrow it more often," I suggested.

The look on Cousin Riley's face told me he just might take me up on that.

"By the way, what's with the cat litter?"

"The what?" Riley turned to see what I was pointing at. A ten-pound sack of cat litter rested next to the right wheel well. It had been in the truck when we borrowed it. Unfortunately, one of the tree branches had poked through near the bottom of the bag. A small pile of loose clay spilled out. "Oh, that. Uh . . ."

"Did you get a cat?" I asked. My cousin had never expressed an interest in getting one.

Riley turned toward Esther. "Oh, uh, Esther, I've got your, uh . . ."

I narrowed my eyes as the scene unfolded.

Esther dropped her broom and dustpan and hurried over as fast as a septuagenarian—who to my knowledge had never set foot in a gym in her life—can, and carefully took the bag. Gray cat litter spilled over her boots. She carried the litter to the back door.

I held my tongue.

"Care to join Mom and me in a little tree-decorating session, Riley?"

"Thanks, but I'd best be going."

If I wasn't mistaken, he seemed in a sudden hurry to beat a hasty retreat.

"If you say so."

With that, he jiggled his keys, gave me a quick hug, and Esther, who had resumed her sweeping, a shout, then climbed into his pickup and chugged off.

I called to Esther as she dumped a load of fir needles in the dustbin along the edge of the back fence, "What about you, Esther?"

"What's that?"

"Care to join me and Mom? We're going to decorate the tree and have some food and drink. It's a family tradition."

"No, thanks. I've got things to do."

"Are you sure?"

"I'm sure." Esther banged the broom against the dustpan, then carried them into the storeroom. She took off her apron, tossed it under the sales counter, and started up the steps.

"Don't forget your sack!"

Esther paused, gripped both bannisters, and reversed course. She picked up her cat litter, careful to keep the puncture at the top, and started back up to the second floor. Halfway there, she stopped and caught my eye. "What are you looking at?"

"Nothing. Nothing at all," I replied. I mean, come on, the woman was holding ten pounds of cat litter—was she still not going to admit to hiding a cat in her apartment?

Esther drew the bag closer to her chest. "It's clay and it's cheap. The same stuff they use for them fancy facials at spas but at a fraction of the price." She turned and took a step. "It makes a great mud mask. You should try it sometime!" With that, she climbed the remaining stairs and entered her apartment.

As much as I was wondering what was going on behind that closed door, I had other things to do.

But there was one thing I would definitely do the minute I got the chance— scan the internet. Could you really use cat litter as a mud mask, or was the Pester, as I like to call her, pulling the wool over my eyes?

If she was trying to trick me, I'd find a way to catch her.

If she was telling the truth, I could save a small fortune on facials . . .

I locked the store and returned to my apartment on the third floor.

Once ensconced in our living room, Mom and I spent the night decorating. She had prepared a Crock-Pot of holiday stew. We filled big, steaming bowls and ate while we worked.

I had brought the tree stand down from the attic and cleaned it off with a rag. It was a heavy piece, made of cast iron and coated in green enamel paint.

Mom had pulled our family Christmas ornaments out of the storage closet. It was good to see them. They were like old familiar faces, friends of the family.

Some, like the tiny white porcelain bells, had been among Dad's favorites. There was one for each of us, featuring a holly sprig with the names Mom, Dad, and Amy inscribed in gold letters. We'd bought them when I was in grade school, from Kinley's Christmas House Village. I shook each one in turn.

The only ornaments new to the tree this year were a glass cardinal and a bluebird, gifts from one of my distributors.

We wound down over mugs of hot cocoa and marshmallows on the sofa and admired our handiwork. Cousin Riley had had to lop off a section of the tree at the bottom to get it to fit against the ceiling. I was planning to use the leftover branches, now lying in a pile in the corner, around the apartment to add to the holiday ambience. Already, the apartment smelled exactly like Christmas should.

I wiggled my toes and scooped up a tiny gooey marshmallow with my tongue. While we decorated, I had filled Mom in on what I'd learned about the murder investigation thus far.

"I can't stop thinking about what you told me Robert LaChance said about Christmas House Village," Mom began. She pulled the Christmas throw up to her chest. It was bright red and covered with white snowflakes and reindeer. "I'm as puzzled as you are."

"The first thing that crossed my mind was that he wanted to tear it down and put up a car lot."

The corners of my mother's mouth turned down. "You could be right. I still remember what he tried to do to you."

I nodded, deep in thought. When Birds & Bees was just starting out, Robert LaChance, Gertie Hammer, and our illustrious new mayor, Mac MacDonald, had tried to get my house. Their intention had been to tear it down and replace it with a parking lot and franchise Italian restaurant.

Fortunately, they'd failed. "He's selling Christmas trees," I said. "Maybe he wants to take over the entire Christmas market now, too."

"I hate to say it, but there's no law against that, Amy."

"Unless you kill to achieve your ends," I pointed out. "Maybe Robert murdered Mrs. Johnson when she refused to sell her share to him." I had told Mom that it now appeared that Virginia Johnson may not have died by her own hand.

"To kill an old woman like that . . ." She grabbed my upper arm. "Who would do such a thing?"

"That's what I'd like to know. And why strangle Finch and then try to make it look like he hanged himself?"

"Somebody wanted everyone to think he hanged himself," Mom said.

"Exactly," I said. "The same as they wanted everybody to think Virginia Johnson hanged herself." I clamped my hands over my thighs. "Which leads me back to Robert LaChance and Gertie Hammer."

"Gertie? What's she got to do with any of this?"

I explained how I'd seen her on a bench at Christmas House Village the other evening. "If you ask me, her behavior was suspicious."

Mom smiled patiently. "Amy, I know you've had your difficulties with Gertie but, at her age, I can't imagine her hanging anybody."

"Maybe not," I said, "but Robert could be doing her dirty work for her."

"Mr. LaChance might be greedy and he might be devious, but would he stoop to murder?"

"I don't know."

"Besides, her death wouldn't and didn't put Christmas House Village out of business, anyway. You told me it went to Tyrone's kids."

"True. But somebody did—stoop to murder, that is. That same someone may have murdered Mr. Finch."

Mom shook herself. "I still can hardly believe it."

I had some more ideas. "Speaking of Tyrone's kids. You must be about the same age as Tyrone Kinley's children, Mom. Did you know any of them?"

Mom picked her ceramic snowman mug off the end table and cupped her hands around it. I held the Mrs. Claus mug. It had always been my favorite. Dad's Santa mug sat in a place of honor under the tree. Aunt Barbara had made the three of them for us ages ago.

Mom took a moment before answering. "Not really. We didn't travel in the same circles. I don't believe the Kinley children even went to the same schools as the rest of us."

I frowned. "How is that even possible, Mom? Ruby Lake is so small."

Mom took a sip and a foamy brown line appeared on her upper lip.

I pointed. "You've got a little something there."

Mom smiled and licked at her lip. "That's the best part." She set her mug on the coffee table and picked up the tray of gingerbread cookies she and her friend Anita Brown had whipped up earlier that day.

"Thanks." I took a fat one and balanced it across the top of my mug.

"Tyrone's children all went off to private schools."

"We don't have any private schools here, do we?"

Mom shook her head.

"You mean boarding schools?"

"That's right."

"Wow. The Kinleys must have been well-off." Three kids in boarding school couldn't have been cheap.

"I suppose."

"And you don't know where they are now?" My eyelids felt like they were being weighed down with cast-iron skillets. I gave my neck a twist and stretched my legs over the coffee table.

"I believe they are all out of state. The closest one, as I recall, may be in South Carolina."

I yawned. South Carolina wasn't necessarily all that far. The Town of Ruby Lake was closer to some parts of South Carolina than it was to parts of North Carolina.

23

At the store the next day, I enlisted Kim's help in moving our entire order of birdseed ornaments to Finch's Christmas House Village. I could have used Cousin Riley for the job, but I wanted to keep Kim busy.

I had other plans for Kim, too. She had talked to Dan the night before and learned that the latest incident at Christmas House Village had been phoned in directly to the police rather than reported to store management.

If it had been up to management, the entire incident probably would have been swept under the proverbial rug. The police wrote it up as criminal mischief, but didn't expect to find the culprit.

Personally, I couldn't help wondering if culprit and killer weren't one and the same person.

"Did you and Dan pick out a Christmas tree?" I asked as we gathered everything up in the back room.

"Yep." Without my asking, Kim pulled her phone from the pocket of her skirt. Her finger played over the phone's screen a moment, then stopped. "Here."

I drew her hand closer. It was a real beauty. I pushed her hand away. "Not bad."

"And you?"

"Yes. It was so big we had to cut it in two pieces to get it inside the apartment." A slight exaggeration.

Kim looked dubious. "I can't wait to see it."

I gulped. "I'm looking forward to it." We carried box after box of ornaments out to the minivan, which I had backed up to the storeroom door.

"I can't tell you how happy I am that Eve Dunnellon is honoring our contract for these." Kim was looking better. Not radiant, but her face held a note of brightness and cheer that had been lacking.

"Me, too. We can use the extra sales." Plus, with our Birds & Bees tags on the bottom of each package, I was hopeful we'd see an increase in our own foot traffic throughout the year. "Sleep well last night?"

"Better," Kim answered. "I'm not looking forward to visiting Christmas House Village though."

I clapped her on the back. "It will be good for you. Hop in."

Kim went around to the passenger side and climbed in the minivan. I drove to Christmas House Village and was happy to see that the only crowds that had gathered were crowds of holiday shoppers.

I pulled into the alley behind Santa's House and followed it along to Elf House. "Wait here," I told Kim. "I'll go see where they want these boxes."

Kim nodded. "That suits me just fine." She pressed her legs together. I noticed she wouldn't even look at the house. The memory of having discovered Franklin Finch swinging from a rope was still too fresh in her mind.

I left the minivan running so she wouldn't freeze to death and went around the front of Elf House, expecting to find Eve Dunnellon in her office there.

She was out, but one of her clerks told me to take the merchandise directly to Santa's House. That made sense. Santa's House was where Eve had told me she was intending to display the birdseed ornaments.

I hurried to the minivan and explained to Kim what we were doing. "The clerk said she would call ahead and there would be someone there to unload for us."

"Fine by me."

Looking carefully over my shoulder, I backed down to Santa's House and cut the engine. "Here comes somebody now."

A big-shouldered man in a long brown coat and cap met us at the rear. He was pushing a green handcart.

Kim and I stepped out to greet him.

"Hello. Mr. Sever, right?"

"Good morning, ladies." William nodded and rolled the handcart to a stop at the rear doors of the minivan. He looked at me as he pushed his glasses up his nose.

"This is my friend Kim Christy."

"My pleasure." He clapped his hands together. "It's cold out here. I'm told you have some boxes to unload?"

"Of course." I scrambled to open the doors.

"If you want to wait inside, someone will be along to write you a receipt." He picked up a box and dropped it lightly on the handcart. "I'll take care of these. If you like, I can move your truck up to the office when I'm done. I'll leave your keys with whoever's working the register downstairs."

"That would be fine. Thanks." There were three reserved parking spaces directly behind Elf House: one for Finch, one for the manager, and one for the employee of the month. Maybe I'd get employee of the month. "Do you know where I can find Ms. Dunnellon? I didn't see her in the office."

William held a box to his chest. "Last I heard, she was in Santa's Workshop. We're having a bit of a problem with it."

That explained the two HVAC company vans I had noticed on the premises. "Santa's Workshop, got it. Uh, where is Santa's Workshop?" I racked my brain but couldn't remember ever having seen it.

"Everywhere." William set the box on the handcart, atop the previous one, his breath coming out in clouds.

"Everywhere?" Kim asked, slipping her gloves over her hands.

"Some time ago, the individual heater units were replaced with one central unit. It runs under Christmas House Village, connecting all the houses. It's off-limits. If you want to talk to Ms. Dunnellon, you ask somebody to fetch her."

I shrugged my shoulders at Kim. William wasn't the friendliest elf in Christmas House Village. "Thank you, William. I'm pleased to see that you've got your job back."

William ran a hand over his forehead. "I never actually left."

"But I thought Mrs. Fortuny said—"

William stuck up his hand. "Irma says a lot of things."

"Yes, well, don't let us slow you down. Come on, Kim." I grabbed my friend by the elbow and pulled her across the side yard toward the house. "Did you see that?" I mumbled.

"See what?" Kim swung her head around.

"Don't look!" I admonished her.

"Fine." Kim pushed my arm away. "But what is it you want to know if I saw, and don't want me to look at?"

I waited until we were in front of the house before answering. "William wasn't using a cane."

"So?"

"So, every time I've seen him before, he's had his cane."

Kim pursed her lips. "Come to think of it, the day the employees were out front protesting on the street—"

"The day Irma Fortuny clobbered you," I added.

"Yes," Kim said, her hand going to the side of her head, "thank you for reminding me, Amy. I do remember that William had a cane. But so what?"

"If you ask me," I said, urging her toward Elf House, "it means our Mr. Sever is perfectly capable of strangling somebody with two hands and then stringing them up. Very possibly, capable of stringing up two people."

"You mean Virginia Johnson?"

I nodded.

"My tree is almost that big," I quipped as we passed the giant outdoor Christmas House Village fir.

"You are so full of it, Amy."

"Possibly," I admitted. I took Kim's wrists. "Now," I began, "I want you to think back to the day Mr. Finch was killed."

"Not on your life, Amy." Kim tried to pull free but I held her.

"Please," I said. "This is important. You want to find out who murdered Franklin Finch, don't you? The sooner his killer is caught, the sooner life around here can get back to normal. Maybe people will stop looking at you funny, like you've been complaining about."

Kim pouted. "Let Jerry do it."

"Jerry? Really, Kim? You really think Jerry Kennedy is going to solve Franklin Finch's murder—and probably Mrs. Johnson's too, if it's not too late—without help?"

The corners of Kim's mouth inched down. "Probably not." She shook her head. "But he's got Dan, plus the others."

"Okay," I said. "Let's give them all the help we can then. There's nothing wrong with that, is there?"

"I suppose not. What did you have in mind?" Kim eyed me with suspicion.

I let her loose. "I want to take you back to the day that you found Mr. Finch in his loft."

Kim groaned. "What for? I wish it had never happened. I'm trying very hard to forget that it did, Amy."

Several shoppers moved past us, giving us odd looks.

I ignored them. "Trust me. Maybe you'll remember something or somebody that you saw." I looked around the cluster of houses. "Or maybe you'll recall something you might have heard."

Kim grabbed a tissue from her purse and wiped her nose. "Like what?"

"I don't know. But let's try. Please?"

Kim crumpled the tissue and dropped it in a trash bin at the edge of the walkway. "Fine."

"Good." I pulled her over to a bench and we sat. "What time did you get here that night?"

Kim sighed wearily. "About eight thirty, I suppose. I'd been at the diner earlier with Mr. Finch. Like I said, it hadn't gone well."

"What did you do next?"

"I went to the biergarten and had a glass of wine. Or two."

"Then what did you do?"

Kim folded her hands in her lap. "I drove downtown and walked around. Did some window shopping. All the time, I couldn't stop thinking about Christmas House Village and how mad everybody was at Finch, at me, and Mr. Belzer."

"So that's when you decided to talk to Finch again?"

"Yes." Kim looked straight ahead, not at me. "And like everything else I've done lately, I wish now that I hadn't. The man was unhappy enough as things stood."

Kim's regret was understandable under the circumstances. But all this moping and self-pity weren't getting us anywhere. I nudged the conversation forward. "Okay, you walk over to Christmas House Village, right?"

"Right."

"And it's about eight thirty?"

Kim nodded.

I squeezed my brows together. "Who knew you were going to see Mr. Finch?"

Kim shrugged. "Only my boss."

"Mr. Belzer?"

"Yes, I think I told you about that already."

"He was here?"

Kim shook her head. "I telephoned him at home. I hated to bother him. He was hosting a party for underprivileged children, but I wanted to get his advice."

A slow sigh escaped her lips. "I only wish I had listened." She turned and faced me. "He told me I should go home, forget about talking to Mr. Finch, and forget about Christmas House Village. He told me that he had been on the phone with Mr. Finch earlier, who'd had some rather unflattering things to say about me." Kim sniffled and pulled out a fresh tissue. "I guess Mr. Finch didn't take too kindly to me, as Mr. Belzer put it, *badgering him* about his business." She ran the tissue along the bottom of her nose.

"But you went anyway." I couldn't help grinning despite the fact that there was no humor in the situation. "Okay," I said. "You arrive at Christmas House Village against all common sense and advice, and nobody else knows you're coming, and who do you see when you get here?"

I had a feeling wine may have played a significant part in her decision-making process but saw no point in bringing it up.

Kim shrugged once more. "Customers. That's about it. And Santa."

"Sidewalk Santa? The one collecting for charity?"

"That's right." She turned toward the entrance. "The same one that's there now, I guess. Though . . ."

"What?"

"Actually, there were two of them when I got here. Must have been a shift change or something."

"Okay, let's move on from Santa. What else do you remember? Anything else out of the ordinary?"

"Well," Kim began with obvious hesitation, "there was one thing."

"Spill."

"I saw Randy."

I jerked my neck. "Randy as in Randy Vincent?"

Kim nodded.

"What was Randy doing here?"

"I don't know, Amy. It's not like I was going to ask him."

"Was Lynda with him?"

"No, he was alone." Kim's voice had grown small.

"Well, what did he say?"

"Nothing. The truth is, I avoided him. I saw Randy walking toward me as I was walking in." She lowered her chin. "I didn't want to see him, so I ran over to that porch over there." Kim pointed to the porch of Frosty's House. "I don't think he even saw me."

I decided to let the subject of Randy go. "Okay"—I made moving-on motions with my right hand—"let's get past Randy." I'd deal with him later. "After Randy passed—"

"After Randy passed I went to Elf House."

"Who else was there?"

Kim shrugged. "Nobody."

"Nobody?"

"Not a soul." Kim quirked her brow. "Except for maybe Franklin Finch's soul, considering he was dead."

"If the man even had a soul," I grumbled.

Kim sniffled and pushed her tissue against her nose. "I called out and nobody answered, so I went upstairs to the office. There was nobody there either."

"So you decided to check upstairs?"

"Yes, I mean, I might have gone up anyway, maybe not, but I thought I heard a noise and figured that Mr. Finch must be up there. So up I went."

"What kind of a noise?"

Kim squeezed her eyes shut, then opened them. "Sorry, Amy," she said, facing me. "Just a noise. Like a clatter, maybe?"

"I have a hunch the clatter you heard was the sound of Franklin Finch going for a swing, not the clatter of reindeer hooves up on the rooftop."

Kim visibly shuddered. "Must you be so . . . vivid?"

"Sorry." I stood and pulled her up from the bench. "My butt's getting cold. Let's go."

"Good idea." Kim allowed herself to be pulled to her feet. She moved one way and I moved the other.

"Where are you going?" I demanded.

Kim turned around and faced me. "Where are you going?"

"To the loft. Come on." I waved her on.

"Are you completely mad, Amy? You want to go poking around in a room where a man was murdered mere days ago?"

"That's the general idea." I put my hands firmly on Kim's back and pushed her forward. She squawked every step of the way, but complied.

24

We followed the path to Elf House and went inside.

"It's freezing in here," complained Kim. She had unbuttoned her tan cashmere coat and was now quickly buttoning it back up.

"I know," I said. "It was like that when I came in a few minutes ago." I tapped a friendly looking sales elf on the shoulder as she waved goodbye to a mother and daughter with a large shopping bag between them. "Why is it so cold in here?"

"The boiler is on the fritz. There are people working on it," she said perkily. "We have hot cider and hot cocoa in the kitchen!" She pointed over her shoulder. "Hey, weren't you here a few minutes ago?"

I nodded. "Ms. Dunnellon asked me to drop some papers off on her desk." I patted my purse as if that meant something.

"Okeydoke." She spun on her elfin feet and went in search of needy customers.

"Come on." I started for the stairs with Kim right behind me. The sounds of voices came from the second-floor offices. I tiptoed to the last flight of stairs and beckoned Kim to keep up.

"What if the door's locked?" asked Kim as we climbed.

"Shh. You worry too much," I whispered.

"Did you ever think that maybe your problem is that you don't worry enough?" she whispered right back.

Friendship is a wonderful thing.

At the top of the stairs, I paused and strained my ears. I couldn't hear a thing except for the sounds of Christmas carols rising from the first floor. I tried the doorknob.

It wasn't locked. I stuck my tongue out at Kim, turned the doorknob, and went inside. Kim hustled in behind me, bumping into my backside.

"Careful!" I said softly. But there was no need. The loft was deserted. I pulled the door shut behind us.

"This is really creepy."

I waved away her concern.

"What if we get caught?" Kim pressed.

"There's no crime-scene tape."

"That doesn't mean we should be here. What are we doing here, anyway?" Kim held her arms wrapped across her chest, but I didn't think it was due to the coldness of the room.

I walked slowly around the perimeter while Kim stood near the door, watching me. Except for the missing noose, the room appeared unchanged.

"I don't know," I answered in reply to my friend's question. "I was hoping being here might jar your memory."

"It's jarring, all right."

"Ha-ha." I crossed over to the antique rolltop desk. The computer was gone and the nearby space heater was turned off. "I wonder who's going to live here next?"

"It wouldn't be me." Kim finally removed herself from the vicinity of the door and joined me at the desk.

"Maybe Franklin's ex-wife." How would she feel, moving into a space in which her husband had been murdered? Happy, sad, or indifferent?

"Not a chance," Kim replied. "According to Mr. Belzer, she's decided to sell."

"Since when?"

"Since this morning. I overheard him talking to her when I stopped in the office. Apparently, she feels like Christmas House Village is nothing but trouble and she's happy where she is." Kim stamped her feet against the cold. "I don't blame her. Can we get out of here now? It's cold and creepy."

"Fine." A drawing protruding from one of the slots in the desktop caught my eye. "What's this?" I slid it out and held it open using both hands.

Kim peered over my shoulder. "It looks like something a kindergartner would draw."

I nodded. "It's pretty rough. But what is this? Look." There were six poorly drawn squares, a line down the middle, and a big rectangle to the right filled with lines. I planted a fingernail on the rectangle filled with lines. "Is that supposed to be a parking lot?" I tapped the sheet of paper. "I think it is. And these squares are Christmas House Village."

Kim pulled a face. "That's not a parking lot, that's the Antiques Mall."

"Maybe our Mr. Finch had designs on turning it into a parking lot."

"Christmas House Village could use some on-site parking. Was he going to call it Santa's Parking Garage?"

I rolled my eyes.

What?" Kim added as I gaped at her. "I'm just saying."

"I'm saying let's go to the Antiques Mall and see if anybody knows anything about this."

"Polly Carter owns the Antiques Mall," Kim said. "She'll probably be in. She usually is."

I went to the attic window and looked down. A black-and-white cat scooted along the edge of the fence and disappeared in a crack between the boards.

A tiny thread of something outside the window caught my eye. I unlocked the window and pushed up.

"What are you doing, Amy? It's freezing in here. Shut that thing."

I waved her complaint away and bent lower. "Look at this." Several thin strands of hemp had become wedged in a splinter.

"A splinter?" Kim said, unimpressed. "Call maintenance."

"Not the splinter, what's in it."

"Some I-don't-know-what. Crud." Kim's face was close to mine.

I fingered the slender bits. "I think it's hemp."

Kim arched her brow in question.

"Hemp as in hemp fibers like the rope Finch's rope was made of. Just like the bits of it that were here on the floor the day you found him."

"Maybe it's from an old bird's nest."

"Maybe." Kim was right. "A bird might have used the bits of hemp to build a nest sometime in the past. But I don't think so. Besides," I said, "that wouldn't explain the bits that were on the inside of the window."

Kim stood. "What's it doing there then? What does it mean?"

I rose and latched the window. "I have no idea."

We left the loft not much the wiser except for the possibility of Franklin Finch wanting to add a parking lot to his Christmas empire.

I had just pulled the door closed behind us when a voice called up from the stairwell.

"What are you two ladies doing up there?"

I looked over the rail. It was Max, the surly young security guard, and he looked even less happy than usual. I cleared my throat and started down the stairs, dragging Kim with me. "We were looking for Eve Dunnellon. Have you seen her?"

Max stood in the center of the step, his hand gripping the banister, preventing our passing. "That's private quarters. Off-limits."

I gulped. "Sorry. We'll be going now. Mr. Sever stated he would be bringing my van around. Is it here?" I eyeballed his arm.

After a moment, he dropped it and stepped closer to the wall to let us pass.

Kim hurried after me. Glancing over my shoulder, I noted that Max was following closely.

We hurried outside. I was relieved to see that Max wasn't still on our tail. We crossed the grounds of Christmas House Village and entered the sprawling Antiques Mall, which was a collection of smaller sellers under one roof. The Antiques Mall, like so many businesses in town, had been around at least as long as I had been.

"Thank goodness, it's warm in here." I unbuttoned my jacket and Kim did the same to hers.

Kim led the way to Polly Carter's office in the rear of the store. The door marked OFFICE stood open, so Kim knocked on it as she went in, and I followed. A woman in her sixties, by my guess, sat behind a decidedly contemporary desk of stainless steel and glass. In fact, the entire office was filled with furniture of a modern age rather than the vintage merchandise that filled the indoor mall.

"Ms. Carter?" Kim began.

The woman looked up from her computer. "Yes?" Small lines ran the edges of her mouth and under her pale blue eyes. Half-rimmed glasses balanced on her nose. Her hair was blond going to gray. "You're with Belzer Realty, aren't you?" She wore loose blue jeans and a floppy red sweater lined with colorful nutcracker soldiers.

Kim nodded. "I'm Kim Christy. This is Amy Simms."

The woman bobbed her head and motioned for us to sit.

"That's okay, we don't want to take up much of your time," I said, remaining standing. "We were wondering if you were planning to sell the Antiques Mall."

Ms. Carter pulled her glasses lower. "Is that why you're here? Are you hoping to get a listing?"

"No, it's nothing like that," Kim said hastily.

"We heard rumors," I said, "that Franklin Finch was looking to maybe buy your business."

"Ahh." Polly Carter smiled and laid her glasses on her desk. "That man." She shook her head. "What a pain in the patooty." She rubbed the sides of her face.

"So he did want to buy the Antiques Mall?" Kim asked.

Polly Carter nodded. "I started getting letters from the man, quite insistent letters, before he'd even arrived to take possession of Christmas

House Village." She grunted. "As if I would ever let anybody turn the Antiques Mall into a parking lot!"

"You told him no?" I asked, to be certain.

Ms. Carter's brow flew up to her hairline. "Of course, I told him no. And I kept telling him no. I saw what he'd done to Christmas House Village. You should hear some of the words that Toby used to describe Finch when he found out what his plans were and how he was operating."

"Toby?"

"Toby Kinley."

Alarms went off in my brain. "Would that be one of Tyrone Kinley's children?"

Polly nodded. "His youngest."

"And you've talked to him?" I pressed.

"Sure, me and the Kinleys go way back. Whenever one of them is in town, we get together."

"He's in town now?" Kim asked.

"That's right. Staying at the motor inn." She rose. "Now, if you don't have any more questions, this is the height of the busy season."

"Of course."

We left as quickly as we'd come.

"A fat lot of good that did us," Kim complained as we started back for the minivan.

"We learned that Toby Kinley is in town."

"Are you suggesting he may have murdered Mr. Finch?"

"Let's find out."

I went inside Elf House to grab my key ring while Kim waited on the porch.

"Can we get out of here?" Kim stomped down the steps to the walk. "Frankly, I don't care if I ever come back to Christmas House Village for as long as I live."

"I don't particularly like the way you phrased that, but I agree with your sentiment."

25

I drove straight to the Ruby Lake Motor Inn on Lake Shore Drive.

Built in the so-called neon era, the L-shaped lodging contains an office and a small diner in the shorter line of the L, with the rooms spreading out in the longer section. A row of small, rustic cabins with kitchenettes had been added later behind the inn.

Rust-pitted thirty-foot-tall steel posts held up the giant ruby-red neon sign. A smaller amber sign braced high up between the posts proclaimed that the inn was full for the night. People had suggested for years that the inn expand. There was nowhere to expand, but they could have built up, adding floors. The owners said they liked it the size it was.

"Look," I said, pointing to a black Toyota sedan, "South Carolina plates. What do you want to bet that car belongs to Toby Kinley?"

"I'd say I see at least two more cars with South Carolina plates and tell you that you were wrong," replied Kim, "except that one does have a Christmas House Village decal in the rear window."

I hadn't noticed, but I wasn't going to tell her that. I pulled in under the portico. We found Dick Feller, the inn's front-office manager, resting on a stool behind the counter. He's a thin man in his early forties with receding dirty-brown hair, skin the color of flour paste, and espresso-brown eyes. One hand held a sturdy coffee mug, the other a copy of the *Ruby Lake Weekender*, our local paper.

"Sorry, full for the holidays, folks," he said, without turning around.

"Hello, Dick," I said.

He turned. "Howdy, ladies." Dick's Southern drawl was thicker than cold molasses in winter. "What brings you to the inn?"

"My Kia," I quipped with a smile.

Kim punched me in the shoulder.

"Ow!" I glared at her and rubbed my upper arm. "We're here to see Toby Kinley. The thing is . . ." I drummed my fingers against the polished wood surface of the counter, "we forgot what room number he said he was in. Didn't we, Kim?"

Kim, ever slow on the pickup, said, "Uh, yeah?"

Dick slid off his stool and stood at the counter. He wore a long-sleeved white dress shirt with thin gray and brown stripes and a pair of cuffed dark brown trousers. "Listen here, Amy. This isn't the first time you've tried to get me to tell you what room somebody or another is in."

"And it won't be the last." I grinned at him. He frowned back. That wasn't the way it was supposed to work.

"A person's room number"—he pulled himself up to his full height, which wasn't saying much—"if that person is or is not staying here, is privileged information."

"Please?" I whined.

He shook his head. "I could lose my job breaking a rule like that."

I felt a hand push me aside. It was Kim. I'd almost forgotten she was there.

"Couldn't you help me," Kim purred, "just this once?"

Dick swiveled his eyes from her to me and back again. "Now, Kim, I already explained to Amy. You heard me," he sputtered. "We have procedures." He tugged at his shirt collar.

"Please?"

"But—"

Kim batted her eyelashes.

I frowned as the man started blabbing. Every time I batted my lashes at a man, they invariably asked me if I had something in my eye.

To make matters worse, he offered to walk us down. As if two grown women couldn't find their way in a straight line from the office to Toby Kinley's room at the opposite end.

"Are you sure it's not too much trouble, Dickie?" Kim asked rather disingenuously, though the manager hadn't seemed to pick up on her tone.

"No trouble at all. I'll be happy to make the introductions." Dick pulled on his overcoat, came from behind the counter, and hurried to open the office door.

Kim stopped at the door as Dick held it for us. "Aren't you coming, Amy?"

"You go ahead. I'll catch up. I need to make a stop in the ladies' room." There were public restrooms between the office and the inn's restaurant.

"Suit yourself," Kim replied.

I waited until they were some distance away, then scurried behind the counter to the computer. It didn't take me long to find Toby Kinley's registration. "Bingo." Toby had checked in on the day of Franklin Finch's murder. He had given an address in Spartanburg, South Carolina, as his residence. That was no more than a couple hours' drive.

The jingle of sleigh bells alerted me to the front door opening. I grabbed the mouse, clicked out of the screen, and spun around. "Oh, hi." I hoped my face wasn't too red. "Back so soon?" Dick held the door as Kim stepped inside.

"He wasn't in his room. At least, he wasn't answering," explained Kim.

"But his car—"

"Gone."

"Oh."

Dick leaned over the counter at me. "What are you doing behind the counter?"

"I-I was checking the newspaper. I placed an ad for the store. We're running a big holiday sale and I wanted to see how it looks."

Dick pulled open the swinging gate and motioned for me to leave. "If you please?"

"Thanks for your help, Dick," I said, moving out to the front. "Would you let Mr. Kinley know that we stopped by, if you see him?"

"Oh, you can be certain of that." Dick's words sounded very much like a threat. His hand went to the *Ruby Lake Weekender* at his desk.

I hustled Kim outside.

"You placed a store ad?" she asked.

"No. Let's get out of here before Dick figures out I was lying."

Once in the minivan with the heater running, I explained to Kim that Toby Kinley had checked into the inn the day of the murder.

"Why would Toby Kinley, or any of the Kinleys for that matter, want to kill Franklin Finch?"

I pulled onto Lake Shore Drive with the intent of returning to Birds & Bees. "Maybe they weren't happy with what he'd done to the family business. Maybe they wanted to buy it back."

"You can't buy something from a dead man."

"No," I had to admit, "but you can buy it from his widow."

"That's true." Kim gazed out the window. "Drop me off at the real estate office, would you?"

"Sure. What's up?"

"I promised Mr. Belzer I'd come in and work the floor. Not that I feel like it."

That explained the gray wool suit she was wearing. "It will be good for you to keep busy."

"I know. To tell you the truth, I'm not sure how much longer I can keep doing this, Amy."

"You mean real estate?"

Kim nodded.

"What would you do instead?"

"I don't know. Go back to school? Leave town? That's probably best." She sighed. "I don't know. I'll figure something out. Speaking of which, where are you going next?"

"Back to the store. I want to see if I can get a line on Bobby Cherry."

Kim frowned. "That's one character I think you should let the police handle."

"I promise, any information I find I will turn over to Jerry. Okay?"

"Okay," Kim answered. "But knowing you, and I do, you're bound to do something stupid first."

I kept my eyes on the road and fumed. I hated it when she was right.

Several minutes later, I pulled into the lot of Belzer Realty. "Look at that," I said as I turned off the main road.

"What is that?" Kim leaned toward my window.

"It looks like somebody spray-painted your sign."

Kim frowned. "Mr. Belzer isn't going to be happy about that." Jagged streaks of black paint crisscrossed the real estate agent's sign. "Is it ever going to end?"

"Yes, and soon, I hope." And I hoped I was right. I stopped outside the office and Kim climbed out.

"See if you can get a line on Bobby Cherry from your boss."

"I will," promised Kim. "But it's a longshot."

"Longshots are all I have to go on at this point. By the way," I said with a smile. "I hate you."

Kim laughed. "Because I have a way with men like Dick that makes you green with envy?"

"Yes," I said through gritted teeth.

"Love you, too." Kim giggled and wiggled her fingers.

I nodded and waved as she slammed the door shut behind her.

* * * *

I had told my best friend a small white lie. I wasn't going back to Birds & Bees, I was going to Vincent Properties. I wanted a word with her former boyfriend.

Randy and Lynda Vincent operated their business out of a small log cabin near the lake, convenient to several of their rental properties.

I saw Randy's black-and-chrome Harley out front. There was no sign of the silver pickup that he also sometimes drove. I hoped that meant that Lynda was out. It was going to be awkward enough seeing Randy. I didn't need to see Lynda, too.

I parked and killed the engine, letting the CD player run for several minutes to delay the inevitable. I'd been listening to the soundtrack to *Miracle on 34th Street: The Musical.* I waited for the song "Expect Things to Happen" to conclude.

I needed to make things happen. Maybe if I expected them to happen, they would.

I pushed open my door and went inside.

Randy was seated at his desk, which angled toward the door. An identical desk mirrored it on the other side of the small cabin. Presumably, it belonged to his wife, Lynda. A flagstone fireplace separated the two.

"Amy." Randy stood. "This is a surprise." Randy is a wannabe rebel biker and his wardrobe today was no exception. He wore baggy black denim jeans, black motorcycle boots, and a black leather jacket. His only nod to the weather rather than the image was the blue flannel shirt that hung loose over his pants.

"Hello, Randy. Do you have a minute?"

"Sure." He brought a chair over from the wall and set it in front of his desk. "Have a seat."

"Thanks." I unbuttoned my parka and looped my purse over the back of the chair.

"What's up?"

"I'm sure this is uncomfortable for the two of us, so I'll cut to the chase."

"Okay." Randy returned to his big leather chair. "Shoot." He leaned back and squinted his green eyes at me. Randy has a broad face and a narrow chin. He keeps his black hair short, probably for fear of helmet head. His fancy motorcycle helmet sat perched on the corner of his desk.

"Kim mentioned that she saw you at Christmas House Village the day Franklin Finch was murdered. Not long before he was killed, as a matter of fact."

"Wow, you don't mince your words, do you?"

"Was she right?"

Randy cocked his head and glanced out the window before turning his attention to me. "Sure. I was there." He picked out a pen and tapped out a beat. "What of it?"

"Did you see anything? Hear anything?"

"Nope."

"Can I ask why you were there?"

He smiled at me. "You just did."

"Do I get an answer?" The man was getting under my skin and not in a good way. I'd never known what Kim saw in him.

"I had an appointment with Finch."

"What for?"

"He had called here earlier in the day. He wanted me to take a look at Christmas House Village and give him a bid."

"A bid?"

"He was looking to do some sort of maintenance contract."

I nodded thoughtfully. "Cash Calderon had been providing those services for years."

"I know." Randy squirmed and set his pen down.

I whispered a prayer of thanks because the incessant tapping had been driving me crazy.

"This is a small town. I felt uncomfortable coming in and taking work from Cash. He's good. Christmas House Village had been lucky to have his services. And that's what I was going to tell Finch. Besides," added Randy, "that sort of work isn't really what we do."

"How did he take it?"

"He didn't. I never saw him. I went to Christmas House Village but he wasn't in the office. Nobody knew where he was, so I left. I figured if he wanted to talk to me, he knew where to find me." The cell phone on Randy's desk chirped. He turned the screen toward him and took a look. "End of story."

"Do you know a young man named Bobby or Robert Cherry?"

"No. Should I?"

"Bobby's local. He had been renting the room over the garage at Virginia Johnson's house until she was murdered."

"Murdered?" Randy dropped his elbows on his desk and leaned closer. "That's news to me."

I cleared my throat. "That hasn't actually been confirmed yet." At least, not that I knew of. "Anyway, I was wondering where he might have moved to afterward."

"And since I own rentals, you thought maybe he was renting from me?"

I nodded. Randy rolled back his chair, stood, and crossed to an oak filing cabinet along the wall. "Cherry, you say?" he asked as he thumbed through some hanging folders.

"That's right."

"Sorry, I don't see him." He pushed the file drawer shut. "Any special reason you're trying to get ahold of this guy?"

"No. I think the police might like a word with him."

"Well," Randy said, "if I run into him, I'll be sure to let *the police* know."

I felt my cheeks heat up. "Thanks for your time."

"Anytime."

I rose, picked up my purse, and started for the door. Randy followed me.

"How's Kim holding up?" Randy asked, his hand on the door handle.

"Fine," I replied. "In fact, she's doing great."

Randy ran his fingers across the top of his head. "She's a great girl."

"That she is. How's Lynda, your wife?"

Randy's lips twitched. "She's good."

"Glad to hear it. Tell her hello for me."

Randy pulled open the door and I couldn't wait to get out of there.

That was one man who wouldn't be getting so much as a lump of coal from me for Christmas.

26

There was no Robert Cherry in the phone book and a search of the internet revealed his address as being Virginia Johnson's house. I'd hit another dead end.

From the van, I dialed Birds & Bees to see how everything was going. With Esther's assurance that everything was fine, I told her to hold the fort and promised I'd be in as soon as I could.

She explained that Riley was out front hanging Christmas lights and that my mother was working the cash register. "And I sold our most expensive spotting scope to Frenchie McNeil."

I frowned at the screen of the phone. "Frenchie? What would he want a spotting scope for?" I knew Frenchie. He'd been my dentist until his eyes got so bad he had to take an early retirement.

"To spot birds, of course," Esther snapped.

"But the man can barely see."

"He knows that," Esther said rather impatiently. "Gotta go! Customers just walked in!"

The line went dead.

Birds & Bees seemed to be in capable, if batty, hands.

I drove downtown to the public parking lot. The streets were crowded. It was a cold but blue-sky day and everyone seemed to be enjoying it. The Finch's Christmas House Village banner still hung over the entrance to the shopping village. I was surprised someone hadn't torn it down by now.

I walked briskly to Harlan and Harlan, the strong wind whipping me in the face.

To my astonishment, Gertie Hammer, bundled in her big green parka, stepped out the door. A rotund man half her age accompanied her.

"Gertie!"

"Simms." The old woman didn't look happy to see me. But then, that was nothing new. The man glanced curiously at me, then said to Gertie, "Shall we stop at the mayor's office?"

"Good idea." Gertie scooted past me and rounded the corner in the direction of the town square.

"Would you mind closing the door, please?" A woman's voice, smooth and chilly, reached me.

I turned. Ben and Derek's receptionist slash secretary, the latest in a long line of such persons, sat at the front desk. "Sorry." I'd been so amazed to see Gertie at Derek's office that I'd been standing there with the door open to the elements. Those elements being of the frigid variety. Not unlike Mrs. Edmunds, who sat behind the mahogany desk.

In the short time that I'd known Derek, the office had gone through a number of front desk staff. Mrs. Edmunds seemed to have staying power.

"Hello, Mrs. Edmunds." I secured the door shut behind me and smiled. "Is Derek in?"

"Yes, he is." The coolly elegant woman favored skirt suits, and today was no exception, this one being brown tweed, matching the brown hair that fell ever so perfectly from the top of her head to the bottom of her neck, as if sprayed in place. Her skin was so pale, I had a feeling she only went out after dark.

"I just need a quick word with him." I unbuttoned the top button of my coat and started for the hall. Mrs. Edmunds beat me to it, blocking my path. "Have a seat, please." She motioned to the bank of plush chairs near the door. "I'll let Mr. Harlan know that you are here, Ms. . . . ?"

"Simms," I said, dropping into a chair. There was no sense arguing with the woman. "We have met—several times."

She smiled and picked up the phone on the corner of her desk. "There's a Ms. Simms to see you, Mr. Harlan."

I squelched the extreme rolling of the eyes I felt coming on. If I didn't play nice, Mrs. Edmunds would likely find a way to block my visit.

"You may go back now, Ms. Simms. Second door on the left."

"Thank you," I said. Once in the hallway and out of earshot, I muttered a few words I'd learned from Karl and a couple more that I had picked up from Esther.

I found Derek seated at his desk, a stack of papers in front of him. He looked worn—still good, but worn.

He rose and kissed me. "This is a pleasant surprise, Amy. Have a seat. Can I get you anything to drink? Mrs. Edmunds brought in homemade eggnog."

"No, thanks. I'm not interrupting anything, am I?" I took a seat across from the desk near the outside wall.

"No." Derek returned to his leather chair and swiveled it in my direction. "I've got some time."

"Are you sure?"

"Yep. What's up? I don't have another appointment for nearly an hour."

"What did Gertie want? I saw her leaving the office as I came in."

"I'm afraid I can't say." Derek slid some typed papers into a big brown envelope and set it in the left-hand drawer of his desk. "It was a personal matter."

"Was that her son with her?"

"A friend. I'm afraid I really can't say any more, Amy."

"I understand. Maybe you can help me with something else."

"What would that be?"

"I'm trying to find this Bobby Cherry character. So far, I've had no luck."

"Does he have a criminal record?"

"I don't know. From what I've heard about him, he ought to."

Derek pulled his laptop closer and his fingers went to work on the keyboard. "Let me check something."

I listened to the clicking of the keys. "Well?" I asked when he stopped.

"Nope. I don't see any Robert Cherry around these parts with a criminal record of any sort."

"Are you sure? You can tell that?" I leaned closer. "Can I see?"

Derek lowered the lid of his laptop. "Sorry. Confidential."

I pouted. "Fine. Be that way." I folded my hands in my lap. "How do you propose I go about finding him?"

Derek leaned back. "Assuming he still lives in Ruby Lake, as I understand from what you told me, he was working at Christmas House Village until recently. Somebody there should be able to tell you where he's living."

"That's true. Yet when I asked Eve Dunnellon, the manager, if she knew where he was living, she claimed she didn't."

Derek shrugged. "Maybe she doesn't. Ask somebody who works in payroll or human resources."

"That's very tempting, but I can't think of what reason I could give them for wanting to know."

Derek shrugged. "There is that." He locked his hands behind his neck. "How is Kim holding up?"

"So-so. I hate to see her so depressed, especially during the holidays. I keep hoping that things will get back to normal soon. I believe that once Mr. Finch's killer is caught, everybody's spirits will lighten."

"I hope you're right. Are the police any closer?"

"Not that I've heard. I also found out that Toby Kinley, one of Tyrone Kinley's kids, was in town the day Finch was killed."

"I doubt if that means anything."

"Did you know that Finch had been trying to buy the Antiques Mall?"

"No, I didn't."

I explained how Kim and I had found a rough sketch in his loft and then talked to Polly Carter, owner of the Antiques Mall. "He wanted to turn the spot into a parking lot."

"It sounds like Franklin Finch was a real go-getter."

"Yeah," I said, rising, "until somebody decided he'd gotten enough."

* * * *

I left Derek to his work and walked across the square to the Coffee and Tea House. I ordered a cup of chai tea and a blueberry scone and dialed Kim on my mobile phone. After exchanging greetings, I said, "Did you ask Ellery about Bobby Cherry?"

"Mr. Belzer wasn't in. He's out showing a big client some properties, and then he's going by Christmas House Village."

"What is he going there for?"

"We got a call that it was time for another toy pickup. Every time the toy collection box is full, they call and we go pick up."

I sighed. "That's too bad. I mean, about Bobby. I'm afraid I've hit a dead end when it comes to finding him."

"Not so fast, Amy," Kim replied. "Mr. Belzer wasn't in the office, but I did some digging."

"You found him? How? Where?"

"I called some of my contacts. One of them owns two small apartment complexes; furnished, monthly rentals, and they're low priced."

"And Bobby Cherry?"

"He's renting a furnished one-bedroom at the Olympia Apartments on Crawford Avenue."

I wasn't familiar with the street. "Give me the address, quick!"

Kim rattled off the address.

"Wait," I said. "Let me get a pen and paper." I smoothed out the paper napkin I'd been using, then rummaged around and came up with pen. "Shoot." Kim shot and I wrote. "I'm going to go check it out."

"Wait a minute, Amy."

"What?"

"You told me you would turn anything you found out over to the police. Particularly when it comes to this nefarious Bobby Cherry character."

"And I will," I promised as I carefully folded the napkin and stuffed it in my coat. "As soon as I do find out anything. Right now, all I have is an address and a lot of questions."

"Amy . . ." My best friend said my name like it was a warning.

"What? I'm only going to drive by. Then I will call the police myself and tell them where they can find him."

"Promise?"

"Scout's honor." I pressed two fingers over my heart. Not that she could see them, or that they were crossed, which everybody knows negates the whole promissory aspect of the oath.

"Fine."

"Great." I was anxious to hang up. "Bye."

"Wait a minute!"

I sighed. "What is it now?"

"You're welcome."

"What?"

"I said: You. Are. Welcome."

Understanding, though it often came late, finally dawned on me. "Oh, right. Thanks."

* * * *

The poorly kept apartment building sat mere yards from the weed-infested train track. The track had been abandoned decades ago when the last freight train had discontinued service.

The apartment building itself was a nondescript rectangle of cracked vinyl siding, with four apartments on the ground floor and four above. Each apartment had an outside entrance. Concrete walkways ran along the front. I wouldn't have trusted my life to the rusty iron railing running the length of the second floor.

A patch of blacktop in front of the apartment building contained several older vehicles, a small boat on a trailer with one flat tire, and one shiny, new, modernistic blue motorcycle.

I pulled to a stop beside the boat trailer and looked toward the second-floor windows. One holiday-minded renter had hung a Christmas wreath on their door. I was pretty sure that wouldn't be Bobby's place—unless he'd stolen the wreath from Christmas House Village.

A definite possibility.

The curtain fluttered in the third window over, and a face peered down at me. A moment later, that face disappeared.

I removed my keys from the ignition and slipped the key ring into my coat pocket. A bank of built-in mail slots sat at the foot of the stairs. There was no name on the box marked 203, Bobby's apartment.

I knew I had told Kim I would only drive by and then call the police. But we both knew I hadn't meant it. I climbed the stairs and approached the scuffed brown door of apartment 203. The curtains were closed. No sound came from within.

I knocked. "Hello?" A face had looked down at me from that window moments before, so I knew somebody was in. I tried again, banging my knuckles a little harder. "Bobby? Can I talk to you for a minute?"

I pressed my ear to the door. All I got for my effort was a cold ear.

Then I had an idea. "I'm Amy Simms from Birds and Bees, a store in town. A friend of mine told me you were looking for work. I could use some part-time help through the holidays." I strained to listen. "Bobby?"

The door flew open and I jumped back, hitting the railing. It wobbled as I locked my hands over the top rail.

"What friend?"

I turned around quickly. Bobby Cherry was everything that Kim had described—black hair, an acne-scarred complexion half-buried in the start of a beard, and blistering dark eyes. "More of an acquaintance really. Her name was Mary something."

I peered past him into the apartment. It was small, sparsely furnished with pieces that could have come from a thrift shop. There was no art on the walls and no TV set that I could see. Nothing personal to mark his presence. "May I come in a minute?"

His eyes raked over me before he answered. "I guess." The black leather motorcycle jacket hanging open off his shoulders appeared a couple sizes too big for his slender frame. There were more zippers on his jacket than I had in my entire wardrobe. Underneath the jacket was a purple football jersey.

Bobby stepped away from the door and, despite the alarms going off in my head, I entered, closing the door behind me. Not that it helped much. It was almost as cold inside the dingy apartment as it was outdoors.

The young man smelled like bargain-bin cologne and tobacco. Bobby threw himself into a threadbare chair and picked up a pack of cigarettes on the cluttered side table.

I stood a couple of steps inside the entrance. The main room was no more than two hundred square feet. There was a small galley kitchen toward the back to my left. Off a short hall, I could see a bathroom with white subway tile walls and floor. The bedroom, which shared a wall with the outside, was to the right. The bedroom door stood open, but all I could see was the unmade end of a bed.

"So what's the job?" Bobby stuck a cigarette between his thick red lips, pulled a cheap plastic lighter from the pocket of his jeans, and lit up.

"General help around the store." I took a step back as he blew a cloud of smoke toward me. "I heard you used to do that sort of thing at Christmas House Village."

My mention of Christmas House Village was accompanied by the twitch of his brow.

"In fact," I pressed, "didn't you formerly rent a room from a family friend of mine?"

He pushed his brows together and sucked loudly on his smoke. "And who would that be?"

"Virginia Johnson." I clutched my purse close against my belly. The room was dark and close and filling with cigarette smoke. I was dying to open a window. The pale green carpet looked like it had died decades ago.

"Yeah. I lived there. Until the old lady killed herself." He plucked the cigarette from his lips, inspected it, then took another puff. "I don't remember even once seeing you there." He leaned forward, elbows on his knees. "What did you say your name was?"

"Amy." I coughed and resisted the urge to wave a hand in front of my nose. "Amy Simms."

"Mrs. Johnson never once mentioned you to me."

"That's funny. Well"—I smiled—"you know how old people can be."

"I guess." Bobby mashed the cigarette into a dented beer can on the table.

"A pity, her dying the way she did."

Bobby reached for his next cigarette. "Yeah. Rough."

"I heard you were the one who found her."

Bobby's countenance darkened considerably as he sucked hard on his cigarette, the end glowing like molten ore. "You ask a lot of questions, lady." He stood, towering over me by several inches. "I thought you were here to talk to me about a job?" He thrust his empty hand in the pocket of his leather jacket.

"I-I am."

"That's funny." He jabbed his cigarette at me. "Because it sounds like you're being snoopy."

I took a step back in the direction of the door, without taking my eyes off him. He could very well prove to be a killer.

Times two.

"I didn't mean anything, Bobby—"

Anger flashed in his eyes. He flicked his cigarette toward the kitchen, where it landed on the linoleum and smoldered.

"I wasn't even there when Mrs. Johnson died. I was in Asheville. Ask anybody," Bobby said defiantly. "I came home and found her. I was the one who reported her dead! Bet you didn't know that, did you, Miss Nosy?"

I suppressed a frown. The snotty kid was right. I hadn't known that. But I did now.

"I'm sorry. I didn't know." I swept a lock of hair from my eyes. "About the job. You would need transportation." As I blathered on, I wondered if Bobby could hear how shaky my voice sounded. "Is that your motorcycle outside? It's very nice. Blue is my favorite color."

Bobby pulled his hands free and pointed one of them at me. "Don't go anywhere. I'll be right back."

I nodded quickly. "Okay."

Bobby went through the bedroom door. "I've got something I want to show you." He closed the door behind him and shouted, "You're going to like it."

I debated turning and bolting, and every bone of wisdom screamed at me to run for my life. But curiosity won out and I waited.

And wondered.

After several moments of waiting in fear and interest, hearing nothing but the sound of my heart thumping and blood rushing in my ears, I tiptoed to the bedroom door.

As I did, I heard the roar of a motorcycle coming to life. "Bobby?" I opened the door.

The window screen had been tossed on the bed. The bedroom was empty. Bobby had gone out the open window. I ran to the window, which stood ajar, letting in the force of winter. Bobby was astride his motorcycle and already heading down Crawford Avenue. Soon he disappeared from my sight completely.

"Rats." What an idiot I'd been. First, to come alone to his apartment, second to enter it alone with a criminal, and third, to let him get away.

I frowned and pushed the window shut, not that it mattered.

The tiny closet with accordion doors hung open. A few cheap long-sleeved cotton shirts hung from black plastic hangers. Two pairs of blue jeans lay in a heap on the carpeted floor beneath them.

In the battered bureau, I discovered a mixed bag of socks and underwear. If there was anything lurking underneath, I'd never know because there was no way I was touching any of it.

The bottom drawer was empty. Once again, there was little in the room to reveal the personality of its occupant. Then again, maybe that said scores.

A flash of red and white under the bed caught my eye. I bent and took a peek. Uncertain what I was looking at, I gave the material a tug.

My brow went to the ceiling.

It was a Santa Claus suit.

All red and white and fluffy and fake furry.

"What the devil?" No matter how hard I tried, I could not envision the Bobby Cherry whom I had learned about, and now met, playing Santa Claus to a bunch of smiling, hopeful children.

If anything, I pictured him as the Anti-Santa, sliding down chimneys and removing all the toys from under each and every Christmas tree in Ruby Lake.

27

I rose early the next day determined to put in a full day at the store.

"You're really going to work for the *whole* day," Mom said with a twinkle in her eye as she picked up our breakfast dishes.

"Very funny, Mom." I pushed my hands through my hair. I had thrown on a comfortable pair of brown corduroys and a cable-knit sweater featuring a cockatiel in an elf costume perched on a snowman's head.

"Speaking of funny . . ." Mom tugged at the fabric of my sweater.

"I know. It is tacky, yes, but it's the spirit that counts. Besides, I bought it on clearance a year ago and haven't had the opportunity to wear it yet."

"Or the guts."

"Ha-ha."

I left Mom to her jokes. She had the day off from store duty. At the apartment door, I thrust my feet into a nice pair of knitted boots with faux fur cuffs and green and blue laces. Perfect for the holidays. While I expected to stay inside where it was clean, dry, and warm, there had been a dusting of snow overnight and these boots provided good grip.

I arrived downstairs a few minutes before opening.

Esther stood near the door and turned at the sound of my steps on the stairway. "It's about time."

"Good morning, Esther. Is everything ready? Have you started the coffeepot?" I always liked to have the coffee brewing before we opened our doors. The smell of coffee added to the shopping experience, in my opinion.

"Never mind the coffee," Esther said, sounding surlier than her usual self.

"What's wrong?" I opened the cash register and checked that we had plenty of cash on hand. I wasn't in the mood for a trip to the bank. "Did you miss your coffee and cookie this morning?"

Esther is fond of strong coffee and sugar-packed cookies, especially when they're on the house. That house being mine.

"Just come here, would you?"

I banged the register shut and grabbed my apron off its hook behind the counter. "Fine, but if this is about the snow, I've already seen it."

"Yeah," snapped Esther, stepping away from the front door, "but have you seen this?" She wore a pale blue frock decorated with horizontal rows of two-inch tall white snowflakes.

I jolted to a stop. "Oh, dear."

A neatly tied rope noose hung from the eave, dancing on the breeze.

A chill shot through me. I bit my lip and inched closer to the French door. "Is this somebody's sick idea of a joke?" I spun around. "Where's Paul?"

In addition to owning the biergarten next door, Paul was renting the apartment next to Esther's on the second floor.

Esther pulled a face. "Do you actually think he'd pull a stunt like this?"

Paul could be annoying and he could, indeed, be a bit of a clown. But hanging a noose on my front porch went beyond even his juvenile idea of a joke. "No," I was forced to admit. I pressed my nose to the glass. "Have you telephoned the police?"

"No." Esther stuck her hands in her frock. "I figured that was your job."

I shot her a look. Sure, suddenly something around here was my job. "I suppose I'd better call then."

"You'd better do something," quipped Esther. "A thing like a noose hanging from your door is bound to scare the customers away."

There wasn't a doubt about that. "Too bad our midnight visitor didn't leave a nice Christmas wreath instead."

* * * *

The big man himself arrived in response to my call. I unlocked the front door the minute I saw his squad car pull up to the curb.

It was well past the time to open our doors but, as Esther had suggested, not a customer had appeared. Jerry spoke into his radio then extracted himself from his car and headed up the brick path to the porch, shaking his head side to side as he came.

I stepped out on the porch to greet him. "Good morning, Jerry."

"Simms." He stopped several feet from the porch steps and stared at the noose. "Damn. That's something you don't see every day."

I had thrown a coat over my sweater. "It's not the same kind of rope that was used to hang Franklin Finch."

"I can see that." Jerry climbed the steps, his breath coming out in tiny white clouds that quickly disappeared. He craned his neck and examined the noose. It had been expertly knotted but the rope was much thinner than the rope I'd seen around Finch's neck. This white rope looked like what my mother used to hang between the trees in our yard to dry our clothes on. The rope was attached to a nail that I sometimes hung feeders from.

"Any idea who might have left you this little Christmas present, Simms?"

"Not a clue."

"Well," Jerry sighed, "I'll send Pratt over to take pictures and check it out. I don't expect we'll come up with anything though."

"I'd like to get it down as soon as possible. Esther says it might scare the customers away."

Jerry stamped his feet. "It's cold out here. Let's go inside." He pulled open the door and led the way.

I walked to the seed bins arranged on the front wall. Customers could buy various types of birdseed by the pound and mix their own varieties if they chose. I also prepared some blends that I mixed myself and sold in prepackaged bags. I grabbed a bag, picked up one of the two metal scoops I provided, lifted the plastic lid of the peanut bin, and shoveled a generous portion into the bag.

I handed the bag of peanuts to Jerry. Jerry had a habit of helping himself to my peanuts. I'd long given up trying to stop him.

To prevent his eating dangerously into my profits, I had come up with the idea of scooping him up a small bagful preemptively. So far, my plan seemed to be working.

"Thanks." Jerry opened the bag, gave it a shake, and pulled out a handful of shelled peanuts that he chewed quickly.

I could see and hear Esther preparing the coffee in the kitchenette.

"What did Bobby Cherry have to say for himself?" I had called Dan at the police station after returning to Birds & Bees.

"Nothing." Jerry ran the back of his hand over his lips.

"Nothing? Didn't you haul him in for questioning?"

"I might have if he'd been there. When we got to Olympia Apartments, he was gone." He was looking at me like it was my fault.

I squirmed. An argument could have been made that he was right.

"We staked out his apartment and he didn't come back all night."

"I saw a Santa suit under his bed."

"Yeah, we saw it too. Ho, ho, ho." He looked toward the back of the store. "Coffee ready?"

"In a minute!" Esther hollered. "Hold your horses, copper!"

Jerry glowered but didn't dare respond. I couldn't blame him.

"Bobby told me he was in Asheville at the time Virginia Johnson died."

Jerry shook the bag of peanuts and stuck his hand in. "That's right. He was in Asheville at the time. Witnesses confirmed it, not that we were looking at murder at the time. But he was there all right. If Virginia Johnson was strung up, it wasn't by him. He was in Asheville all that day until he came home and found her."

"That reminds me, I saw some strands of rope outside that window that had been left ajar in Franklin Finch's loft."

Jerry narrowed his eyes at me and buried his right hand in his back pocket, which I figured was better than placing said hand on the grip of his pistol. "What were you doing there, Simms?" Bits of chewed peanut spilled out his mouth and landed on his boots.

"I, that is we, Kim and I, went to see Eve Dunnellon . . ."

"The offices are on the second floor. What were you *and Kim* doing on the third floor?"

"Look, Jerry, I think you should check it out."

"You want me to check out every rope in town?"

"It couldn't hurt," I shot back.

"No, but it could take a lifetime."

"There's a coil of rope in Santa's Reindeer Barn."

Jerry snorted. "Yeah, and there's bells on bobtails."

"Very funny. There's a killer loose and hanging threatening nooses on people's doorsteps, and you're making jokes."

Jerry shook his head. "We saw the rope in the shed. The hardware store also sells that rope, as does the lumber yard, so do any number of other stores in this county alone."

He balled the bag of peanuts up in his hands. "I know how to do my job, Simms. What you need to focus on is doing yours." He swiveled his head toward the kitchenette. "That coffee ready?"

Esther scooted over with a lidded to-go cup in her hand.

"Thanks." Jerry took the cup. He went to the door and opened it. "If you have any more trouble, give me a call."

"If I have any more trouble," I muttered, crossing my arms over my chest, "you are the last person I'm going to call."

Jerry stopped at the threshold. "What's that?"

I smiled. "Thanks, Chief!" If he got himself caught up in that noose on the porch as he passed by, I wasn't sure if I would help him or not.

Fortunately for him, I didn't have to make that life-or-death choice. He bent his head and stepped lightly under the noose on his way to his squad car.

I planted my hands on my hips. "Somebody better get here soon and take that thing down." I turned the CLOSED sign to OPEN, not that I expected any customers under the circumstances. Maybe if I wrapped some sprigs of mistletoe around the noose . . .

"Thanks, Esther. That was a smart move bringing Jerry his coffee in a to-go cup."

"I figured if I did, the man would get the message and go."

I had to admit, though I never would to her, the woman had some slick moves.

Esther grunted. "I guess I'll fill those stockings now."

"Good idea." We had ordered several dozen Christmas stockings with various species of birds on them. We would fill the stockings with an assortment of bird-themed items, from seed to socks. I hoped customers would agree that they made great Christmas gifts for their bird-loving friends.

"Amy?" Mom stood at the bottom of the stairs. She'd changed her robe and slippers for a wool skirt and slate-colored sweater.

"Hey, Mom. What's up?" I moved to check the levels of the seed bins.

"Mr. Calderon called a few minutes ago," Mom explained. "I thought you'd like to know. Well"—she brushed her hand against her sweater—"maybe *like to know* isn't quite the way to phrase it."

"Oh?" I picked up a bag of millet and topped off its bin.

"I'm afraid it isn't good news."

I set the bag down and reached for the safflower seed. "What do you mean?" I had more important things on my mind, like nooses on my doorstep.

"He had the estimate on the house repairs."

"And?"

"He says he has given you the absolute lowest price possible," Mom prevaricated. "And a very generous discount."

"I'm sure, Mom. Go ahead, hit me with it."

"It comes to just over twenty thousand dollars."

"Twenty thousand dollars?"

"Just over," corrected Esther from the corner where she'd laid out a dozen or more red and green Christmas stockings.

I snapped my head in her direction. "Thank you, Esther." When had the carousel been installed under the floor? When had the floor started spinning?

How could I make it stop?

Mom rested her hand on my shoulder. "Are you all right, dear?"

I gulped. "Yes." It looked like I would be needing a trip to the bank after all. But not to get small change for the cash drawer—to apply for a huge loan.

28

I hate going to the bank. That's probably because I'm in my thirties and have almost no money in one.

The Bank of Ruby Lake's lobby had been elegantly decorated for the holidays with a perfect fake tree covered in silver and gold tinsel. Wreaths hung from every available space. Electronic Christmas music played at an almost inaudibly low level in the background. It seemed to be putting the lone security officer near the door to sleep. He leaned against a marble Ionic pillar, his head tilted to one side.

After cooling my heels for several minutes, I was ushered into the small office of a loan officer named James Latimore, a lanky man in a gray suit, white shirt, and blue bow tie. I had a loan application in my hand that had taken me half an hour to wade through and fill in the myriad blanks.

By the time I had finished, I felt like I was swimming in paperwork and drowning in debt.

I took the proffered chair and sat, my expectations running high. As much as the idea of being an additional twenty thousand dollars in debt scared me, I knew, as my contractor had frequently reminded me, it wasn't a question of if I made the necessary repairs but when. The key word being *necessary*.

"Thanks for squeezing me in."

"No problem, Ms. Simms. We are always happy to meet with one of the town's local business owners."

I smiled. That sounded good. That's what I was, one of the town's local business owners. An upstanding, hardworking and much-needed, job-providing local business owner.

I crossed my legs and waited as Mr. Latimore, who didn't look any older than me, turned each page of my application with slender, manicured fingers.

Mr. Latimore inhaled deeply as he came to the last page of my application and turned it over in the pile. "I'm afraid it isn't possible at this time to provide you with the funds you require, Ms. Simms."

"Sure it is," I said glibly. "Don't you keep all your money right back there in the safe?"

Mr. Latimore smiled at my weak joke. "Without any collateral—" He arranged my application and tapped the papers against his expensive walnut desk.

"But I do have collateral. I have my store."

He raised a brow. "Already mortgaged. Quite heavily, I might add." He handed me back my application. "Do you have any other collateral?"

"We own a trailer," I said. We being Birds & Bees and Brewers Biergarten. "Shaped like a giant birdhouse. Free and clear."

The truth was, it was only half mine and that half I didn't even want. Without my permission, Paul Anderson had bought it for the two of us. So far, it had proved more trouble than it was worth. Not to mention, that it had once belonged to a friend of mine who had died a violent death. If you asked me, it was cursed.

The loan officer seemed unimpressed. "Perhaps a cosigner to the loan?"

The corner of my mouth turned down. I could ask my mom or even my aunt Betty, but they'd both already loaned me startup money.

I rose. "Thank you for your time, Mr. Latimore."

"Of course." He stood and adjusted his tie. "If there is anything else we at the Bank of Ruby Lake can do for you, or if your financial circumstances change, please come see me again."

My financial circumstances had changed, only not for the better. "Thanks. I'll keep that in mind. As for the loan I need for the repairs, I guess I'll have to take my chances."

I stepped out into the lobby, feeling suddenly drained and morose, but I was determined to look on the bright side. It was the holidays, after all.

And the truth was, things could be worse.

The sad truth was, they probably would be.

To my surprise, I saw several faces I recognized in a small conference room at the opposite end of the lobby. At a long table sat Gertie Hammer, Robert LaChance, the younger man with Gertie at Derek's office . . .

And Derek himself. Ben Harlan was there as well, seated at Derek's side. There were two others who were unknown to me.

Derek noticed me and jerked his head in surprise.

I cocked my head in question and he acknowledged me with a nod of the head before returning his attention to the others seated at the table.

* * * *

I left the bank and drove to the toy and hobby store. I already had a box of bird plush toys in the back of the van. I spent another hundred dollars buying various educational toys and hobby kits. I took my gifts to Belzer Realty at the opposite end of town.

There was no sign of Kim's vehicle but Ellery's was in its usual spot near the door. I parked and went inside, carrying my box and bags.

"My client is prepared to pay ten percent over—" Ellery Belzer looked up as I came in. He smiled and held up a finger. "Excuse me, someone has walked in. I have to go. I'll phone you later. Yes, that's correct, ten percent. Bye."

I set the packages on an empty chair at the nearest desk.

Ellery waved me over to his desk. "Sorry about that."

"No problem. Business is business."

"I'm glad you understand. Not everyone does." Ellery set his elbows on the desk and rested his chin on his fists. "What can I do for you?"

I pointed to his chest. "Nice tie."

Ellery looked puzzled, then his hand went to the bright green Christmas tree–shaped necktie around his neck. "Thanks." He smoothed it back down. "There's a battery tucked into the inside that makes the lights blink. You don't think it's too much?"

"Not if you don't think this sweater is too much." I unbuttoned my coat to reveal my Christmas cockatiel.

"Wow!" Ellery chuckled. "I guess we're even. Can I get you some hot cider?"

"No, thanks. I can't stay. I only wanted to drop off some presents for the children's toy drive."

Ellery's face lit up. "That's very generous of you." His look then turned wistful. "I only hope the tradition continues once I'm gone."

"Gone?"

Ellery nodded somberly, splaying his fingers across the papers on his desk. "Didn't Kim tell you? I've decided to retire."

"No." I pulled myself straighter. "She didn't." I looked around the office. "What about Belzer Realty?"

"Closing its doors."

"But why? I mean, after all these years."

Ellery began to frown. "This is a people business, Amy. People have to like you, trust you . . ." He bit his lower lip. "Respect you."

"People around here feel exactly that way about you, Ellery."

He shook his head. "I'm afraid not. Not anymore. Business is already suffering." He raised his arms and let them fall again. "Nope. It's time to retire. Move away."

"But I heard you on the phone just a minute ago, you still have clients—"

The real estate broker was shaking his head as I spoke. "Not enough to sustain a business."

Silence reigned between us, but for the sound of Christmas carols from the speakers and the crackle of the fire in the fireplace.

"What about Kim and the other agents?"

"I'm sure they'll land on their feet. I've given them all glowing referrals." He lifted the pile of letters in his hand.

The phone at his desk rang and his hand leapt for the receiver. "I'm afraid I'd better take this."

"Of course." I rose and buttoned up my coat. "I hope you'll reconsider." Ellery's only answer was a brief smile.

* * * *

I was relieved to see that the noose and all evidence of it were gone from Birds & Bees on my return. I spent the day dealing with customers.

Around five o'clock, I telephoned Derek's cell number and got his voicemail. I dialed his office and got Mrs. Edmunds.

"Mr. Harlan is gone for the day," she informed me, with a voice like ice. I pictured icicles where her vocal cords ought to be.

"Do you know where he went?"

"Mr. Harlan has not authorized me to say."

I made a face at the phone, hoping she'd see it. "Please tell him I called." I hung up and telephoned Kim.

"Hello?" She sounded as if she'd been napping.

"Hi, Kim. Mom is making chicken potpie and insists you come for dinner. Be here at seven. Bye." I hung up before she could refuse.

I ran upstairs. Mom was reading a library book in the living room. "Can you whip up a chicken potpie for dinner? Seven o'clock?"

Mom pulled her reading glasses down her nose and stared at me. "I don't have chicken or half the vegetables we need—"

I waved her off. "Never mind. I'll pick one up at the market." Lakeside Market carried freshly made potpies, beef and chicken. "I'll run to the store and pick up a chicken pie for tonight and a beef one that we can freeze for another time."

"What's the occasion?"

"Nothing. It's only a bribe to get Kim here."

"Then you'd better pick up a dessert, too." Mom pushed her glasses back up her nose and returned to her book.

I grinned and started for the door. "I like the way you think."

Downstairs on the sales floor, I found Esther in the act of pulling down a roosting pocket and handing it to a familiar face.

"I remember you. Swan Ridge. You're the receptionist at Dr. Ajax's office."

"That's right. Shirley, Shirley Beagle."

"It's good to see you again, Shirley." I walked with her to the register. Esther tagged along. "What brings you here?"

"I thought I would check out your store. Plus, all the talk of Christmas House Village got me thinking that I haven't been there in years. Thought I'd take one last look."

"What's the news in Swan Ridge? Are you still staring at protestors all day?"

"No, they're gone."

"That's good news."

"Good news for me, great news for you."

I knitted my brow. "What do you mean?"

"I mean, it looks like Ruby Lake is going to be getting the new hotel instead of Swan Ridge." She handed me her credit card and I ran it through the machine and handed it back.

"Are you sure? I haven't heard a single soul talking about it. You'd think it would have been talked about in the newspaper at least." I bagged her purchase and slid it across the counter.

"That's the way it is." Shirley shrugged as she picked up her package. "That's why the protestors gave up. Rumor has it that Cozy Towne Inn pulled stakes and decided to build here instead. Thanks again. Say hi to your mother for me. I'm off to pay my respects to Christmas House Village."

"What a strange woman," Esther quipped as Shirley retreated through the front door.

While it was an odd statement coming from the Queen of Strange, it wasn't any the less true.

What was also odd was that somebody had told me that Max Poulshot had recently worked at a hotel in Black Mountain. Could that have been a Cozy Towne Inn?

* * * *

The store closed at seven and Kim showed up on the dot. The potpie came out of the oven piping hot and I set it down gingerly on the kitchen table between Mom and Kim.

"Smells good," Mom exclaimed.

I cut us each generous servings and we dug in. Kim and I washed our food down with merlot. Mom stuck to water. We ate dessert, fresh cranberry pie, on the sofa in front of the TV, watching *Broadway Christmas Musical.*

When the show ended, Mom went off to bed, leaving me and Kim to finish the bottle of wine.

Kim brought her wineglass to her lips. "I didn't want to say anything with Barbara here, but my tree is definitely bigger than yours."

I threw a pillow at her, missing by inches. She stuck out her tongue at me.

"What's this about Ellery retiring and closing the business?"

Kim shrugged and took a sip.

"What are you going to do?"

"There are other real estate agencies in town."

I nodded. I couldn't argue with her there. "Has Dan said anything about closing in on Franklin Finch's killer?"

"Not a word." Kim pulled her lips tight as she picked up the wine bottle and tipped the remaining liquid into her glass. "On another gloomy subject . . ."

"Yes?"

"I heard from your mother that Birds & Bees needs some TLC."

"Twenty thousand dollars' worth of TLC."

"Any idea what you'll do?"

"No more than I have an answer to who murdered Franklin Finch." I stretched my arms overhead, then stood resolutely. I went to the Christmas tree and grabbed a remnant of wrapping paper that lay on the skirt beside a stack of presents.

I grabbed a pencil from the junk drawer in the kitchen and returned to the sofa. I turned the paper over to the plain side and smoothed it out.

"What are you doing? I'm not in the mood for tic-tac-toe or *hangman*," she added rather pointedly.

I wrote Max Poulshot's name at the top and followed with William Sever, Irma Fortuny, Eve Dunnellon, and last but not least, Bobby Cherry.

"What's that?" Kim frowned.

I let go of the paper and it curled up on itself. "Our list of suspects." I grabbed my mom's book and laid it along the edge of the wrapping paper to keep it reasonably flat. "Who do you like?"

Kim sighed as if put out. "I don't know. Bobby Cherry, I guess. But what's his motive?"

I began to frown. I liked him, too, but he didn't appear to have a motive. I wrote *motive* and put a question mark next to it at Bobby's name. "William could have done it. And he was at Christmas House Village. He seems very protective of Irma."

Kim tipped her glass and drained it. "He might have been mad enough at Mr. Finch to strangle him for firing her."

"I agree." I underlined both their names. "They could have plotted together."

"What's Eve's name doing on your list?"

I doodled on the paper. "It has always struck me odd that her arm was in a sling right after the murder."

"You think she injured it fighting with Finch?"

I shrugged a shoulder. "It's a possibility, isn't it?"

"I suppose. She might have hurt herself hoisting up with that rope."

"Exactly." I rubbed my hands together. "And that leaves Max." I told Kim how I'd just learned that a hotel that was planning to build in Ruby Lake had once been Max's employer.

Kim looked doubtful. "Cozy Towne Inn? That's a big chain. I've stayed in one of their properties a time or two myself." She pulled her legs up under her. "I'm not sure that means anything, Amy."

I leaned back on the sofa and tossed my legs up on the coffee table as I pressed my palms against my temples. "I don't feel like we are any closer to knowing who murdered Franklin Finch and why than we were the night it happened."

"I agree."

"Maybe Mr. Belzer is right."

"About what?"

"About closing up shop and moving."

Kim picked at some imaginary lint on her sweater. "Maybe that's what I should do, too. Sell my house and move someplace far away."

I slapped my hands on my thighs. "I have a better idea."

"What's that?"

I told her.

She thought it was crazy, but then she thought all my ideas were crazy. It had never stopped her from going along with one before—and it didn't stop her this time either.

29

It was lunchtime at Jessamine's Kitchen and the gang was all there.

"Good job," I said, turning to Kim with my hand shielding my mouth.

The staff had grouped several tables together and a host of Finley's Christmas House Village employees had gathered with me, Kim, and Ellery Belzer.

While two waiters scooted around the collective tables, I stood and began. "Thank you all for coming to lunch today." Which I was paying for, and would be paying for—for months to come, on my monthly credit card bill.

"Why are we here exactly?" shot Irma Fortuny, digging into the basket of cornbread. William Sever sat beside her like an armed guard.

Karl Vogel sat between me and Kim. I had asked him to come and be another set of eyes and ears. With him being a former law officer, he might notice something about one of our guests that I would miss. When I called to invite him, he had filled me in on what he had learned about Irma Fortuny and William Sever, which was very little—and nothing that directly pointed to their involvement in Finch's murder.

I started a smile. "I—we," I corrected, motioning to Kim and her boss, Mr. Belzer, "invited you all here, in the spirit of Christmas, to air our grievances and clear the air." I turned my eyes on each person in turn. "Isn't it time to forgive and forget? Let bygones be bygones?"

"I'd like to be gone," Max quipped.

Several other Christmas House Village employees snickered.

"Where's Eve Dunnellon?"

"The police came for her this morning," one of the employees said.

"Came for her?"

"Arrested her for the murder of Finch." Irma Fortuny pulled a tube of lipstick from her glittery gold purse and applied it roughly to her lips.

"First I'm hearing of it," snarled Karl.

"You're kidding! Eve?" I'd had a few doubts about her but hadn't put her high on my list of suspects. "Why would she murder him?"

"Maybe because he fired her," quipped one man at the other end of the table.

"And after having sex with the woman, too," Irma sniped.

"Sex? Excuse me?" I felt myself blushing.

Karl chuckled. "I'm sure glad you invited me to lunch, Amy."

"I caught them going at it myself," Irma purported. "Upstairs in his loft. On the carpet. Can you believe it?" She looked to William, who shook his head.

I looked to Kim for help, but none was forthcoming. She had turned pale and was staring at her empty plate. Ellery was fingering his necktie.

We were interrupted by a young woman who burst through the door, tossed off a red wool scarf, hung it from the coat tree, then threw her coat on top of it. "Sorry I'm late." She squeezed in across the table from Max. "Car wouldn't start."

"That's okay. Lizzie, right?" I said.

The young raven-haired woman nodded and picked up her glass of water.

"We were just starting. Listen, everyone." I cleared my throat. "Christmas House Village has been sold. We can't do anything about that."

Grumbles and a few swear words followed my statement. I raised my voice above the others.

"But especially now that it appears Franklin Finch's killer has been caught. Let's let that be the end of all this unpleasantness. I mean, can't we?" I gazed around the table, then stopped on Max's stepsister.

"I suppose—" one older woman grumbled.

"Wait." I held up a hand and turned to Lizzie. "I thought you didn't drive, Lizzie." I looked questioningly at Max, her stepbrother.

Lizzie's brow went up. "Only when the car won't start. That's what I get for buying a junker."

Which probably meant she'd bought it at LaChance Motors. I turned to Max. His face had turned bright red and he refused to make eye contact with me.

We both knew that he had lied to me about being at Christmas House Village the night of Franklin Finch's murder because he had to give his stepsister a lift.

But I wanted to rub it in. "So Max doesn't give you a ride to and from work?"

Lizzie snorted. "Max? Please, like he'd lift a finger to help me."

"That's no way to talk about your brother, Lizzie," Irma Fortuny snapped.

"Yeah, yeah." Lizzie flicked her hand toward Mrs. Fortuny. "Just because he's your favorite nephew doesn't make him a favorite of mine." She took a swig from her class. "And that's *step*brother."

I put a hand on the back of my chair to steady myself. Max was Mrs. Fortuny's nephew? Why didn't I know that?

Before I knew what was happening, the entire restaurant erupted in raised voices, accusing one another of all things imaginable. I couldn't decipher half of what was being said because of the babble.

Kim and Ellery Belzer hunkered in their seats, looking miserable. I couldn't blame them. I had failed.

I felt a tug at my sleeve. It was Karl. "I hate to say it, Amy, but, if you ask me, any one of these folks is off their rocker enough to be a killer." He lifted his hand to catch our waiter's attention.

Jessamine Jeffries hurried over, looking hot and bothered. "Please, Amy," she implored. "Your group is creating quite the disturbance." She motioned for me to look around the restaurant.

Jessamine was right. People were looking at us and whispering to each other. So much for the Christmas spirit. I had to put a stop to it. "I've got this," I assured her. She nodded and went to have a word with a customer at the door.

I picked up an empty glass and slammed it against the table. "Listen, everybody. The police are wrong."

All eyes turned to me and everyone stopped talking.

"Eve Dunnellon did not murder Franklin Finch."

"But the police said—" Ellery piped in.

I shook my head at him. "The police are wrong, Mr. Belzer." I planted my palm on the table. "Because I know who the real murderer is."

A murmur of wonder and disbelief went around the table.

"And I intend to prove it."

"That's ridiculous," replied Mrs. Fortuny. "The police are far more capable than you, young lady." She stared hard at me. "The police have their killer, and I say you should mind your own business."

"A murder in Ruby Lake is all of our business," I answered.

Kim whispered, "Amy, what are you doing?"

"How are you going to solve Finch's murder, assuming the police are wrong? Not that I think they are." That was William.

Max was noticeably quiet.

"Sorry," I replied. "But I'm not prepared to reveal that just yet."

Mrs. Fortuny chuckled and several others joined her.

"You'll all see. By the end of the day."

"Impossible!"

"I think not. Because the real killer has left evidence behind. Enough evidence to hang himself for murder." Which was only fitting.

"Him?" Lizzie asked.

"Or her." I opened my purse, pulled out my wallet, and threw way too much money down on the table. "Enjoy your lunch, everyone." I'd had enough Christmas spirit for the day.

Karl, Ellery, and Kim followed me outside to the sidewalk.

Karl scratched his head. "Eve getting arrested is news to me. You think Jerry's wrong, Amy?"

"I think something is wrong, Karl."

"What are you up to, Amy?" Kim asked.

Ellery leaned into a gust of wind that had sprung up. "Have you got something up your sleeve?"

"Yeah, just what do you have planned?" Karl's eyes danced with interest.

I sighed and looked back at the folks seated inside. "I wish I knew."

But I didn't have anything up my sleeves but bony elbows.

30

The first thing I wanted to do was verify what I'd been told about the police arresting Eve Dunnellon for the murder of Franklin Finch.

Chief Kennedy was on the phone at his desk when I walked in. Dan was typing at his computer. I went to his desk and he spent thirty seconds trying to pretend he didn't see me.

"I can see you, Dan. So I'm pretty certain you can see me."

Dan pulled a face and looked over his monitor at me. "We're kind of busy around here, Amy. Now is not a good time."

"Is it true that you have arrested Eve Dunnellon for the murder of Mr. Finch?"

Dan's hands hovered over his keyboard. "I'm afraid I cannot comment on an open investigation. Sorry, Amy."

"I get it."

"How's Kim?"

"Miserable. Did you know she's thinking of quitting?"

"She did mention it. I don't think she's serious."

"You don't know Kim as well as I do. She's even talking about leaving town."

"Permanently?"

I shrugged. I glanced toward the back of the office. "Jerry's off the telephone. I think I'll go wish him a Merry Christmas."

"I wouldn't if I were you."

I shot him a wink and extracted his promise to give Kim a call the first chance he got.

"Go away, Simms," Jerry snarled at me from six paces away.

I didn't let it stop me. I reached his desk and plopped down in a chair across from him. "Is it true that you arrested Eve for Finch's murder?"

"I can't talk about that."

"Why not? Half the town is already talking about it, Jerry!" We glared at one another.

"Fine." He thumped his elbows against the desk. "Yes."

"And you have proof?"

The corners of Jerry's mouth turned down in a decidedly ugly manner. "I am not in the habit of arresting people without proof. If I did, I'd have locked you up long ago!"

"For what?"

"For the fun of it!"

I tried a fresh approach. Juvenile antics were getting us nowhere. "Has she confessed?"

"No," admitted Jerry. "She hasn't. But she has no alibi and we found rope that appears to be the same type used to hang Finch in her potting shed."

"Did she say what it was doing there?"

"She said she never saw it before. She claims it must have been in there when she bought the house along with a bunch of other stuff the last owners left behind. And, she has no alibi for the time of death. The lady says she was home alone. With her cat." The chief shook his head. "Oldest, lamest excuse in the book."

"It could be true."

"It could be a bald-faced lie!"

I made an effort to keep my voice calm and steady. "Why would she have killed Mr. Finch?"

"Lover's spat. Plain and simple." Jerry reached for his mug and walked to the coffeepot. "She strangled him, which explains her sprained arm, then hanged him." He filled his cup and brought it back to the desk. "Women can be downright ornery."

While I was fuming on the inside over the sexist remark, I decided to let it slide. "She told me she fell taking out the trash."

Jerry snorted. "Yeah, she took out the trash, all right! Get it? That trash was Franklin Finch, who took her to bed and then fired her."

According to Irma Fortuny, he'd taken her on the rug, not the bed, but it was a technicality not worth quibbling over with Jerry.

"Why did she strangle him and then two hours later string him up? And why didn't anybody see her at Christmas House Village?"

"Maybe she was wearing a disguise." Jerry ran his fingers through his scalp. "I don't know. As to why, she isn't talking. She's called a lawyer."

"Derek or Ben?"

"Nope. Somebody's coming over from Charlotte."

"I still don't understand why she waited maybe two hours to hang him. It doesn't make sense."

"It does if she wanted to give herself an alibi," countered the chief. "And my guess is that she wanted it to look like Finch hung himself. What better way to do that than to have him swinging from that beam when he's found?"

"Yeah, but how did she know Kim would be coming?"

Jerry could only shrug. "Maybe she didn't. Maybe she only waited until she saw somebody coming and roped him up to make it look like suicide."

"A rope!" A light bulb went off in my head.

"A rope?" Jerry turned his chair sideways, avoiding my eyes.

"A rope, Jerry. That's how it was done."

Jerry harrumphed like a dyspeptic cow. "Of course, it was a rope," he said, spinning back around. "Most hangings are."

"You know those bits of rope that I saw on the window ledge and on the floor?"

"Yeah. What of it?"

"I think somebody, not necessarily Eve," I said, wagging my finger at him, "used a rope to make Finch's death appear to be a suicide."

Jerry rolled his eyes. "Just how did they manage that?"

"Our killer tied one end of a long rope loosely around a leg of the stool, placed Finch on the stool, tossed the rope out the window to the attic below.

"Think about it. It explains the strands of rope, the stool lying on its side, the open window. Everything!"

"Sounds farfetched to me, Simms."

I ignored him. "Then, when our killer figured somebody was on their way upstairs . . ."

I put my hands together and made a violent jerking motion with my arms. "Our killer pulls the rope and BOOM!" I slapped his desk. "Finch goes for a swing."

It made sense. But I still didn't believe Eve was guilty of anything—except poor taste in bed partners.

"Preposterous!"

"Have you got a better theory?"

"I'm working on it." He jabbed a finger toward the back. "I'm holding Eve Dunnellon on suspicion. I'm figuring by morning she'll be ready to confess."

"Oh, please." As far as I was concerned, we had the how but not the who or the why.

"Max's stepsister—her name is Lizzie—drives, Jerry. She said she drives herself to work every day. Max lied to me. He told me he drives her to and from work every day because she doesn't drive. There's no love lost between those two either. And there's rope at Christmas House Village just like the kind used to hang Finch."

"So is the one in Eve Dunnellon's potting shed. If anything, you're making your friend look guiltier."

I waved off his comments. "And Max was at Christmas House Village the night of the murder. I saw him myself, Jerry."

Jerry went through his case file. "I have no record of him being there or one of my officers speaking with him."

"He told me that the police told him to stay away."

"Then why don't I have a record of it?"

Incompetence came to mind, but I knew better than to suggest it. Besides, Max had probably lied to me about talking to the police, too. "Can I see Eve?"

"No."

"Just for a minute?"

Jerry held up his index finger. "Not for one second."

"What about Bobby Cherry?"

"Still on the loose."

"Don't you think it's important to catch him?"

"I wouldn't mind a word with him." Jerry rubbed his jaw. "Though, so far, the boy hasn't done anything wrong, except run from you, and I can't say that I blame him."

"Eve told me he'd been sabotaging things at Christmas House Village. That's why he was fired."

"The word of a murderer."

My blood was hotter than Jerry's steaming coffee. I stood. "Merry Christmas," I cursed.

"Thanks," Jerry replied. "I'll take a new shotgun or maybe a new set of golf clubs." He threw his feet up on his desk.

I threw myself out the door.

* * * *

When I returned to work, the store was busier than usual.

"Good news," said Esther, grabbing me as I came through the storeroom door. "I managed to sell that big purple-martin house that's been gathering dust instead of birds."

"That's great." I smiled, removed my coat, and tossed it over a box.

In one of my more optimistic moments soon after opening Birds & Bees, I had ordered the deluxe twenty-four-gourd purple martin kit. It came with an eighteen-foot pole that employed a winch and pulley system to raise and lower it. It retailed for over five hundred dollars and, as Esther so aptly put it, had been gathering dust and little interest, since arriving in the store.

I followed Esther out to the sales floor. There were several customers wandering the aisles. The big space where the purple-martin gourd rack had hung suspended on its pole was blissfully empty. "The store practically looks twice as big with all that space now."

Esther nodded.

I rubbed my arms. "Why is it so cold in here?"

"That's the not-so-good news." Esther followed me to the thermostat.

I read the display. "Sixty-two? Esther," I said, reaching for the controls, "that's practically freezing. You'll chase all the customers away."

"Don't blame me. The heater's broken again. I set the dial to eighty and still nothing." That explained the thick knit cap she had pulled down over her ears.

I squinted at the tiny gray display. Sure enough, it called for eighty. We should all be toasty and warm and we were chilled to the bone instead.

I sighed. "Let's make sure there's plenty of hot beverages for the customers."

"Already done," snapped Esther, turning on her heel to come to the aid of a customer who was ready to ring up his order.

I went to check on the other customers and make sure they were finding everything. I still was not quite sure how I was going to make good on my promise of catching a killer that day. Unless he planned to walk in the door of Birds & Bees and introduce himself, Kim and I were going to have our work cut out for us.

And we'd possibly be putting our lives on the line.

I was considering the wisdom of my big-mouthed boast at that afternoon's disastrous lunch get-together when Derek surprised me with an appearance at the store.

He looked elegant and handsome in a dark blue suit and long black wool coat. He waited with his hands behind his back as I rang up a short line of customers.

I went out from behind the counter then, and kissed him. His lips were warm. "This is a nice surprise."

"I had a few minutes and thought I'd stop by. It looks like business is good."

"We've had a good day."

"Why is it so cold in here?"

"There's a problem with the furnace."

"Again?"

I shrugged. "How about a hot drink to warm you up?"

"You warm me up enough."

I grinned and took his hand, leading him to the kitchenette, where he chose a cup of hot tea with local honey. I took a cup as well.

Derek removed his winter coat and laid it over the bookcase. We sat in the rocking chairs. I filled him in on my failed détente between Kim, Ellery Belzer, and the Christmas House Village staff.

Derek nodded but remained oddly quiet as I talked. I set my cup on the floor, reached over and rested my hand on his knee. "You're awfully quiet. Is everything okay?"

"Huh? Yeah, sure." He raised his cup and drank.

"What is it?"

"All this effort to fix things at Christmas House Village, make everybody happy . . ."

I pulled my hand back. Something weird was going on and I couldn't figure out what it was. "What's wrong with that?"

"Nothing. Nothing is wrong with it, Amy." The corners of Derek's mouth twisted downward. "It doesn't matter."

"What is that supposed to mean?" My hands gripped the arms of my rocker.

Derek appeared saddened. "Because there's not going to be anymore Christmas House Village—not Finch's, not Kinley's. Nobody's."

"I don't understand." I felt the ground slipping from beneath me.

Derek ran a hand along the side of his neck. "Cozy Towne Inn is purchasing the business from Finch's ex-wife."

I pushed my eyebrows together. "Why on earth would the Cozy Towne Inn Corporation want to buy Christmas House Village?"

Derek looked at me. When he saw that I still didn't get it, he filled me in. "Because they intend to tear it down and build a new Cozy Towne Inn."

"What?" I gasped as if I'd been hit in the stomach with a sledgehammer. "You mean, right here in downtown Ruby Lake?" That couldn't be possible.

Derek took my hand. "I'm sorry to be the one to tell you, Amy."

My mouth went dry. "What about the town? What's everybody else going to think?"

Derek's lips pulled tight. "It won't matter what they think. The property doesn't belong to them."

"But is that possible? Doesn't the town have to approve a transaction like that? I mean, don't they have to approve the development? A hotel—" I couldn't come to grips with the news yet. "That's quite a change from a quaint village of historic homes."

"It's all perfectly legal. There was nothing the planning and zoning commission could do to stop it."

I fell into a chair in disbelief. "It's one thing to imagine Christmas House Village with somebody else's name on it. It's impossible to imagine it gone!"

"I know. I'm sorry. I wish I had some good news, but I don't."

"Wait," I said. "You knew all about this, didn't you?"

Derek paced in front of me. "You mean about the pending sale?" I nodded and he said yes.

"Why didn't you say something? Why didn't you tell me?" Why did I feel like I had been stabbed in the back?

"Because it's my job, and I owe my clients my complete confidentiality. They trust me."

I jumped to my feet. I felt a tightening between my eyes. "I trusted you, too."

Derek stepped toward me but I backed away. "You can still trust me, Amy." His hand reached for mine, but I left him hanging until he pulled his hand back.

There was softness in his voice, but I wasn't hearing it.

"No, I don't think I can, Derek." I snatched his coat and thrust it at him.

Derek lowered his head. "I'm sorry you feel that way, Amy." He gripped my hands in his, then let them go. "If you change your mind, you know where to find me."

My heart lurched as he walked away.

31

I sat alone in my apartment and I moped. When I was done moping, I moped some more.

I would have kept on moping except that it was seven o'clock at night and Kim was banging on the apartment door.

I rose, zombielike, and let her in.

"Come on in."

Kim wore a bright red scarf and a black wool coat open to the waist. Underneath, she wore a bulky white sweater and blue jeans. "Are you okay?" she asked as she unwound her scarf and let it drop to the floor.

"Good as it gets." I sniffled. I had already shared my news with her on the telephone. I had settled on a pair of dark blue corduroys and a blue wool sweater. The color matched my mood.

"Have a seat." I waved to the sofa and went to get a bottle of wine and two glasses. So far, I'd been feeding my sorrow on chocolates. I had already devoured three-quarters of a box of Otelia Newsome's best assorted from Otelia's Chocolates, located conveniently across the street.

"Are you sure you want to go through with this?"

I extended my hand and Kim took one of the glasses I held by its stem. "Yep. Everything's ready. Riley brought the suit."

I gestured toward the big canvas sack on the floor, leaning against the kitchen counter. "He made me promise to have it back by tomorrow." I unscrewed the cap on the sangria and poured us each a glass. "He also made me promise not to mess up the costume. The Christmas show starts tomorrow. It won't be much of a show without Santa."

I had asked him to borrow the Santa Claus costume for me. He'd gotten it from the community theater. His butt was on the line if I let anything happen to it.

"Let's hope there are no bullet holes then." Kim filled her glass and drained it in a matter of seconds. "Are you sure you wouldn't like to stay in? We can drink away our troubles."

I took a drink to show my support. "That's all well and good for tonight, but what about tomorrow and the next day?"

Kim shrugged and refilled our glasses. "We could move to Florida."

"Florida is for snowbirds. I prefer real birds."

"And I prefer burying my head in the sand like an ostrich," groused Kim.

"That's a myth." I laughed.

"Really?"

"Really. What would happen to you if you buried your head in the sand?"

Kim thought for a moment. "I'd suffocate?"

"Bingo. Ostriches have got to breathe, too."

Kim nodded solemnly. "I never thought of that."

"Last one," I said, lifting my glass. "I have to drive." Chocolate and sangria in small quantities might be good, might be very good, but all that chocolate and sugar sloshing around in fruity alcohol was beginning to do strange things to my stomach.

And my head.

We sat in silence a moment. It was just the two of us. Mom had gone with her sister to do some volunteer work at the high school where she'd once taught. They were helping supervise the school's Christmas float construction.

"Have you talked to Derek, I mean, since . . ."

I felt a tear roll down my cheek. "No."

Kim snatched her purse from the cushion beside her and pulled out a pack of tissues. She handed me one.

I ignored the flimsy tissue and grabbed the pack. "Thanks." I pulled a couple of tissues loose and wiped my runny nose. "I don't think I can trust him anymore."

"He was only doing his job, Amy," Kim said softly. "Do you think Dan tells me everything that happens at his job? He's a police officer. There's probably a lot more that he doesn't tell me. More than I'll ever even know."

My lips drew a straight line. "Derek's not a cop. He's a lawyer."

"Who has to respect his clients' privacy."

"Not helping." I rubbed the ball of tissues under my nose.

"I talked to Mr. Belzer today. He confirmed that Mr. Finch's ex telephoned him this afternoon, as a courtesy, to tell him that she has decided to sell to Cozy Towne Inn." Kim swirled her glass. "I guess she felt running Christmas House Village was more trouble than it was worth. Especially with her being so far away."

I nodded sourly. "Like Tyrone's kids. Only worse. Now, instead of a name change from Kinley's to Finch's, Christmas House Village will be razed to make room for Cozy Towne Inn. Speaking of Tyrone's kids, I still can't figure out what part Toby Kinley might have played in all this."

"Maybe his being here is only a coincidence," suggested Kim.

"Maybe."

"But it's the end of an era, all right."

I huffed out a breath and set down my wineglass. I didn't like coincidences. "Are we going to talk or are we going to do this?"

"You can't avoid this conversation forever, Amy." She stood. "And you can't avoid Derek."

Kim was right but I was sure she knew that, so there was no point in my telling her.

I went to the kitchen and picked up the big sack containing the change of clothes. "Ready?"

Kim nodded and I helped her swap her street clothes for the Santa suit. Kim held up the fluffy white beard. "Do I really have to wear this?"

"You want to blend in, don't you?"

"What I want to do is disappear." Kim grumbled but hooked the beard over her ears.

I giggled.

Kim glared at me. "That's it, I'm taking it off! In fact, it's all coming off!" She grabbed angrily at the black vinyl belt around her waist.

"No." I grabbed her arms. "You look cute. Adorable. Really." She stopped resisting and I released her arms.

We walked downstairs and out to the minivan. I hopped behind the wheel and Santa climbed in beside me. It was all I could do to stifle my laughter.

"What if they won't let us in?" Kim asked as I drove.

"Who's going to stop us? Eve Dunnellon is in the town jail and Mr. Finch is dead. I'll bet we can go anywhere. Especially with you in that Santa suit."

Kim tugged self-consciously at her outfit. "It makes me look fat." She glanced at her reflection in the windows. "And hairy."

I couldn't help myself. I snorted. Kim thumped me in the upper arm.

"Careful!" I admonished her. "I'm driving!"

Without further ado, we made it to Christmas House Village, lights aglow, shoppers buzzing around with gift bags. Had they heard the news? Did they know that this was to be the last Christmas at Christmas House Village?

The lights were on in Derek's apartment. I had told myself I wouldn't look, but I rarely listen to myself.

I drove slowly into the alley behind Elf House and cut the engine.

"Why are we parking here? Anybody could see us. We're in Eve's parking spot."

"That's the point. I want everybody, or at least the real killer, to know *exactly* where I am."

Kim shook her head. "I still think you're crazy to want to make some killer come after you. You could get hurt. Seriously, as in dead."

"Don't remind me." I pushed my hat down over my head, extracted the key from the ignition, and locked the minivan behind me while Kim climbed out the other side.

We left the alley and followed the dimly lit path between Elf House and Reindeer House.

"Here's where we part company," I whispered.

"I don't know about this." Kim shivered and I didn't think it was only because of the near-freezing temperature.

"Just follow the plan. Walk around. Blend in."

"Fine." Kim started to move away.

I grabbed her sleeve. "Remember to keep an eye on me."

Kim gulped and nodded. "I will. But you're putting a lot of faith in me, Amy. I hope it isn't misplaced."

I grinned at her. "I'm sure it isn't. Have you got your phone?"

Kim nodded. "In my front pocket." She had left her purse at my apartment.

I watched from the pathway as Kim headed out to mingle with the shoppers. There was a crowd full of parents and their children in the area of Candy Cane Corner, where the petting zoo filled with sheep, goats, and llamas, was set up behind a white picket fence from Thanksgiving through New Year's.

The first thing I wanted was a better look at the alley and the window that had played a part in setting the scene of Franklin Finch's suicide by hanging.

The back of the house was poorly lit and the attic itself was dark. But it wasn't all that farfetched to imagine someone spotting another person entering the house. Due to the pair of oval windows along the wall of the staircase, that same person could fairly easily see anyone passing the second floor on the way to the attic. All they had to do then, was yank a rope—a rope that maybe if looped loosely enough would slip free and slither out the window. Leaving no one any the wiser.

It would look to any casual observer like Finch had just hung himself.

At least, that appeared to have been the plan.

And it hadn't been a bad plan.

Though it had taken a bad person to devise it.

I felt fingers digging into my left shoulder and screamed. "Hey—" I spun around, flailing my arms as I did.

"Whoa!"

"Oh, it's you!"

"Are you okay, ma'am?" It was Leo, one of the security guards. He held a flashlight in his left hand.

I tasted blood in my mouth. I had bitten my tongue. "Yeah, sorry. Are you okay?" I had clobbered him pretty good.

Leo nodded and ran his beam along the fence. "I was leaving for the day and saw you standing here. I thought maybe you were lost."

"No. I was on my way inside."

"If you're looking to do some shopping, I'd hurry if I was you. Christmas House Village closes in less than an hour."

I thanked him and watched him disappear around the corner. After that, I hurried toward the front. Not that I was scared, but there was nothing further to see in the alley.

There was no sign of the killer and no sign of Kim. Hopefully, she was nearby.

In case she was, I gestured to Elf House and pointed upward, indicating that I was now, as I had explained earlier, about to head upstairs to the loft.

I hoped I knew what I was doing. I hoped the murderer was watching and would follow.

And I hoped like I've never hoped for anything before in my entire life that Kim called the cops and they caught the murderer before the murderer caught me.

I had Christmas presents to wrap, to say the least. Being murdered would put a definite crimp in my plans for my future. Not that that future appeared to include a certain lawyer any longer . . .

The shop was busy, the elves were busy assisting customers, and nobody paid me any attention. I walked around the interior for a few minutes and was relieved to see Santa on the front porch. I waved and Santa gave me a thumb's-up.

I also saw Max, in uniform, prowling the walkway.

Mrs. Fortuny was working the cash register. She gave me a puzzled look but otherwise was too busy to pay me any mind.

I unzipped my puffy pink parka and sauntered over to the stairs and started climbing. I heard some soft sounds coming from the offices but ignored them and continued up.

I paused and looked out one of the windows between the second and third floors. It was dark but I was certain I could be spotted from the alley.

On the third floor, I stopped outside the loft. I was having second thoughts followed by third and fourth thoughts.

What if Finch's killer was inside? What if they had a rope and were waiting to tighten it around my neck?

I bristled and felt a cold wind sweep over me—odd, considering I was indoors and the wind couldn't reach me.

Before I lost my resolve completely, I wrapped my fingers around the door knob and turned it. The door opened with a creak I normally only heard in horror movies.

"Steady, Amy," I whispered. "There's nobody here and you don't believe in ghosts."

I stepped into the dark loft. Besides, Kim should be inside now, mingling on the first floor, waiting to see who came up after me.

Then all she had to do was call the police and all I had to avoid was having my throat wrapped in a rope necktie.

I crossed the silent room to the window and looked down, resting my hand on the window sill. The alley was deserted.

I turned at the sound of feet. A tall figure stepped through the open doorway and flicked on the lights.

It was William. He wore a Christmas House Village outfit and was dressed like a giant nutcracker. Hadn't Kim noticed him?

A nutcracker with a very sturdy cane in his hand.

I stayed near the window. "William! What are you doing here?" My heart raced like it knew there was going to be no tomorrow.

The big man leaned against his cane. "Irma told me you were here."

"I just wanted to . . ." I couldn't come up with a plausible excuse for being there.

"This is private property, Ms. Simms. I'd hate for you to make it necessary for me to—"

"To what? Murder me? Like you did your boss, Franklin Finch?" Hopefully, Kim was listening outside the door, as we had planned.

William began to smile. "Somebody must have spiked your eggnog." He waggled his cane in my direction. "You're talking crazy now." His voice filled the room.

"You would do anything for Irma, wouldn't you?"

William blinked at me. "Why, yes. Yes, I would," he replied evenly. "Now, if you don't mind?"

It might have been stupid, but I said, "And if I do mind?" I folded my arms over my chest.

William's hands went into the front pocket of his trousers. He held up his cell phone. "Then I'll have to call security."

I blew out my breath. "Fine, I'm leaving." I took a step, then paused and extended my arm. "You first." No way I wanted that big guy standing behind me with a deadly cane just waiting to whack me in the skull when I wasn't looking.

William shrugged and moved to the door, turning only to make sure I was following. I clumped down the stairs after him and moved outdoors. Through the porch window, I saw him inside conferring with Irma Fortuny.

I wished I could read lips.

I turned and scanned Christmas House Village. I spotted Santa across the way on the lawn between Nutcracker House and Sugarplum House. In the distance, my ears picked up the clang-clang of the sidewalk Santa at the street as he rang his bell.

Where was our killer?

Had Kim found something? Or someone?

I waved and headed over, lowering my head into the cold wind. I had forgotten my hat and gloves.

Kim raised her hand and went farther back between the houses, which were lined with large bushes. I lost sight of her in the darkness.

Out of the corner of my eye, I saw Max make a beeline in that direction. My heart quickened. So did my steps.

This was not working out as I'd hoped. The killer was supposed to come after me, not Kim!

I started jogging, pushing my way through the crowd. I stopped once I reached the backyard that connected Nutcracker House and Sugarplum House. My lungs burned and I was out of breath.

I squinted into the darkness. "Kim?" I whispered. "Where are you?"

I strained my ears but the only sounds were of shoppers and the gentle melody of Christmas music playing from the speakers scattered around Christmas House Village. I still couldn't wrap my head around this quaint village being turned into just one more nondescript, cookie-cutter Cozy Towne Inn.

"Kim?" I moved slowly over the dark ground. As I rounded the corner past the shrubs at the corner of Sugarplum House, a tiny flash of red, blinking slowly, caught my eye.

What was it? The blinking came from a dark shape near the ground. I was pretty sure it wasn't Rudolph the Red-Nosed Reindeer.

I approached cautiously and bent for a closer look. "Max!"

It was the uniformed security guard. He was sprawled out on the snow-covered ground. He groaned but remained unmoving. The light came from the walkie-talkie hooked to his belt.

"Max!" I dropped to my knees and touched his chest. "Are you okay?" I placed a hand gently behind his head and felt a warm stickiness. Even in the darkness, I knew that it had to be blood!

"Don't worry, Max!" I gently removed my hand and reached for the walkie-talkie. I unclipped it and pushed the talk button. "Hello! Hello!" I called desperately. "Can anybody hear me? Max has been hurt! Hello! Hello!" I pressed my ear to the device but heard no reply.

"Don't worry, Max." I unzipped my parka and draped it over him. "I'll get help! I'll be right back!"

Then I heard the scream and I jolted to my feet. There was only one person in the world with a scream like that. I would recognize it anywhere.

"Kim!" Her cry had come from the direction of Santa's Reindeer Barn. "Hang in there, Max!" I shouted as I took off. "Help's on its way!"

At least, I hoped and prayed it was.

I ran full speed into the alley and, by the glow cast by the spotlights at the corner of the work shed, discovered two Santas locked in mortal combat, steps from the open shed.

"Hey!" I slid across the icy surface, tumbled and rolled. I hoisted myself back up. "Hey! Hey, stop it!"

"Amy! Help!" one of the Santas called. I recognized Kim's voice. The second Santa, who seemed to have the upper hand, glanced at me, then broke Kim's grip on his arm and punched her.

Kim went down in a heap.

I saw a snow shovel leaning against the side of the shed and picked it up. I ran at the second Santa and took a swing. He leapt backward and took off running. I hurled the snow shovel at him but missed by a country mile.

"Damn!" I ran after him. Santa was fast. In seconds, he'd reached the space between Sugarplum House and Frosty's House. He was probably hoping to get lost in the crowds. Sure, he was in a Santa Claus suit, but there were several on the grounds this time of year.

I gave it my all. Santa had been slowed by a dense crowd of children who headed for him. He pushed them away but they were hampering his progress.

He crossed the central walkway and headed toward the big Christmas tree. I went around the other way, hoping to surprise him.

And I did. He froze, then turned and started back the way he'd come. I let out the biggest yell of my life and dove at him the way I'd seen linebackers do on TV.

"Ooph!" Santa and I went down in a tangle of arms and legs.

"Mom! Mom!" I heard a high-pitched voice squeal. "That lady's beating up Santa Claus!"

"Hey, hey, you!" A purse whomped me across the back. "You leave Santa alone, you hear me?"

Santa struggled to his elbows and tried to rise, but I locked my arms around his legs and held on for dear life. Santa kicked at me, the unseen mom pounded on me, and voices around me were cheering and jeering.

32

I wasn't sure how much longer I could have lasted, so I was glad it was over.

There was a tight circle of people surrounding us. Santa had stopped kicking and the crazy lady had stopped whacking me.

I pushed myself up, breathless and sore.

The crowd had parted. Officers Sutton and Pratt approached. For a second, I thought I was hallucinating because they looked like giant, goofy elves in red coats and tight-fitting, green-and-white striped pants. Their heads were bare. Both officers had strapped their gun belts around their waists.

"We were helping with a Christmas event at the orphanage when we got the call." Dan lifted me to my feet and Al Pratt picked up Santa.

Santa's beard had come detached and hung loose from one ear.

"Mr. Belzer!"

"Well, well, what do we have here?" asked Officer Pratt. He grabbed Belzer's arms as he made to flee.

"Dan!" I grabbed his arms. "Kim is around the corner. Ellery hit her. She's over by the work shed."

"Thanks!" Dan started to move.

"Wait! Max, the security guard, is lying on the ground between Sugarplum House and Nutcracker House. I think he was struck in the head."

Dan nodded. "I know. That's why we're here. The ambulance is already on its way. Somebody in the Christmas House Village office heard your call on the walkie-talkie. They called it in."

I gulped.

"That was you, wasn't it?"

"Yes. I'll explain later. Go!" I said. "Help them!"

"Out of the way, everybody!" The crowd split wide and Dan bolted for the alley.

I turned to Ellery Belzer. "If you've harmed Kim in any way—"

Ellery hung his head. "I'm sorry, Amy. Believe me. I never meant for any of this to happen."

"Let's go," Officer Pratt ordered. He slapped a pair of cuffs around Belzer's wrists and led him away. It was a sorry sight watching a giant elf lead a beaten Santa Claus away in handcuffs. I only hoped it would not overly traumatize the children. Christmas was a time for joy and giving, not mayhem—that was what after-Christmas sales were for.

Two squad cars, lights flashing, sat at the street. As I watched, it was joined by a third. It was Jerry, and he was in uniform.

Glancing up across the street, I saw Derek's silhouette in his apartment window. The tip of a glittery Christmas tree glowed behind him.

I watched until the shadowy shape stepped to the side and pulled the curtains.

* * * *

The next morning, Kim and I gathered in the corner of Birds & Bees before opening. The Christmas tree near the sales counter was a sad reminder that it was nearly Christmas. So much had changed, and not for the better, since the day the tree had arrived and we had decorated it with smiles on our faces.

The dull throbbing of my heart was a reminder of the Christmas tree upstairs that I purchased in the company of Derek and Maeve. Would I ever see either of them again?

Would things, could things, ever be the same?

Kim sat in a rocker. I sat on the floor, cross-legged, wishing I'd worn thicker underwear—the house was still painfully cold. Though, as fate would have it, the refrigerator in my apartment was on the fritz and as warm inside as a summer's day. We were storing our frozen foods on the window ledges outside. I could only hope the fridge was working again before the squirrels and birds discovered our stash.

Kim had been kept in the hospital overnight for observation. I had picked her up first thing in the morning and brought her back to the store for coffee. Eve Dunnellon had been immediately released from jail.

Kim explained to me, as she had to the police, that she had seen Max and Santa, whom we now knew to be Ellery Belzer, fighting. Max was recovering in the hospital and told the police that he had been following the Santa because he'd seen two Santas following me and had gotten suspicious. Of course, the other Santa had been Kim.

Max had confronted Mr. Belzer and the two men fought. Max had knocked Mr. Belzer to the ground, but Mr. Belzer had come up swinging with a stone in his hand. Mr. Belzer clobbered Max in the back of the head. After getting the better of Max, Belzer had gone after Kim.

"If you hadn't shown up when you had," Kim had said, "I might have been a goner."

It had been kind of her not to mention that if it wasn't for me she wouldn't have been in such a dangerous predicament in the first place. I had no doubt that at some date in the future, I'd be getting an earful.

Once again, that's what friends are for.

I had suggested that Birds & Bees take over the annual toy drive that Belzer Realty had started, and Kim thought that was a great idea.

The coffee machine gurgled and hissed on the counter. Mom had made mini-fruitcakes in a muffin tin, and I had carried them downstairs to the store on a festive ceramic dish, designed to look like a Christmas wreath.

Esther joined us moments later. I swear, the woman can sniff out free food. I don't care what scientists say about senior citizens, they have all their faculties and then some.

"Why all the glum faces?" Esther tugged at the sash of her robe. Apparently she wasn't planning on working right away. Her hair was in curlers. Gray slippers that looked like mutant dust bunnies clung to her white-stockinged feet.

"Didn't you hear, Esther? Ellery Belzer was arrested last night for the murder of Franklin Finch," Kim explained.

"Yeah, and he might have killed Max, Kim, and me, to boot." I rose from the floor and reached for the coffeepot.

"And Christmas House Village has been sold," Kim sniffed. "Again."

Esther shook her head and rolled her eyes. "Old news."

I poured coffee for all of us and handed around the mugs. "*Again*, Esther. Christmas House Village has been sold *again*." I sipped from my mug, then handed around the platter of fruitcakes.

Esther stuck her hand out and took the first one.

"They're going to tear it down and put up a Cozy Towne Inn," Kim said morosely. "Can you believe it?"

"No," Esther said firmly. She peeled the paper from around her fruitcake and chomped down.

"No?" I raised my eyes in her direction. "What does that mean, Esther?"

"No, as in I don't believe it." She chomped down again and two-thirds of her fruitcake was now gone. "Because it's not true."

"It's true, Esther," I said. "Believe me."

Esther snorted. "Believe you? Are you kidding me? You're wrong half the time," she quipped, batting at fruitcake crumbs on her robe, including bits of cherries and pineapple, mindless of the fact they were now on my previously spotless floor.

Kim and I shared a look as Kim mouthed, "Senile."

"I saw that," snapped Esther. She reached for a second fruitcake. She treated the store's food and drinks like her personal buffet. Soon, there would be none left for our customers.

Kim decided that was a good time to throw me under the Esther the Pester bus. "Amy broke up with Derek."

Esther paused, fruitcake halfway to her lips. "See? The woman's a fool. Where's she ever going to find another man?"

I glared at her. "I'm right here, you know. And I can so find another man."

"Do you want another man?" pressed Esther.

"No," I admitted, "I want that one."

Esther rolled her eyes at me. "As for Christmas House Village—" The frustrating woman paused, ever so slowly peeled the wrapper from her second fruitcake, and took a big bite. I was certain she had left us hanging just to get my goat.

And she had succeeded.

I grabbed her arm before she could take another bite. "What about Christmas House Village, Esther?"

"Yes, what is it, Esther?" Kim added.

"It's been sold, all right. But not to Cozy Towne Inn."

"To who then?"

Esther shrugged, broke off a bit of walnut-heavy fruitcake, and glared at me as she popped it in her mouth. "I can't say."

"What?" Kim half rose from her rocker. "Why not? Who—"

Esther raised a hand to silence her. "What I can tell you is that Finch's Christmas House Village is now, or at least will be shortly, Kinley's Christmas House Village."

Kim and I started talking at once. I threw my hands up and called for silence. Once I had it, I said, "Esther, are you sure?"

"Of course, I'm sure."

"Who told you?"

"Can't say."

Kim and I looked at one another.

"Are you really certain of this, Esther?" That was me.

Esther nodded. "It's getting late. Shouldn't we be getting to work? I think I'll go get dressed."

I jumped in her path. "Not until you tell us what's going on."

Kim joined me in blockading her.

"Fine." Esther caved. "Gertie Hammer, Robert LaChance, and Tyrone Kinley's children offered to buy Finch's Christmas House Village from his ex-wife."

"What about Cozy Towne Inn?" I persisted. What would Gertie Hammer and Robert LaChance want with Christmas House Village? Did they have their own plans to raze it and put up a shopping mall or something?

"It seems she was going to sell to the hotel chain," Esther told us. "Belzer had been pressing her to do it all along."

"That beast!" Kim gasped.

"After what happened with Belzer, she decided to go with the local offer instead," Esther said. "Besides, Cozy Towne Inn has backed out. Too much bad publicity."

Esther started to go, but I pressed my hand lightly to her chest. "How do you know all this?"

Esther plucked my fingers from her chest. "I have my sources."

"What sources?" Kim asked, eyes filled with wonder.

"Karl Vogel, for one. He called me this morning and told me that Ellery Belzer was the one behind all of Christmas House Village's troubles. He paid Bobby Cherry to stir up trouble, too."

I nodded. We had already learned from the police that Bobby Cherry had been picked up in Black Mountain, where he had been staying at a Cozy Towne Inn. They had spotted his motorcycle in the parking lot—a motorcycle bought with the money that Ellery Belzer had been paying him for his dirty work.

Cozy Towne Inn. I remembered now. It was their website that Finch had been looking at on his computer the night he was killed.

Bobby Cherry was being brought back to Ruby Lake by the state police for questioning.

"Belzer had been trying to sell Christmas House Village to Cozy Towne Inn forever. Not only would it mean a big commission but he was going to get a kickback from Cozy Towne Inn's territory manager. Only he had to make the sale by the end of the year. Otherwise, they'd build elsewhere."

"Like Swan Ridge," I said.

"That's right, which is where they're going to build now."

I knew one person who would be glad to hear it: Dr. Ajax's receptionist.

"But what messed things up for Belzer was Kinley's kids deciding to sell to Finch instead. All that could save the deal with Cozy Towne Inn at that point was to convince Finch to sell and sell fast."

"That's why he upped Bobby Cherry's involvement."

"That's right," Esther said. "Belzer was paying Bobby to sabotage the business, hoping that Finch would give up and sell. When that didn't happen fast enough to suit Belzer—"

"He took matters into his own hands. Literally," I finished.

Kim's voice was filled with disbelief. "He was the only one who knew I was going back to see Mr. Finch that night."

Poor Kim. Her boss intended her to be his unwitting witness to Finch's suicide. My theory about how the stage had been set was correct. Belzer had strangled Finch, then saw an opportunity to frame Kim when he learned she was going to pay him a visit that night. Belzer's house wasn't far from Christmas House Village. Belzer admitted that he ducked out of his party, raced to Christmas House Village ahead of Kim, arranged the noose, tying one end of the second rope loosely over a leg of the stool. He then waited from his vantage in the alley for Kim to arrive. When he saw her through the stairway window . . . bam! He yanked the rope, sending Finch swinging and leading Kim and everybody else to believe he had just hanged himself.

Kim's hand went to her throat. "I'll bet he killed Virginia Johnson, too."

"I wouldn't be surprised. Though the police might never be able to prove it," I replied. He'd also hung the noose on my porch in an attempt to frighten me. "Getting rid of Virginia Johnson was the first step in clearing all the obstacles to his sale of Christmas House Village to Cozy Towne Inn."

"He almost got away with it, too," Kim said before sipping from her mug. "To think, I worked with that man."

Esther made to leave and I stopped her once more.

"Just a minute, Esther. So it was Karl who told you that Gertie Hammer, Robert LaChance, and the Kinley kids are buying Christmas House Village?"

Esther shoved an arm between me and Kim and wedged her way between us. "I never said that. Now, I'm pretty sure we have work to do. It's less than ten days to Christmas."

"Please, Esther. I've got to know . . ."

Esther let out a sigh that smelled like fruitcake and sounded like I'd just asked her to donate me her last kidney. "You aren't going to let this go, are you?"

I raised a hopeful brow.

"Fine." Esther thrust her hands in the pockets of her robe. "My sister told me."

"Your sister?" This was the first I was hearing of such a person.

"I didn't know you had a sister," Kim said. At least I wasn't the only one who'd been in the dark. "Who is she?"

Esther's jaw tightened. "Gertrude is my sister. My *older* sister."

"Gertie is your sister?" I felt my world crumbling. Derek had been holding meetings with Gertie and Robert.

And Toby Kinley.

"Of course she's my sister," scoffed Esther. "You don't think I'd stay in a house with a complete stranger, do you?"

I refrained from reminding her that she and I had been strangers when I bought the house with her already in residence.

"But you're a Pilaster! She's a Hammer!"

"And you're a kook who gave up the best guy she could ever hope for in the whole world. What's your point?"

I bit down hard on the inside of my cheek in a monumental effort to remain conscious.

"Speaking of work . . ."

Esther and I stopped at Kim's soft interjection.

"What is it?" I asked.

"I have an announcement to make." Kim set her mug down on the counter and clasped her hands. "I'm quitting real estate."

"Why?" Esther and I asked as one.

Kim shrugged. "Because of the murders and bad memories. And, it's not fun anymore."

I gave her a hug. "Even after the peace offering from Irma?" William had dropped off one of Irma Fortuny's famous Christmas plum puddings as a peace offering. We hadn't dared cut into it yet. Mrs. Fortuny's plum puddings were famous for containing more suet than raisins. I had suggested we save it for the birds.

"I'm afraid so," Kim answered.

"What will you do?" I asked.

Esther couldn't help putting in her two cents. "I hear Christmas House Village is hiring!"

Kim visibly shuddered. "Never."

"I don't blame you," I said. I shot Esther a warning look.

"Maybe I could use you around here, part-time, that is," Esther said, rubbing her chin between her thumb and forefinger.

Kim drew herself up and planted her fists on her hips. "I'm already a partner, Esther."

Esther looked at me, hurt in her eyes. "How come she gets to be a partner and I'm only assistant manager?" Her arthritic hand fiddled with her assistant manager nametag. Yes, she even wore it when she was in her bathrobe. Possibly even when she was in the bath. She probably pinned it to her shower cap.

"Because Kim invested startup money in the business. You didn't."

Deep lines formed in Esther's face as she frowned. "How much would I have to invest to make me a partner?"

Kim and I looked at one another.

I so wanted to say that there was not enough money in the world for that to happen.

Before I could form any words at all, Kim blurted, "Twenty thousand dollars!"

Esther threw her right hand up. "Sold!"

"What?" I felt my knees buckle.

"I said sold!" Esther threw both hands up in the air this time.

Kim was dancing. "Twenty thousand dollars! Yea! Not only can we make all the necessary repairs, now we can really expand this place!" She squealed loudly. "And I can work here full-time!"

"No, no twenty thousand dollars!" I attempted to jump between them. They had actually joined hands and were doing some ridiculous jig. "*No* sold!"

"What's sold?" Mom had appeared at the bottom of the stairs. Her hand clung to the rail. Her brow was etched in furrows as she looked first at Esther and Kim doing their crazy dance and then at me.

I was doomed and I knew it.

There was only one answer to Mom's question.

I hung my head. "My soul, I think."

Please turn the page for an exciting sneak peek

of J.R. Ripley's next

Bird Lover's mystery

FOWL OF THE HOUSE OF USHER

coming soon wherever e-books are sold!

1

It all started innocently enough. Life is like that, at least, mine is. I was rearranging boxes of merchandise in my storeroom to make space for an expected shipment later in the day when I saw it.

There was a dead body in the middle of the floor.

A rat.

I yelped and dropped a case of squirrel-proof birdhouses on my feet—squirrel-proof because the clever feeders contained a mechanism that effectively shut the seed ports. That didn't stop the hungry squirrels from scooping up every morsel the birds dropped. And they seemed to drop as many seeds as they consumed.

My yelp turned to a curse that would have caused my mother to blush had she been present. Fortunately, she wasn't. Because she probably would have laughed, too.

I repeat: A RAT.

No, not an old boyfriend, ex-lover or cheating husband. A real rat. Cash Calderon, he's my contractor, had warned me that once he starting ripping open walls—we were in the middle of some extensive renovations—we could expect to see some critters who were being driven from their residences deep within the nooks and crannies of my three-story Queen Anne Victorian-era house.

Those critters had, thus far, included rats, gray squirrels, a raccoon and two snakes.

Plus, the brown rats. I had a feeling some of those rats were direct descendants of the house's Founding Rat Fathers.

And I was alone in the store with the beastie.

Not a pleasant thing, alive or dead.

With the number of creatures popping out of the woodwork, I could have opened a pet shop rather than a store selling bird food, bird houses, birding gear—everything for the bird lover.

In addition, a small section of the store was devoted to beekeeping. Depending on the season, we also carried a selection of plants specific to supporting local bird and bee populations.

I moved the fallen box out of my way and limped toward the ripe rodent remains.

This rat didn't look homeless. And it didn't look like it had succumbed to old age. This rat looked like it had been...I wrinkled my nose and bent down for a closer look...gnawed.

"Esther," I muttered.

Esther Pilaster, or Esther the Pester as I sometimes called her when she was out of sight but in the forefront of my mind whenever she did something particularly irksome, had a cat.

She denied it but I was sure of it. Each time I broached the subject of her hiding a cat, she stalwartly repudiated my claim. That did nothing to lessen my conviction that she did.

Now the evidence was right here in front of my eyes.

Maybe it was circumstantial but, under the circumstances, that was good enough for me.

"Let me see you get out of this, Pester," I grumbled to no one but the walls and the walls had long ago stopped listening to me. If they had been listening, they would have done a better job of keeping out the rats.

And the cold.

Esther lived on the second floor. When I'd bought the building that would become my home and home to my planned business, Esther had been a tenant. One of the owner's conditions of the sale to me was that Esther's lease would be honored. I now had a second renter, Paul Anderson, also on the second floor. Mom and I lived on the third.

The rats had no floor preference. They apparently lived everywhere.

I retreated to the hall closet for the broom and dustpan. I'd scoop up the dead critter and give it the best burial I could considering how frozen the ground was outside. I snatched my charcoal down jacket off the nail by the rear door and bundled up, popping a knit cap over my head and gloves on my hands.

It was winter. In western North Carolina that meant temperatures dipped and we got our share of snow and ice. Nothing like the northerners got, sure, but that was their fault for choosing to live in such climes.

I set the little dead guy down outside and went to the toolshed against the back of the building. I pulled out a garden shovel that probably hadn't been expecting to see duty again until nearer to spring.

I spied around for a nice spot to bury the rat and settled on a space near the holly along the back fence that separated the shops on Lakeshore Drive from the single-family homes behind us.

The hard ground gave way slowly. Fortunately, rats don't take up much space. I laid the little guy inside a shallow hole and covered him up.

I returned the shovel to the shed and hurried back to the relatively warm interior of Birds & Bees. I removed my outerwear and walked to the front of the empty store. The original fireplace in what had been the house's living room had long ago given up the ghost. The chimney stack had been sealed shut with cement.

The simple stone fireplace had a narrow wood mantle and slate hearth. We now used the fireplace as display space. Currently, that display was winter-themed and featured roost boxes, suet and a couple of heated birdbaths.

Happily, somebody along the way had added a woodstove in the rear of the first floor, in the space that now held a small kitchenette and seating for customers to relax, enjoy a drink and a snack and read from our small library of birding books and magazines.

As I approached the sales counter, Mrs. Gruber came in waving a photo of an owl. Her nose glowed red from the cold. As gelid as the tip of mine felt, it was probably glowing, too.

"Look!" Mrs. Gruber flapped the letter-sized paper in front of my face. "I shot a photograph of a barn owl in my backyard."

She set the picture on the counter and turned it around to face me. Mrs. Gruber was a mature woman and enthusiastic backyard bird watcher. She wore a knee-length, multicolored houndstooth wool coat, red gloves and a red hat that covered the tops of her ears.

"It's a great shot," I replied. "But I'm afraid it's not a barn owl." I handed her back the photo of the mottled brown and white bird.

"It's not?" Mrs. Gruber's face fell.

"No. This is a *barred* owl." The medium-sized owl was perched on a branch up against the trunk of an oak. Its eyes were closed. "The barn owl is much more ghostly in appearance and has a heart-shaped face. Your owl has a rounded head. Did you hear it speak?"

Mrs. Gruber shook her head in the negative. "I believe it was sleeping. It never moved the whole time I watched." She studied the picture more closely. "Is it a male or a female?"

"I can't be sure. There isn't much difference in plumage or coloration between males and females of the species. If you see two of them together and one appears larger than the other, it's likely that the larger bird is the female."

"I'll keep that in mind. We get a lot of birds in our yard. We back up to a nature preserve."

"Lucky you." I lived in the middle of town. With my business also being home, and that business relying on the presence of people, I needed to be someplace that the people frequented, not necessarily the birds. If it hadn't been for the need to be where the action was, albeit small town action in a place the size of Ruby Lake, North Carolina, I'd have chosen something more rural for myself as well.

"If you see the bird again, they have a distinctive call. People say it sounds like 'Who cooks for you? Who cooks for you?'"

Mrs. Gruber laughed. "I do all the cooking in my house. The mister can barely toast bread."

I grinned. "Being single, nobody cooks for me either." That wasn't strictly true. Mom lived with me and spoiled me with her home cooking.

Mrs. Gruber held the photograph in front of her nose. "Now that you mention it, Amy, on occasion I've heard a sound like 'who cooks for you' coming from the woods."

She matched her eyes with mine. "During the daytime, however."

"That's not unheard of," I said. "Put the picture on the bird board. The others will love to see it."

Mrs. Gruber's bird photo wasn't exactly headline material but that particular bulletin board was for posting bird photos. I should know, I'd hung it there myself on the thick support beam in the center of the store. The board was an excellent way for myself, my staff and customers to let others know what birds they were seeing and when.

"I will."

"Good." I handed her a felt-tipped pen. "Don't forget to write down the location, date and time of day of the sighting."

Mrs. Gruber filled in the data and tacked her photo proudly to the bulletin board.

"If I had a trained barn owl like that one in the store at night, I wouldn't have to worry about the rats," I quipped.

Mrs. Gruber pulled her purse close to her chest as her eyes darted anxiously across the floor. "You have rats?"

"Huh? No, I was only joking," I assured her.

I wasn't sure Mrs. Gruber quite believed me because she did the remainder of her shopping very quickly and beat a hasty retreat.

Esther came down to work at noon and would be staying until closing. She's a small, narrow-shouldered woman with long, uneven teeth, a hawkish nose, sagging eyelids, and silver hair habitually worn in a sharp four-inch ponytail. Wispy white eyebrows sit atop her gray-blue eyes.

Esther had never married, at least so I thought. For a woman who didn't like to keep her opinions to herself, the septuagenarian was the keeper of a lot of secrets, including the cat.

Esther not only worked for me and rented from me, she was now a partner in Birds & Bees. Truth be told, it was her recent investment in the business that was allowing us to go forward with the long-needed and heretofore unaffordable repairs to the property.

Esther once thought I was a killer. I once thought she was a pain in the patooty. In the months we had gotten to know one another, we had gotten past those initial first impressions.

Well, mostly.

Mom was out and I didn't feel like eating alone upstairs. It would only mean peanut butter and jelly or baloney sandwiches with a side of baby carrots and cheese puffs, anyway. I'd been there, done that a hundred times or more already since returning home to Ruby Lake.

"I'll be back in an hour or so, Esther." I was running next door for lunch at Brewer's Biergarten. "Can I bring you back anything?"

"No, thanks. I'll take my lunch upstairs when Kim gets here."

"Okay, see you soon." I grabbed my wool coat from the coatrack by the front door and wrapped a cashmere scarf around my neck.

This time of year, I kept a coat at the front and rear of the store. Not only did it facilitate going in and out, I often helped customers to their vehicles with some of the heavier items, like bulk birdseed. "Please let Kim know I'll be back in an hour or so."

"You got it." Esther popped open the register and began counting the cash money in the till. She was a stickler for knowing how much was in the register when she started each day.

The Kim in question was Kimberly Christy. Kim's a long-legged, blue-eyed blonde. My shoulder-length hair was the color of chestnuts roasting. My eyes were blue but not as blue as Kim's. I had all the same parts that she had, somehow those parts just seemed to look better on her.

While we rarely shared our wardrobes, we shared the same age, thirty-four.

Kim and I had grown up together. She was my best friend and proverbial partner in crime. She was a literal partner in Birds & Bees, too. She had started out as a small investor, helping me out when the store was nothing but a crazy idea in my head. Recently, she had quit her real estate gig and asked to work full-time with me at the store.

How could I say no?

How the store was going to manage the additional payroll I, as yet, had no clear idea.

I opened the door and closed it quickly behind me. The air was cold and the wind was hard. My house is on Lake Shore Drive, one of Ruby Lake's main thoroughfares. Many of the town's businesses, like mine, occupied the road, especially those catering to tourists because Lake Shore Drive was the road most of those tourists drove in and out of town on.

Across the street to my left was our namesake Ruby Lake with a lovely park and marina. Directly across the street was the quaint Ruby's Diner.

I slogged down the brick path to the sidewalk, avoiding the icy patches that refused to disappear. I'd asked Cousin Riley over and over again to do something about them, but he hadn't gotten around to the job yet.

From Birds & Bees, it was only a matter of steps to the entrance of Brewer's. Brewer's used to be a garden supply store. Now it was a brewpub and a thriving one at that. The space between Birds & Bees and the main portion of Brewer's Biergarten had been transformed from an outdoor plant sales area to an outdoor dining room.

I couldn't help but be a little jealous. I had opened Birds & Bees long before construction of Brewer's Biergarten had begun, but judging by the often filled to capacity seating and the lines out the door most Friday and Saturday nights, their business was booming.

It seemed there was more money in beer than birds. No matter, I loved my birds and if I wanted a beer I could buy one.

I approached the front door of the brewpub. A waiter at the door pushed it open and welcomed me. "Hi, Amy. Table for one?"

The cozy outdoor seating area was open except during the worst weather. In the winter, like now, large propane heaters generated plenty of warmth. Nonetheless, I opted to sit indoors. "Hello, Mitchell. Inside, please."

Mitchell took a quick look and escorted me to a small two-top in the middle of the dining room. There were plenty of seats at the bar but I avoided sitting there alone. I had learned that being a woman alone at a bar was a man magnet.

I wasn't looking to attract any.

I had one. His name was Derek Harlan. My mother liked to tease me that I had come home to Ruby Lake and I had found my own jewel.

She wasn't wrong.

We'd had a slight hiccough in our relationship before the holidays. I thought he had been keeping things from me. The truth was he had only been doing his job. He'd had a client whom I thought might be involved in a murder. When I found out later that this person had been Derek's client and was innocent of any crime, I felt Derek should have told me up front.

Of course, I was wrong.

And I might have gotten mad. And I might have stormed off. But I prefer to rewrite history and remember it as nothing more than a bump in the road, the growing pains of any relationship.

I had to get used to the fact that Derek, as an attorney, was sometimes privy to information that wasn't for public consumption—even if that public was me and I really, really wanted the dirt.

I took a look at the lunch menu and ordered the portabello melt and a diet lime soda. Behind me, a couple of men were throwing darts.

Halfway through my melt, a manicured hand gripped my shoulder from behind and squeezed. "Hey, hey, hey. Look who's here!"

I turned and spat out a mouthful of mushroom, lettuce and brioche bun. "Craig?"

"Hi, Amy."

I jumped to my feet and took a step back to be sure I wasn't hallucinating. "Craig, what are you doing here?"

In front of me stood Public Enemy Number One. Well, Amy Simms Enemy Number One—with a bullet.

Craig Bigelow was my ex-boyfriend. He and his cheating ways had played a big part in my decision to return to Ruby Lake.

It was bad enough that he and his partner, Paul Anderson, had opened Brewer's Biergarten not only in my hometown, but right next door to me, now Craig was standing right in front of me.

As was his custom, he was wearing black designer jeans and a black t-shirt, neatly tucked, of course, and a black leather belt with a silver buckle. Up close, I caught a whiff of his cologne: eau de lying scum.

A member of the biergarten's cleanup crew scooted between the two of us with a dustpan and broom and swept up my mess.

"Sorry," I muttered to the industrious young man.

"Paul's on vacation. Didn't he tell you?" Craig was smirking in a major way. He took a step in my direction as if threatening me with a one-armed hug. His right hand held a foaming beer mug.

I pulled back further, almost getting clipped in the cheek by a passing dart that flew by like a missile or some exotic insect far from its Amazon rain forest home.

"Sorry, lady!" its thrower called.

"Yes, he told me." I planted my hands on my hips. I was even watching his black and tan hound dog, Princess, for him while he was away. "He also told me that he had somebody coming in to manage the business while he was gone."

Gone being a three week trip to the Bahamas. And, no, I wasn't jealous, I merely hated him for his good fortune.

"That's me." Craig thumped his chest with his thumb.

"Whatever." There was nothing I could do about it anyway. Except kill Paul for not warning me about Craig's arrival. The big chicken.

"Don't think for a minute that you are going to be staying in Paul's apartment though." Like, I said, Paul rented an apartment on the second floor of my house. A few months back, I'd allowed Craig to share that space for a day or two, against my better judgment.

I wasn't about to repeat the mistake.

"Don't think for a minute that I intend to," Craig replied. "We rented a house."

"We?" I furrowed my brow.

"Hi!" A perky woman with perky breasts appeared from the doorway leading to the restrooms and oozed up alongside my ex-boyfriend. Dark jeans clung to perfect legs and a white cashmere sweater laid across her chest like snow atop the peaks of the Alps.

I began to frown. It was the bimbo blonde, the latest long-legged, curvy cutie with whom Craig had cheated on me last before I caught him and dumped him.

Okay, so she was a redhead and had a master's degree in psychology. She was still a bimbo in my book. I mean, anybody with a master's in psychology ought to know better than to get involved with a lying, two-timing, two-faced, cheating bit of scum like Craig "the gigolo" Bigelow.

Her name was Candy something.

Craig snaked his arm around her impossibly narrow waist. "You remember Cindy."

Cindy, Candy, the whole scene was as sickeningly sweet as the girl ten years younger than Craig and attached to him now at the hip.

"Hello, Cindy." I shook the hand she offered. It was younger, healthier, and better manicured than my own. While her nails were shiny and pink, mine had birdseed crud under them from rooting around in the seed bins earlier and the nails themselves looked like my manicure had been performed by a one-eyed grackle. "I hear you'll be staying in Ruby Lake a while."

Candy, or Cindy, bobbed her head excitedly. I noticed that the middle two fingers of each of her hands held shiny rings. If I wasn't mistaken, that one on the left with the big diamond was an engagement ring. Was Craig getting married?

"Isn't it great?" Cindy rubbed up against Craig. What was she, part cat?

Cindy's layered locks were parted down the middle. Her eyes were blue with a hint of silver-gray. Her nose was so pert that I'm sure a lesser ex-girlfriend than I would have wanted to take a poke at it.

Unlike Craig, her skin was fair; where he was of the tall, dark and, yes I admit it, handsome variety. Craig has deep brown hair, cut short and he has dimples, too, most evident when he smiles, which he likes to do. A lot.

"We rented a house and everything," Cindy explained. "It's up in the mountains and looks straight down on the town."

"Wow." I was impressed that Craig was willing to spend a few bucks for one of the higher end vacation rentals. A house with a view like that could not have come cheap.

Then again, this was winter. It could have come dirt cheap. "What house is it?"

"It's called the Usher house." Craig squeezed his main squeeze's hand. I began to smile. "The *Usher* house?"

"That's right, Amy." Cindy drew a lock of long red hair across her face. "You should come visit sometime. Hey!" Her face brightened and I squinted in the glare of all those big white teeth. "You could be our first dinner guest!" She turned to Craig. "Right, honey bear?"

"Sure." Craig cracked a smile. "We'd love to have you. Bring Kim, too."

"I'm sure she'd love that," I said with a soupçon of sarcasm. I'd caught him ogling Kim on more than one occasion the last time he'd slithered into town.

"Who is Kim?" Cindy asked.

"Amy's best friend," explained Craig. "In fact, bring that other guy. What was his name?" He snapped his fingers thrice. "Dirk?"

"His name is *Derek*, Craig. Derek Harlan."

"Right, him." He planted a kiss of Cindy's cheek. "I'll call you and we'll set something up."

"I'll be looking forward to it," I said with a pasted on grin. "Honey Bear." Not.

"My lunch hour's up." It really wasn't but my appetite was shot and I'd spit half my lunch on the floor. "I need to head next door."

Craig turned to Cindy. "Amy's got a little bird store."

"Ooh," Cindy exclaimed. "I love birds."

"That would explain your attraction to birdbrains," I replied.

"Excuse me?" Cindy blinked.

Craig squeezed Cindy's hand. "It was a joke, honey."

"Oh." Cindy grinned.

I threw some money on the table and left.

The joke was on Craig. Two jokes, actually. Because, number one, I was never in this lifetime going to accept that offer. And, number two, everybody in town knew that the Usher house was haunted.

ABOUT THE AUTHOR

In addition to writing the Bird Lover's mystery series, **J.R. Ripley** is the critically acclaimed author of the Maggie Miller mysteries and the Kitty Karlyle mysteries (written as Marie Celine) among other works. J.R. is a member of the American Birding Association, the American Bird Conservancy, and is an Audubon Ambassador with the National Audubon Society. Before becoming a full-time author, J.R. worked at a multitude of jobs including: archaeologist, cook, factory worker, copywriter, technical writer, editor, musician, entrepreneur and window washer. You may visit jrripley.net. for more information or visit J.R. on Facebook at facebook.com/jrripley.

J.R. RIPLEY

A Bird Lover's Mystery

First in a
new series!

DIE, DIE
BIRDIE

J.R. RIPLEY

A Bird Lover's Mystery

TOWHEE GET YOUR GUN

THE
WOODPECKER
ALWAYS PECKS
TWICE

A Bird Lover's Mystery

J.R. RIPLEY